PRAISE FOR
RUNNING SECRETS

It's always a treat to pick up a novel that's so compelling one can't put it down. That's the case with Arleen Williams' *Running Secrets*. It's a great story, captivatingly told, full of secrets, surprises, and complex relationships.

—Susan Knox, Author of *Financial Basics, A Money Management Guide for Students*

Gorgeous Chris Stevens seems to have everything going for her except the will to live. In this delicately crafted story, Arleen Williams explores with sensitivity the inner life of an emotionally scarred woman—and the secrets that threaten to destroy her. *Running Secrets* is a must-read for anyone seeking to understand fear of one's own past.

—Laurel Leigh, Author of the blog Dear Writers

Ms Williams has written a book of secrets—about life, death, family, and resurrection. As she works through the pain of the past, Chris Stevens, the protagonist of *Running Secrets,* uncovers the deepest of family secrets and in it finds something to live for. Williams is a writer who never gives you what you expect, but what she gives you is better than what you expect. This is a very American novel about race and love, about assimilation and reconciliation. As Chris discovers, you never know where you'll find your mother.

—Jack Remick, Author of *Gabriela and the Widow* and *The California Quartet*

Some things I loved about *Running Secrets*: this buddy story features women--Williams pairs a young American with a middle-aged African immigrant, the direct discussion of race and identity through the characters and their trials, Chris Stevens's ascent from despair to creativity, Gemi Kemmal's transformation from rigid to adventurous, and a little romance for all the protagonists.

—Pam Carter, Seattle playwright

Coming off the success of her memoir, *The Thirty-Ninth Victim*, Arleen Williams has written *Running Secrets*, a novel of redemption, rebirth, friendship, and romance. When protagonist Chris Stevens goes wacko and tries to kill herself, helpers appear, bright as angels, to render aid and succor. The story deepens as each helper comes onstage, bringing a feeling of warmth and deep spirit—just in time for Christmas.

—Robert J. Ray, Author of *The Weekend Novelist* and
Murdock Tackles Taos

RUNNING
SECRETS

ARLEEN WILLIAMS

For Melissa,
Thank you so much
for your support. Happy
reading!
AWilliams

Booktrope Editions
Seattle, WA 2013

Cover Design by Loretta Matson

Edited by Katrina M. Randall

This is a work of fiction. Names, characters, places, brands, media, and incidents are either the product of the author's imagination or are used fictitiously. Any resemblance to similarly named places or to persons living or deceased is unintentional.

PRINT ISBN 978-1-62015-191-4

EPUB ISBN 978-1-62015-287-4

Library of Congress Control Number: 2013923195

For
Tom and Erin

Death Wish

ONE

CHRIS SLUMPED AGAINST THE STEERING WHEEL listening
to the steady hum of early evening traffic punctuated by the rhythm
of rain spattering on the windshield. The familiar thought crept up
on her, unbidden and blinding, each time more real than the time
before. And yet it wasn't really a thought, not the kind of thought
she could relate to another, a thought that she could attach words to
and explain. No, this was more of an inexplicable force.

With a slight turn of her head, she checked the rearview mirror
and saw a white SUV speeding toward her. In that split second, there
was only darkness.

... She shoves open the car door and steps into the SUV's path.
The right front bumper tosses her into the air like a limp ragdoll. She
hears the squeal of brakes and scream of tires on wet pavement,
hears the shatter of glass and crunch of metal, hears the chatter of
on-lookers swarming around the crumpled heap of her broken body.

Blood seeps from her skull. Bone pierces her left leg. Her skirt, a
loose navy serge, rides up her thighs. She wants to pull it down, but
her right arm, cocked at an angle, won't move. Her jacket is torn
open, her white blouse, red. Red like the scarf tucked behind the
flight wings on her chest pocket.

The driver of the SUV stands over her. He drops to his knees and
searches for a pulse. Beside him, a little girl in a bright raincoat asks,
"Daddy, what happened?"

"I couldn't stop, sweetie. I need you to be a big girl now and
watch your sister."

"Okay, Daddy."

With a slight shake of her head, Chris glanced at her rearview mirror again as the white SUV sped safely past. Then she stepped out of her car and walked into the post office.

As she entered the squat building, it took a moment to remember why she was there. Stamps. She needed stamps to mail the bills that she'd been carrying around in her purse for over a week. She finger-combed the dark curls from her forehead, glued a flight attendant smile on her face and took her turn at the counter.

Back in her car, she wound the steep hill down Genesee Avenue to Alki Beach. With a turn of her key, she entered her dark condo, dreading the long, lonely night that lay before her.

She headed to her bedroom turning on lights, unbuttoning her uniform and kicking off her pumps. Within minutes she retraced her steps wearing Lycra running pants, Asics and a jacket. Just across the street from her building a pedestrian path ran along Alki Avenue and the beach. Runners were gathering at the miniature replica of the Statue of Liberty – a gift from a local Boy Scouts troop to the City of Seattle. She'd noticed them before, sometimes in the morning, sometimes in the early evening, always on Sunday morning. She lowered her eyes and began her solitary run in the opposite direction.

An hour later, hot water formed rivulets as it traced the curve of her breasts. The steam was thick and comforting. She shampooed her curly hair and lathered her lean body with slow, measured movements until her fingers wrinkled. Later, in flannels and a long sleeve T-shirt, she zapped a frozen dinner, filled a glass of wine and settled into the sofa in front of the television. Surfing channels, nothing caught her attention. She tried to read but was blind to the printed words of the novel that lay in her lap. Despite her fear of nightmares, she went to bed early. She was still awake when the phone rang. Could she cover an early morning departure for a sick call? She accepted the assignment and collapsed into her pillows willing sleep to come, but her mind was invaded by images she could no more control than incurable cancer.

... She flies along West Marginal Way, a fast arterial running parallel to the Duwamish waterway favored by truckers and longshoremen on their way to and from the busy Seattle waterfront and locals headed to SeaTac airport. Mountains of shipping containers line the road under the dim streetlights and heavy rain of pre-dawn.

A semi barrels towards her. With little more than a blink of an eye and a flick of the wrist, she takes the 18-wheeler head-on. Tires scream as the truck jack-knifes across four lanes of traffic and slides to a stop, her mutilated Toyota a postage stamp glued to its front grille. The driver radios for help before leaping from the cab, a cigarette still dangling from his lips. A second later the world explodes. By the time firefighters are able to control the flames, little remains of either vehicle ...

Beads of sweat tickled Chris's hairline. She kicked off the heavy comforter and glanced at the bright face of her alarm clock. Not even midnight yet. She turned on the lamp, reached for the small notebook and pen on her bedside table and began to scribble.

I've got to find another way. Something simple that doesn't drag anybody else into this hell. I can't take it anymore. Nobody involved, just a clean break.

It crept in as a darkness, a long shadowy dark spiral that pulled Chris downward and kept her there. A darkness that hurt. Burying, suffocating, shadowing all meaning, all hope. A lump in the back of the throat robbing food of all pleasure. A tongue so thick, so heavy, words were impossible, thoughts couldn't form. Eyes that burned. A body that ached. A mind that wouldn't slow down, stop, take a break.

She'd felt the darkness before, but never like this, never the inside of a coffin under six feet of heavy, damp earth. In the past, when the darkness came, she played mind games, the perfect death becoming more real than reality itself. But she still functioned. Got up, took a shower, ate breakfast. She put on a smile and went about her daily business. She even ran, but it was never a good run, a mind-clearing run, in that cloud of black.

This time it was different. It was all she could do to force herself out of bed that morning after her third wake-up call. The scalding shower got her to Reagan International on time, but just barely.

The flight from the other Washington was hell. It seemed like an entire middle school was on board, headed home from five days in the Capitol, the White House, the Lincoln Memorial. They wouldn't, they couldn't stop talking, yelling, moving about the cabin. How could that many noisy kids be just one U.S. history class? She thought of being their teacher and shuddered.

But first class was worse. Chris saw her father's face in first class. Those rich bastards ordering drink after drink. Looking right through you like you didn't even exist. Or sizing you up as their next conquest. Invisible or sex object. After a few months of working first class, she'd requested a return to coach. At least the kids saw you when you stood in the aisle to serve them.

After six long flight hours, she was back in Seattle, driving home from the airport. Another slick, cold wintery day. The kind of day best spent in a comfy chair in front of a blazing fire with a good book instead of stuck in rush hour traffic. She avoided Interstate 5 and took the back roads home.

The rain hammered the windshield as she headed north on 35th Avenue, a road with a thirty-five mile per hour speed limit that everyone, cops included, ignored, even as the rain dropped like a curtain. Rain and the pulsating intervals of the dim streetlights: shadow-light-shadow-light. A Morse code of darkness.

The arterial was undivided. The oncoming traffic came hard and fast. Rain and steamed-up windows in old junkers like her battered Toyota made the limited visibility even worse. She no longer paid attention to the traffic around her, to the rain or the slick streets. She accelerated, unaware, staring towards the golf course at the foot of a steep hill. She accelerated in the precise spot where most drivers had a foot hovering over the brake, coasting, ready to brake at any moment. The space closed between her and the car in front of her. She accelerated, and in one swift movement, she pulled the wheel to the right.

The car took flight, jumping the curb, grazing the concrete base of a tall Native American totem pole and plunging headfirst down a steep embankment into the northwest blackberry brambles that covered the hillside. The noise, the crunch of metal and glass, shattered the darkness that was Chris's mind. She felt a sharp pressure on her chest pinning her against the seat as the airbag inflated with the first frontal hit. The car rolled over and over and over again slamming her head back and forth into the side window until it dripped with blood. She rolled for eternity, and then there was stillness.

The warmth of another body inside the crushed car told Chris that she was still alive. Fragments of thought, words, floated through her. His, hers? She couldn't be certain. She wanted to scream, to run. But most of all, she wanted to die.

"Okay, she's free," the voice next to her called out.

Another voice. Far away. "Slide that back board over...Jake, get her waist. One, two, three lift."

Pain ripped through her body. Sharp, searing pain. Darkness and light. Agony and blessed nothingness.

Then, more voices.

"Strap her in for the ride."

"Get some pressure on that head wound...losing blood fast."

"Shit, I know this chick. I mean, I see her running Alki all the time."

"Well, she ain't gonna be doing much running ..."

With the grace of morphine, Chris heard nothing more.

TWO

EARLIER THAT SAME WET, WINDY DAY, Gemila Kemmal pressed the intercom button of Patrick O'Reilly's condo in the upscale Belltown neighborhood just north of downtown. As she waited, she tucked a few black curls back under the edges of her dark headscarf before slipping cold hands into the pockets of a nondescript coat.

When she received no response, Gemi used the key Patrick had given her the day they signed the contract for home healthcare. She entered the building and took the elevator to the twelfth floor where she keyed open another door, crossed the foyer and entered the large living room of white leather, brushed chrome and glass.

The condo was silent. Too silent. It was not unusual for Patrick's partner to leave for work several hours before Gemi arrived. She'd offered to come in earlier on several occasions, but both men assured her it wasn't necessary. Nine o'clock was fine. Still, the silence made Gemi uneasy as she walked down the hallway towards Patrick's bedroom. A classical guitarist by profession, Patrick's passion was music. Usually the condo sang with the chords of Christopher Parkening, John Williams, or the legendary Andres Segovia. Today only silence greeted her arrival.

She pushed open the wide French doors to Patrick's bedroom suite and paused in the doorway. Without approaching the bed, Gemi sensed that Patrick had left this world for what she hoped was a far more gentle and peaceful place than the one he had endured these past months. When she moved towards the bed to take her patient's pulse for the last time, his body was cold to her touch.

Gemi knew death. Her life had been full of death since her earliest years in war-torn Ethiopia. It never got easier. She sank to the chair beside Patrick's bed and lifted the phone to make the necessary calls. First, she called Patrick's life partner at his downtown office to tell him the news he already expected. Patrick's decline had been steady. Death was inevitable. He had chosen, insisted, on dying at home. Her next call was to the Neptune Society. As with so many details of his life, Patrick had prearranged for his own cremation, and Gemi had agreed to make the call when the time came.

Gemi did not leave Patrick's bedside until his partner arrived to take her place. She spent the remainder of the day offering as much comfort as warm tea and gentle words can provide to the bereaved. Only after Patrick's body had been removed, only after family and friends filled his home and enveloped his partner in a collective loving embrace, only then did Gemi slip away. She left the condo key next to the Chihuly bowl on the foyer table and let herself out the front door for the last time.

Once in her car, she relaxed, allowing her body to sink into the old, upholstered seat. She gave herself a few minutes, then collecting her thoughts, she remembered one more call she needed to make. She reached for her cell phone from the large woven basket in the passenger's seat and speed-dialed Peter Bentley. An answering machine.

"Hello Peter. Gemi here with sad news. You will not be needing to come by Patrick O'Reilly's flat for his appointment tomorrow. He passed away this morning. Call me when you have a moment, will you?"

THREE

CHRIS AWOKE TO THE MECHANICAL HUMMING of machines, the rhythmic beeping of the EKG, and the beating of her own heart telling her that she was still alive. She lay on her back and could move little more than her eyes. Her range of vision was too limited to take in the pulsating peaks and valleys of the heart monitor, the IV bags, or the tubes connected to the needles in her arms.

Only fragments of images played in her mind – heavy rain, a golf course, a totem pole. She tried to sit up by forcing her weight onto her elbows, but she couldn't move.

The door opened and a stranger walked in. "I see you're awake."

"Where am I? Why can't I move?" Her slurred voice was tinged with panic.

"Harborview. You've been in a car accident."

"What happened? Why can't I move?"

"You got pretty beat up, Christine, but you'll be fine," the nurse said. "You have fractures in both legs, so you won't be dancing any time soon, but not to worry, Dr. Anderson's the best."

"My legs?" Chris struggled to follow the nurse's voice as she moved around the bed.

"Your mother came by while you were still in surgery. I'm sure she'll be back later for a visit."

"My mother?"

"Just rest now. We'll talk more, later," the nurse said before she slipped from the room.

Darkness settled over Chris as she sank again into oblivion.

"Christine, are you awake?" the nurse asked. "Someone's here to see you."

"Mom?"

Chris opened her eyes for a brief moment, but her lids were heavy, too heavy to hold open. She couldn't focus. She tried again and saw two people but recognized neither. A woman in scrubs stepped back and busied herself with a chart at the foot of the bed. A tall man in some kind of uniform stepped forward.

"Hello, Christine. My name's Jake Bowmer," the man said. "I'm one of the paramedics who pulled you from your car last night. I just stopped by to see if you were okay."

The voice was familiar. Nothing more.

A week later, another nurse was wheeling Chris to the elevator when her mother walked towards them with brisk, firm steps. For the briefest of seconds, Chris felt that warm glow of love that stems from being remembered.

"Where do you think you're taking my daughter?" Ellen Stevens asked as she grabbed the edge of Chris's gurney and jerked it to a stop.

"That hurts," Chris gasped. "Mom, please, just let her do her job."

Ignoring her as though the gurney were empty, her mother spoke to the nurse. "Don't you dare move my daughter one single step from here until I get to the bottom of this."

Chris heard her mother's heels clacking on the hospital linoleum, followed immediately by her surgeon's calm voice. "Good morning, Mrs. Stevens. Can I help you?"

"You can tell me what you think you're doing with my daughter. I believe I made it perfectly clear to you the night Christine was brought into this godforsaken place that she'd be transferred to Rainier Rehab as soon as she could be moved. Then I get a curt phone message telling me she's being taken to some other floor. What part of my instructions did you fail to comprehend, Doctor?"

Listening from the gurney, Chris cringed. That question – she'd heard it so often growing up, but always in her father's voice, angry and slurred. Never in her mother's voice.

"Your daughter's simply being moved out of the ICU," Dr. Anderson said.

"If she's out of intensive care, I want her moved to Rainier Rehab."

"Mrs. Stevens, that simply is not your decision to make unless, of course, you have power-of-attorney."

Chris heard him pause for a moment, waiting for a response from her mother. Receiving none, he continued. "I can't transfer your daughter on your wish or demand. Christine is a mentally-capable adult, and if she wishes to leave the hospital against our advice, she can do so. You have no standing in this matter."

He turned to the nurse beside the gurney and said, "Get Christine up to Ortho immediately and make sure she's comfortable. Let's not make any decisions here in the hallway."

Chris felt her mother's rage, sensed the frustration and helplessness that surged through her manicured body. She knew her mother's façade was thinner than it appeared. She'd seen that helplessness before. Now, caught between her mother's rage and her surgeon's control, she was a child again.

... She nestles in the back seat of her father's Bentley, clinging to her big sister's hand, listening to her father's angry, demeaning voice tearing at her mother in the passenger seat in front of her.

"What part of my instructions did you fail to comprehend, Ellen? I told you to get the cleaners to lighten up on the starch. This goddamn collar is so stiff I can't breathe." Her father curses as he tugs at the silk tie around his neck.

Leaning against Beth, she whispers, "Why does he always yell at her?"

"Shush. Just ignore it, okay?"

She releases Beth's hand but snuggles as close as her seatbelt will allow. She clamps her small hands tight over her ears and shuts her eyes as her father flies over the hills of West Seattle.

He runs the intersection at the foot of Charlestown hill, too lost in his rage to check the cross street for on-coming traffic. A large moving van has the right-of-way and takes it, along with the Bentley that speeds across its path. The car is tossed against a power pole on the opposite corner of the intersection. The front end collapses, sandwiching the bodies of both parents between the airbags and the front seats.

She opens her eyes, uncovers her ears, and unfastens her seatbelt. Together she and Beth climb from the backseat of the mutilated car. Holding hands they walk away, leaving the scream of sirens and their dead parents behind them ...

The gurney swayed as the nurse pushed Chris towards the elevator doors. She saw her mother try to pass the surgeon, saw him block her path as the nurse pushed her into the open elevator. Then he turned to leave, but her mother reached out and grabbed the white sleeve of his medical jacket.

"We're not finished here, Doctor."

Chris watched as Dr. Anderson disengaged her mother's hand from his sleeve and walked away in silence.

"You'll be hearing from my attorney," her mother screamed as the elevator doors closed behind the gurney.

Alone with the nurse in the quiet elevator, Chris was flooded with a sense of relief. She might not be that child walking away from a crash scene, but she knew her mother wouldn't follow her to the sixth floor.

FOUR

"HEY, DAVE, GIVE ME TEN MINUTES."

"Where're you off to?"

"Just gotta check on somebody. I'll be back. Why not grab that coffee you've been moaning about?"

Jake turned towards the elevator, pushed a button, and disappeared, leaving his partner alone at the emergency room entrance. They had just brought in another accident victim. Only minor injuries this time, probably nothing at all. Just another insurance claim. Jake got so fed up with the fakes. There were plenty of good folks out there who needed help in life-threatening situations. It pissed him off when the call was nothing more than a fender bender and some guy wanting the Medic One ride to fortify his whiplash claim.

The elevator opened, and Jake headed to the intensive care nurses' station. He was in luck. The same plump, gray-haired nurse was on duty, the one with the gentle voice who reminded him of Aunt Mattie.

"Back for another look?" she said.

"Guess so."

"Sorry, she's been transferred out. She's up on the sixth floor, I think. Ortho. Let me check." She turned to her computer and clicked a few keys. "Yup. Here she is, Christine Stevens. 632. You'd better get up there if you want to see her. Her mother's been making life miserable for all of us."

"What's the problem?"

"She thinks we aren't good enough for her, I guess. I overheard her telling the surgeon she's moving her daughter to Rainier Rehab.

Pity. A perfect patient. Never a whisper of complaint. Wouldn't mind
more like her, but a few visits from that mother of hers are more
than any of us can handle."

"Thanks for the tip. I'm on my way."

"Good luck. She's awfully pretty, even with all those bruises."

Sixth floor. Another nurses' station. It was empty, so Jake kept
walking. 630, 631, 632. He pushed the door open a few inches, exposing
a view of the bed. A private room. He saw her turn towards the
whisper of movement.

The room was bright with afternoon sunlight through a west
window. The air was heavy sweet. Even Jake could tell that the floral
arrangements covering every flat surface weren't the grocery store
variety.

"Can I come in?"

"I guess." Her voice was soft, just above a whisper, and laced
with a hint of fear.

"Hi. My name's Jake. Jake Bowmer." He saw the lack of recognition
in her eyes. "I was here a few days ago. You were still in the ICU."

"Who are you?"

"I'm one of the paramedics who brought you here after the
accident."

"You should've left me there."

Chris turned her head away from him. Silence filled the room.
He'd walked in thinking himself the hero only to be knocked off his
proverbial white stallion by a damsel who preferred the dragon. He
struggled to find words, something, anything to keep her engaged.

"From the looks of this room, a lot of people would be mighty
disappointed if we'd done that."

Chris shifted in her bed. Jake watched as she looked around the
room. When her eyes returned to his, they were wet with tears.

There are a lot of different types of pain in this world, and Jake
was an expert in dealing with most, but tears left him at a total loss. He
couldn't stop tears with a morphine drip. "I'm sorry. What did I say?"

"Nothing. It's the flowers. They're from nobody."

"Nobody?"

"My mother. Keeping up appearances. No one else knows I'm here."

"I know you're here."

"But I don't know you. And you don't know me."

"True, but I'd like to. I've seen you before. Before the accident, I mean. Down at Alki. You're a runner."

"Was."

Jake glanced at the heavy casts immobilizing both of Chris's legs. His eyes darted back to Chris's – large, questioning, challenging. He saw her fear, her vulnerability. "What does your surgeon tell you?" he asked.

"I haven't asked."

"I'm no doctor, but I know fractures heal. You're young and healthy. You'll heal. I'll see you back on Alki before you know it."

"Alki?"

Jake realized she was struggling to follow his words and wondered how much of this visit she'd remember. The IV was still in her arm, the morphine clicker close at hand.

"Yes, Alki," he said, a new gentleness in his voice. "I've seen you run."

"Why?"

"I'm a runner, too. I hook up with a group most afternoons. We meet at the Statue. You know, that little Statue of Liberty right across from Alki Bakery. I've seen you pass us. You run hard. Fast. I'd never be able to keep up."

"You could now."

"I don't know. You can really move. I'm not sure I'll ever be able to match your stride or endurance. You'll be back. I'm certain."

Chris gave him a hint of a smile. Just a hint, but enough of a reward. Enough to make Jake glad he'd come, but a quick glance at his watch reminded him of where he needed to be. "Man, I gotta go. I left my partner down in the ER and didn't even tell him where I was headed. Can I come back and see you again?"

"Why?"

"Ah, well, I guess cuz I'd like to get to know you."

"I don't even know me anymore."

"Maybe we can get to know you together."

"Maybe."

"I really gotta go or they'll have my ass. I'm supposed to be working. See ya soon."

After Jake left, Chris was awake and very much alone. She tried to relax, breathing slow, deep breaths, the breaths of a distance runner. She steadied the pulse that reminded her that she had failed, that she was, in fact, still living. That awareness, and the dread that came with it, pulled at her like the undertow of a strong wave.

... She rips the needles from her arms. The heavy casts fall from her legs and the bandages unravel from her head. She sits up in a bed no longer surrounded by pea green hospital walls. She stands and walks to her closet. The ugly hospital gown drops to the floor, and she puts on sweats and a fleece sweater. She steps into flip-flops and leaves the condo.

White caps crash against the bulkhead at Alki Beach. She walks down the concrete stairs to the sand and into the black, churning water. The undertow rips her flip-flops from her feet. She feels the sand wash away under her soles and is unable to keep her balance. The undertow drags her deeper and deeper into the cold darkness of Elliott Bay. She does not struggle as the water closes over her, fills her lungs, drags her down. Deep. Darkness. Death ...

Pain tugged at Chris. Pure physical pain. Pain she could feel with every nerve of her battered body. She reached for the call button at the side of her bed. A few minutes later a young aide entered the room.

"Can I help you?"

"My purse," Chris said. "Is my purse here?"

"Yes, your personal items are all right here," the aide said. She pulled open a large drawer in the bottom of the bedside table that Chris hadn't noticed, couldn't even see from her confinement in the bed. "Here you go," she said, handing her the standard issue handbag. "Are you a flight attendant?"

"I don't know," Chris said, confused. "Am I?"

"Looks like it," the aide said. "I've seen these bags before. My sister works at SeaTac and I have to pick her up way too often. Can I get anything else for you?"

Chris tried to shake her head, but it hurt. "No," she said.

"Okay then, buzz again if you need me."

Alone, Chris opened the clasp of her purse. One by one she took out the contents and spread them on her lap. A red wallet, a black day planner, and a small cosmetic case. A cell phone and a set of keys attached to a large pewter C. She fingered the C and remembered. C and B. She and Beth bought them at the Seattle Center Arcade the summer before her sister's sixteenth birthday. What would Beth think of her little sister now?

Chris didn't want to go there. Instead, she picked up the cell phone. The battery was dead. She opened her wallet and took out her driver's license, credit cards, car and medical insurance. The basics that create identity.

She fingered each item. Read the words. Looked at the photos. Then one by one she put everything back into her purse, snapped it closed and sank into her pillows. Something was missing. Some part of her, something she couldn't remember, was not there.

Pain gripped her. She fingered the morphine clicker and conscious thought drifted beyond reach.

FIVE

IT WAS LATE EVENING when Jake slipped the key into the front door of his apartment, stumbled in and closed the door behind him. He was beat. He'd pulled a double shift and hadn't slept more than a few hours in the past forty-eight. Still, he couldn't erase the pain in Christine's large brown eyes any more than he could convince himself that it was the morphine that had said, "You should've left me there."

He'd had a few of the guys over to watch a Seahawks game. It seemed ages ago. "Shit, this place stinks," he muttered as he crumpled Dominos boxes and dirty napkins into a large black trash bag, setting the beer bottles to one side for recycling. He opened the windows and filled the small space with fresh night air. On Avalon Way, halfway between Alki Beach and Fire Station #32, he was just close enough to catch the salt air.

From the living room, he headed to the bedroom where he stripped off his uniform and put on sweats. Then to the bathroom where he grabbed a sponge and some Ajax. He scrubbed with unnecessary force. Scrubbing was something he knew, something he spent idle hours doing between calls at the fire station. The station glistened. So did the bright red and white Medic One aid vehicles. Scrubbing was repetitive and soothing. Scrubbing freed the mind to wander. A few hours later the apartment was spotless, but his mind was still as troubled as when he started.

After a restless night of tossing and turning, Jake made himself a cup of strong coffee and left his condo as though in a dream, his feet taking him where his mind had not yet focused. In the shadows and heavy fog of early morning November, he drove up Avalon Way to 35th Avenue and stopped in front of the tall totem pole. "What in the hell am I doing here?" he mumbled as he climbed from his car. But he knew, just as he knew he wouldn't find what he wanted to see: skid marks, tread on concrete, the telltale signs of someone slamming on the brakes in a futile attempt to stop a fast-moving vehicle, faster than physics would allow.

He hiked the mid-slope of the 35th Avenue Hill – up and then down again – searching. He tracked the trajectory of the car as it left the road, hit the concrete base of the totem pole, took flight over the hillside and rolled into the blackberry brambles that edged the golf course below. But there were no signs that Chris Stevens had braked at all.

Back in his car, he drove into the golf course to the spot where Chris's car had landed. Again, he climbed out as though pulled by an invisible force he'd be hard pressed to identify should anyone question what he was doing there on such an early gray morning. He paced off the area, imagining the car as it tumbled down the hillside and rocked to a stop at the bottom. He identified the tire tracks of his own Medic One vehicle and of the fire engine, as well as those of the tow truck that had been called to handle the wreckage. He fingered the sore, scabbed areas on his lower arms caused by the tangle of blackberry vines that had seemed intent on consuming Chris and her car. The vines were trampled, but not destroyed. Like most people born and raised in the Pacific Northwest, Jake knew that they couldn't really be destroyed. They always grew where you didn't want them with the tenacity of wild salmon returning to spawn each year despite the challenges of environmental destruction.

As he headed back to his car, something caught the corner of his eye, a bit of light, something that didn't belong. He retraced his steps towards an area of matted brambles to take another look, and there it was. "Shit," Jake muttered, reaching gingerly between the sharp barbs.

He extracted a thin, damp notebook. As the sky opened and drizzle began to soak Seattle, Jake shoved the notebook into his pocket, pulled up his hood and walked to his car.

With the car running and the heater cranked, he fingered his find. There was no name on the cover, inside or out. No identifying information. Still, Jake didn't need a name or an address. He knew it was hers. Just as he knew that the wreck had been no accident.

Six

CHRIS HEARD HER MOTHER'S VOICE in the hallway outside her room before she saw her, and a faint groan escaped her lips. She tensed as if waiting for a blow. Only a week had passed since her mother's last confrontation with Dr. Anderson. Now trouble was going to start all over again.

Her mother flung the door open and barreled into the room, a nurse with a wheelchair in tow. "Christine, sit up and let me take a look at you."

"Mom, what are you doing here?"

"I'm moving you out of this disgusting place."

"But I'm fine here. They're treating me well."

Chris felt her mother assess her appearance with the same critical eye she had known all her life. Taking the silk scarf from around her neck, she tossed it at her. "Wrap that around your head, Christine. For heaven's sake, you look ridiculous. And why aren't you wearing the lounge wear I had sent over from Nordstrom?"

The nurse, who had been standing by the door, stepped towards Chris, and with a simple hand gesture, offered to help. With the expertise of experience, she wrapped Chris's head to hide the tender stitches and lopsided haircut. Then she stepped back with a sympathetic smile.

Chris watched her mother glance around the room with a look of disdain. "Let's get moving, Christine. I've got a cab waiting downstairs. Sign those papers for the nurse and let's go. I don't have time to wait for you to change. You'll just have to go dressed as you are."

"But Mom, where? Why?"

Her mother glared at her. "I don't have time for this, Christine."
The ice in her voice chilled the room.

The nurse approached Chris again with a clipboard in hand. "Mrs.
Stevens asked that we prepare these release forms, Chris. You don't
need to sign them if you don't want to transfer to Rainier Rehab."

"Rainier Rehab?" Chris's voice was almost a whisper.

"Yes, Rainier," her mother snapped, glaring at the nurse as she
grabbed the clipboard from her and shoved it into Chris's hands.
"Now sign these so we can get out of here. Your father and I have
done more than enough charity work for Rainier, and we expect to
get some decent service in return."

Chris looked back and forth between her mother and the nurse.
With a sigh of resignation, she took the pen from the top of the
clipboard and signed the forms that allowed her mother to take her
from Harborview.

The nurse removed a long cashmere coat from the Nordstrom
garment bag that hung in the closet, removed the tags, and helped
Chris put it on over her hospital gown. Then she pushed the wheelchair
to the side of the bed and helped Chris slide into it. The three of them
made their way to the front exit of Harborview Medical Center. There
her mother deposited Chris into a waiting cab, paid the driver, and
ordered him to deliver her to Rainier Rehab.

The halls smelled of lunch as an aide pushed Chris's wheelchair
through the open door of a spacious, private room. There was a wall
of large windows beyond the bed that brightened a small seating
area complete with a sofa, easy chair and coffee table. The bed was
near the entrance. A second door led to the bathroom. A rustic wooden
armoire stood in the corner, placed by an astute designer to allow
television viewing from both sofa and bed. The walls were painted a
soft, buttery cream and the bed was covered in sunflowers. Unlike
the hallways that flowed with the lingering smells of institutional
cooking, this room was filled with the strong fragrance of flowers.

"Hold it. Stop right here," Chris said, her voice a bit harsher
than she had intended.

Startled, the aide jerked the wheelchair to an abrupt stop, causing Chris to flop forward. "What is it? Is something wrong?"

Righting herself, Chris scowled at the room. Floral arrangements, large overbearing arrangements, arrangements that Chris knew cost enough to feed a family of four for a month, were everywhere, permeating the air with their sickly sweet scent.

"Get those things out of here immediately," she said. "Please."

The aide stammered, unsure she'd heard correctly. "You want me to get rid of the flowers?"

"Yes. All of them. As soon as possible."

"Are you sure? They're so beautiful. Someone must really care a lot."

"Just get them out of here, okay?" Chris said.

As the young aide began to protest again, Chris stopped her with a stare, just as she had done with unruly passengers on transcontinental flights.

"But, but…what do you want me to do with them?"

"Take them home. Give them away. I don't care. And if my mother has any more sent, do the same."

"Okay, Christine. Whatever you prefer. I guess I can put some in the lunchroom and at the front desk and even in the chapel." She thought for a moment and added, "And I'll take one bouquet to Mrs. Jefferson. She's an elderly woman recovering from a bad fall. I'm sure she'll enjoy them. And I'll put a note in your file to block all floral deliveries from Mrs. Stevens."

"Thank you. And could you also put a note asking people to call me Chris?"

"Sure thing. Now, let's get you settled in bed. I'm sure you're exhausted."

"Yeah, I am tired. But let me try it myself."

The aide pushed the wheelchair next to the bed, locked the wheels, and stood by as Chris used her upper body strength to lift herself from the chair to the bed. She managed to get onto the bed, but she couldn't pull her weighted legs up. The aide leaned over and lifted them without a word.

Settled, Chris looked around the room at the assortment of commercial bouquets. That's when she noticed one that didn't seem to belong – more a pot than a bouquet, with small bulbs set in what looked like a base of clear glass marbles.

"Excuse me. That one, the small one there," she said, pointing. "Does it have a card?"

"Let's see. Yes, here you go." She handed Chris the tiny envelope.

Chris tore it open and took out the small card. "Get well soon from your friends in the air." It was signed by a number of flight attendants she knew. By name. They didn't really know her any more than she knew them. She was the outsider, never socializing at the end of a long flight. Never a dinner together, never drinks in the hotel bar. Instead, she'd always head to her room. Alone. Still, here was this note. This connection to the life she once led.

"Leave this one, okay?" she said, her voice soft with emotion.

The aide set the fragrant bouquet of paper whites on her bedside table and left the room carrying the first of the large arrangements. As she closed the door behind her without a sound, Chris felt the walls close in around her. More than loneliness, the weight of desperation took hold. She felt like a caged animal, caged in her own broken body.

A sense of familiarity crept over her, something about the room that she knew – knew deep in her heart, engraved on her soul. It was just another hotel room, no different from all the other hotel rooms where she'd spent so many lonely nights in distant cities. The bank of tall windows to the far side of her bed allowed a view to the outside world and permitted natural daylight to brighten the inside world, but blocked the flow of fresh air. Loneliness crept into her pores as if infused in the circulating air that couldn't be altered by the freshness of an open window. These windows were sealed tight. She drifted off into a troubled afternoon nap.

SEVEN

AS CHRIS PULLED HERSELF TO A SITTING POSITION the
following morning and looked around, it took her a second to remember
where she was. Her fingers reached up to rub her eyes and finger-
comb her hair – automatic movements, mannerisms common in that
moment between sleep and wakefulness. Her mother's scarf was
now a crumpled ball of silk on her pillow. And there, on the left side
of her head, her hand stopped at the rough incision and stubble. The
wound and the flesh around it were still tender and bruised, the
healing still fresh and unfinished. She dropped her left hand and
fingered the curls on the right side of her head, twisting a lock of
dark hair around her index finger.

Chris had never worn her hair long. Always cut just below her
ears, it shone in bouncy, black curls around her tan face. She couldn't
remember ever having a different style, couldn't remember ever
thinking much about it at all. It was a simple, easy haircut. A shampoo-
and-go hairstyle that always looked great. Until now.

With a light knock, a middle-aged nurse carrying a meal tray
pushed open the door. "Good morning, Chris. My name's Susan. I'm
your day nurse here at Rainier Rehab. Did you sleep well?"

"Fine, thanks." Then, with a grimace, she pointed to her lopsided
hair and asked, "Can I get a haircut in this place?"

"Of course. We've got our own little beauty salon right here in
the building."

"Do I need an appointment?" Chris said, holding a handful of
hair on the right side of her head.

"I'll take care of it. Now eat up. We need to get you strong
enough to face Phil this afternoon."

"Phil?"

"Your physical therapist," she said, and then she was gone.

An hour later Chris was wheeled into a small salon. The stylist stood in front of her, his hands on his narrow hips, his shoulders thrown back, striking the perfect pose of an aging runway model. He took a long, intent look at her, as though sizing up the task before him. Then, he extended a delicate manicured hand and said, "Hello, dear heart, my name's Jamie. What's yours?"

"Chris," she said.

"So, Chris, what did you have in mind today?" He gazed into Chris's eyes with a twinkle in his own, and they both started laughing. Chris couldn't help herself. It felt good to laugh. Strange, uncommon, but good.

"I don't suppose you can make this side grow," she said, pointing to the left side of her head. "So, I guess the best bet is to make me a bit less lopsided."

"'Fraid so, deary. I say we take it all off. Down to about a quarter inch. Then we'll watch it grow."

"Okay, go for it."

A half hour later, Chris stared at herself in the large mirror in front of her. "Bald. I'm almost bald."

"Don't worry, deary. The nice thing about hair is that it grows back. By the time you walk out of here, your scars will be hidden."

"Really?"

"Promise. Now off you go. I bet Phil's going to make you work up a sweat today."

That afternoon another aide wheeled Chris into a large room full of a variety of equipment that she had never seen before. "Not to worry, it only looks like a torture chamber, but it's not really that bad," the aide said. "They'll have you up and walking before you know it."

As the treatment ended an hour later, Chris settled into her wheelchair tired, but invigorated by the exercise. For the briefest of moments, she realized that she hadn't thought about suicide or death since she had woken up that morning. She felt the trace of a smile form at the corners of her mouth just as the aide approached to take her back to her room.

"Okay, let's go, Chris," she said. Then, dropping her voice in a conspiratory tone, she added, "I need to tell you that Susan's going to be expecting you to push yourself around real soon."

"No, problem," Chris said. "It'll be good exercise."

As they were leaving the gym, an elderly woman with a walker approached. "Did I hear this little girl call you Chris, young lady?"

"Yes."

"Chris as in Christine Stevens?"

"Yes?"

"Oh, I'm so glad to meet you. My name is Mrs. Jefferson, but please call me Eleanor. I so wanted to meet you."

"May I ask why, Mrs. Jefferson?"

"Eleanor, please."

"Okay, Eleanor. Why did you want to meet me?"

"Oh, sweetie, I just love the beautiful bouquet you gave me. I used to have a large flower garden, you know. Every spring it was full of tulips and daffodils. The summer brought roses. And in autumn, the garden was full of dahlias and mums in every color you can imagine – just like the bouquet you gave me. Oh, listen to me, just rattling on like an old lady. All I really wanted to say was thank you. You brightened my day more than you know."

Chris was speechless. She remembered asking the aide to get the flowers out of her room the day before, but it never crossed her mind that she'd give her name to the recipients of her unwanted arrangements.

"I'm glad the flowers pleased you, Eleanor," she said and put on her flight attendant smile. For the first time in years, it felt almost real.

EIGHT

GEMI LIVED ON THE TOP FLOOR of a subdivided old house with large rooms and lots of charm. It was a climb but always worth the extra exercise. Sometimes it was the only exercise she was able to fit into her busy schedule – now, not quite so busy since Patrick O'Reilly's death. In fact, not busy enough. She pulled her extra twenty pounds up the steep stairs, promising herself she'd begin a weight-loss program soon.

"Hey there, neighbor, the climb slowing you down a bit?" It was Carolyn, just leaving her apartment at the base of the stairs.

"I really must do something about this old body of mine."

"I suppose we all could use more exercise. Home for lunch?"

"Yes, and what about you? Would you like to join me for some lentils?"

"I wish I could, but I'm supposed to be at some awful meeting. I love to teach, I love working with immigrants and refugees, but I sure hate all the meetings."

Gemi had heard her friend bemoan the college system for years. They both laughed.

"I'll take a rain check on the lentils, okay? I really gotta run. See ya."

Carolyn rushed out the front door, and Gemi unlocked her own door at the top of the stairs. The warmth of bright color engulfed her. She smiled, as she always smiled, when she entered her apartment. She'd painted it herself. Bright yellows and rich reds. The colors warmed her soul, even on a cold, gray winter day.

She clicked the door closed behind her, unwrapped the *shash* from her head and draped it over the ornate hook just inside her front door. Removing her shoes, she felt the warm hardwood floor beneath her feet as she padded into the kitchen. She turned on the gas stove, took a pot of spicy lentils from the refrigerator and stirred it slowly over the heat, the fragrance of roasted green chilies laced with cumin and cardamom filling the small apartment.

Gemi had always lived alone. She needed the space, the quiet, to compose herself. Her work took its daily toll. Most of her patients were shut-ins, victims of AIDS or cancer or just old age. She rarely knew with certainty if she'd find a living, breathing person or a lifeless body as she made her rounds. Still, it was her work, she reminded herself as she stirred her lentils, her assistance, that allowed them to stay in their own homes and end their days as they chose. So Gemi's home was her sanctuary, the place where she retreated at the end of each day, or whenever possible, at lunch time like today, between patient visits.

Although Gemi was born an Ethiopian Muslim, she'd lived more than half her life outside of her homeland, returning only twice in the past ten years to visit distant relatives she barely knew and struggled to understand. Ethiopia was no longer the home of her childhood. Continued violence and the unrelenting passage of time had changed it almost beyond recognition. However it was during those visits that she had been able to collect a few pieces of traditional artwork and tapestry that allowed her to decorate her home with the comfort of cultural memory.

In her apartment Gemi expressed her need for a bit of colorful chaos in her world of sterile, methodical patient care. A floral sofa stood against one deep red accent wall. An ornate Muslim prayer rug, as well as an Ethiopian healing blanket with its five sets of staring eyes both hung from the neutral wall opposite the sofa. There were stacks of brightly colored baskets from the central market in Addis Ababa in one corner of the living room, a floral tea set from London beside her stovetop, and a Haida Indian print on the wall above her kitchen table. Ethiopia, England, and the Pacific Northwest – a merging of cultures in color and artifacts.

The apartment was also home to Gemi's business. In the alcove of her bedroom, with large windows facing west, like so many old homes on Capitol Hill, she had set up a small office area. Here she had her desk, complete with patient files, computer, phone and fax machine.

It was the humming of the fax that caused Gemi to turn off the stove and hurry to her desk. She could almost see the broad smile that spread across her own dark face as she drew the paper from the fax machine. It contained details of a new patient with acceptance of her terms and verification of a substantial down payment.

Gemi returned to the kitchen humming softly to herself. She ladled her spicy lentils into a floral china bowl and sat at the small kitchen table to eat her lunch, knowing she needed to leave within the half hour to reach her next appointment on time. She ate, rinsed her bowl and spoon and set them to dry, slipped on her shoes, and wrapped her head before leaving the apartment.

NINE

CHRIS HEARD VOICES and glanced towards the door. She saw a tall man with the lean body of an athlete and dark, wavy hair talking to the assistant at the front desk. From her spot on the lat pull-down at the far side of the gym, she knew she'd seen him before, but she couldn't place him. It took a second for her to remember. The jeans and T-shirt threw her.

When she looked up again, he was crossing the room towards her. For a split second she panicked. Then her mantra, the lesson she'd learned in flight attendant training, played in her head. "When you put on this uniform you are a representative of the greatest airlines in the world."

At this particular moment, like so many others in her life, she couldn't have cared less about being an airline representative. It was the notion of becoming a different person that gave her solace. She could find confidence in that new person's skin. So in the time it took the man to cross the gym, Chris put on her metaphorical uniform, planted a smile on her face and became the person she believed she could never be without pretending.

"Hi, you're Chris Stevens, aren't you?" the man asked, the green and golden hues shimmering in his hazel eyes.

"Yes. And you're the paramedic who visited me at Harborview," Chris said. She raised the bar to its resting position overhead and dropped her arms to her sides.

"Jake Bowmer," he said. "But don't let me interrupt your workout. I was hoping we could talk, but I can wait 'til you're finished."

Chris didn't notice Phil walking towards them and startled at the sound of his loud, jovial voice. "You're not interrupting a thing, young man. What Chris needs is a break. She practically lives here in my gym. I can't get rid of her."

"You said the harder I worked, the sooner I'd be out of this place."

"True, but there's a limit to everything. Now tell me, who is this young man? A runner, definitely. A friend?"

Jake stepped forward and offered his hand. "Jake Bowmer. You must be Phil, the PT. They told me Chris would be back here working with you."

"Friend or family?" Phil asked.

For a moment, the only noise in the gym was the clank of exercise equipment. "I'm a paramedic," Jake said. "I was on the scene the night of Chris's crash. Just wanted to check in to see how she's doing."

"I wonder why," Phil said with a laugh. "Go on, get out of my gym, kids. Jake, take her to the cafeteria for a soft drink. No, better yet, get her a hot chocolate. We need to get some meat on those bones."

Chris was silent as Phil helped her off the machine and into her wheelchair. When she was seated, Phil swung the wheelchair toward the door and passed the handles into Jake's hands.

"So, there's some kind of coffee shop in this fancy place?" Jake asked as he pushed her through the double doors and out into the hallway.

"That's what they say. I've never been."

"Where do you eat your meals?"

"Usually in my room. They've been pushing me to get out more, so I've been forcing myself to eat in the cafeteria. That might be open."

"Forcing?"

"Sort of," she said.

After a short silence, he changed the subject. "What kind of work do you do?"

"I'm a flight attendant. Well, I was. Now I'm on medical leave."

"It's lucky you're even alive."

"Lucky," she repeated.

"Yeah, lucky," Jake said. "You were in a nasty crash."

"Let's not go there."

Jake stopped a passing aide and asked where they could find a decent cup of coffee. A few minutes later, settled at a cozy table with steaming mochas in hand, Chris began to question Jake with the cheerful tone she might use with a bored passenger on a long flight.

"So, you saved me, you keep checking on me, but I don't know anything about you. For all I know, you're some weird stalker with a paramedic's uniform from that costume shop in Belltown. I hear they've got everything there."

"No stalker," Jake said with a laugh. "The uniform's real, and it's mine."

"And why should I believe you?"

"Why shouldn't you?"

"Because I don't know you. I don't know anyone who knows you. I don't even know if it was you who pulled me from my car. Maybe that's just some story you told me."

"I suppose I could bring you a copy of the accident report. You can check my references by calling Harborview. If you want, I'll even give you my aunt's phone number."

"Aunt?"

"Yeah. I was raised by my Aunt Mattie. You want her number?"

"No, not necessary. I'm not that paranoid," she said.

"Okay," he said.

They sat in awkward silence. Neither seemed to know what to say to the other.

"There's something that's been bugging me, Chris. Can I ask you about it?"

"I guess." She could feel the muscles in her neck and shoulders tighten. She reminded herself that she was wearing her uniform. She smiled, prepared to listen to the complaints of a tired passenger.

"When I came to see you at Harborview you said something that stuck in my head. I can't get rid of it. We were talking about your accident, and you said, 'You should've left me there.'"

With one sharp push, Chris backed her wheelchair from the table with so much force the cups clattered and spilled. She spun around and headed towards the automatic doors. "I've got to go. It was nice of you to visit, but do not come again."

"Wait a minute, Chris. Please. Tell me what's wrong," Jake said. He pushed his own chair from the table and stood to follow her.

She was wheeling away from him as fast as she could, but just as she reached the automatic door, she stopped and turned to face him. "What is or is not wrong is none of your business. You did your job. You saved my life. Now just leave me alone."

"But wait," Jake said. "I found something I want to give you."

"I don't want anything from you. You've done enough already," she said.

"At least let me push you back to your room."

"No," she said with a force that stopped Jake cold.

He stood mute, watching Chris wheel herself away from him. As the automatic door closed behind her, he sank back into his chair at the table. "Christ," he swore to himself. "Me and my god damned, big mouth."

The room was empty as he reached around and took the tattered notebook from the pocket of his jacket hanging on the back of his chair. "Christ, what was I thinking," he cursed himself again. "What was she going to say? Sure, Jake, I drove myself off the 35th Avenue hill on purpose cuz I wanted to do myself in." He mimicked Chris's soft, gentle voice as he opened the warped cover of the small notebook. He didn't want to read it, had no intention of reading the private thoughts he assumed it contained, but he was pulled in, as though Chris herself were calling to him. A siren's song he was unable to ignore.

He leafed through the pages, keeping his eyes floating over each page, not allowing them to focus on the looping curls of the handwriting, not allowing himself to read the words written there. He saw that the notebook was more full than not with dates that seemed to indicate entries. As he flipped to the last page of writing, Jake slumped in the hard, plastic cafeteria chair, hit by the realization that his suspicions were on-target. He was holding Christine Stevens's personal journal. He let his eyes stream down the page, reading Chris's shaky script:

I've got to find another way. Something simple that doesn't drag anybody else into this hell. I can't take it anymore. Nobody involved, just a clean break.

Jake froze. Chris wrote those words only two days before he removed her from her mangled car and rushed her to Harborview. He stared at the page for a long time before he closed the journal, put on his jacket and headed for the exit. As he passed the front desk, he picked up an informational brochure with Rainier Rehabilitation Center in bright lettering across the front.

TEN

GEMI PAUSED, PUSHING A FEW ERRANT CURLS back under the edges of her headscarf while she collected her thoughts. She stood outside the half open door at three o'clock on another gray Seattle afternoon. Gemi knew that almost a month had passed since Christine Stevens had arrived at Rainier Rehab. What she didn't know was whether her new patient would accept her services.

Despite its comfort and beauty, the room felt cold and impersonal. There were no cards, flowers or small gifts – the evidence of a prolonged hospital stay. It was a room devoid of love. A girl–for that's what she looked like to Gemi, nothing more than a very sad, little girl– was stretched out on a small sofa by the window, both legs in heavy white casts. The television was turned off and an open book lay on her lap. The girl's head was covered with short black ringlets, a nasty three-inch scar still visible on the left side.

Gemi watched as Chris looked up from the sofa where she seemed to be half reading, half sleeping. As their eyes met, Gemi imagined how she appeared to the girl as she stood in the doorway– a plump, middle-aged African woman in ill-fitting khakis and a floral tunic top, a yellow scarf wrapped around her head and a large, colorfully-woven basket over one arm. She smiled at the image.

"Hello," she said, hesitant to interrupt the moment.

"Can I help you?" the girl said. Her voice was groggy, and she rubbed sleep from her eyes with the fists of a young child.

"Yes, I am looking for Christine Stevens."

"That would be me, but call me Chris, please."

"Then, I am here to see you, Chris. Your mother sent me. Might I come in?" At the word "mother," Gemi thought she saw a tiny wince. The girl's eyes dropped.

"Sure." Chris said.

"Oh no, child," Gemi said when she saw the girl struggle to sit up. "Please, do not trouble yourself any." Chris stilled for a moment and simply stared at Gemi. "Let me introduce myself. My name is Gemila Kemmal, but please call me Gemi."

"An unusual name. Where are you from?"

"Oh, child, that is a long story for another day. For now, let us just say I grew up in Ethiopia, spent some years in Sudan, and another bit in England before immigrating to America. Now I am here, and I hope you will allow me to assist you."

"Assist me?"

"Yes. Your mother felt you might prefer to go home rather than stay here the expected three months of recovery. She responded to my advertisement for home healthcare, and I was contracted on the spot, so to speak."

"And now my mother cares about what I want?"

Gemi heard the pain drip from Chris's words and wondered what she could say to comfort this girl. "I do not know what your mother cares or does not care about, child. My only concern is what you want. Your mother agreed to pay the sum I requested, so if you want to go home, at least you will be sleeping in your own bed."

"Why would my mother do this?" Chris asked, more to herself than to Gemi. She appeared lost in thought, almost unaware of Gemi's presence.

Gemi waited in silence and mused that she had never actually met Ellen Stevens. It was only a phone call and a faxed contract. It seemed odd at the time, but Gemi was happy for the work. Now she wasn't so sure.

"So, you never actually met my mother in person?"

"No, I never had that pleasure. As I understand it, she and your father are spending the holidays in Hawaii."

Chris began to laugh, a quiet, bitter laugh, as Gemi waited. "I'm sorry," Chris finally said. "It's only my mother. The joke's on her." Then, raking her fingers through her short curls on the right side of her head, she asked, "Do you think you could show me how to wrap a scarf around this?"

"A *shash?*"

"Yes. It's a Muslim scarf, isn't it?"

"Yes it is, child, and I'd be happy to show you how to cover your head. But first, would you like a cup of tea?"

"Tea? I don't think they offer much here in the way of an afternoon tea."

"Do not concern yourself about that, child. I come prepared." She lifted her basket to show Chris.

"That's a beautiful basket," Chris said. "Is it from Ethiopia?"

"No, I bought this basket at the West Seattle farmer's market! I believe it's from Ghana in West Africa, but I find it perfect for carrying my supplies." She lifted a bright cloth off the top of the basket to reveal a small electric kettle, a floral teapot and two cups complete with saucers. She also unloaded a quilted tea cozy, several packets of assorted shortbreads and a small box of sugar cubes. "Let me see now. Where shall we connect?" She walked to the bathroom to fill her kettle and plugged it into a wall socket next to the sink. Returning, she took a small tray from the bottom of her large basket and set about covering it with an embroidered cloth napkin and arranging the teapot, cups and cookies.

There was a whistle from the bathroom telling Gemi her water was hot. She poured the steaming liquid over the loose tea in the bottom of the delicate teapot and covered it with the cozy to prevent cooling.

"Wow," Chris exclaimed as she watched. "Mary Poppins comes to Rainier Rehab."

"Poppins?"

"Yeah, you know, the story of the British nanny. She flies through the air with an umbrella and she's got this bag she pulls things out of, stuff that would never fit in the bag at all." "I am afraid I do not know that story."

"Never mind. It's not important."

"All right then. Let me fix your tea just as you like it. I apologize that I have no cream, but I purchased a bit of milk in the cafeteria when I arrived. Do you use cream and sugar, child?"

"Can't remember ever having tea at all."

"There is a first time for everything," Gemi said, even as she saw the wisp of confusion in the girl's eyes. She let the moment pass and busied herself with the tea. "First, we put a spot of milk in each cup, then a cube of sugar, no maybe two cubes," she said, eyeing Chris's slender body. "Now, we pour the tea and stir. Here you are, child. Would you like a biscuit with that?" She handed Chris a cup and saucer and offered a tempting assortment of cookies.

"I once read that all feasts begin with the eyes. Thanks, Gemi. This is great."

"You are very welcome, child. Now, can you tell me a bit about yourself?"

Together, they relaxed with warm tea and gentle conversation. What is it about talking to someone with an accent, someone from another culture? Maybe it's a bit like being in a foreign country. People say things, do things, they'd never do at home. The anonymity offers a cloak of secrecy. Gemi had experienced this with other reticent patients and suspected that Chris was opening up and communicating with her in a way she probably hadn't done with anyone in a long time. An hour later, it was time for her to take her leave if she was to be on time for her next appointment.

"I am afraid I must be going now, child, and I believe you should be resting. May I return for a visit tomorrow?"

"That would be great."

Gemi noticed the eagerness in the girl's voice as she stood to rinse the cups and pot, and she wondered if she had many visitors. She repacked her beautiful basket with care and said, "All right then, tomorrow it is. It was a pleasure meeting you."

"Thank you for coming. I'll see you tomorrow."

"Three o'clock?"

"Okay."

"Until then, child," she said, smiling back at Chris as she walked out the door.

Leaving Rainier Rehab with her heavy basket on her arm, Gemi walked into the afternoon rain. Despite having lived more than half her life in northern countries, she still struggled to adjust to the early darkness that fell over Seattle during the shortened days of late autumn.

As she walked towards her parked car, she couldn't get the young woman's dark, haunting eyes out of her mind. Here was a person she could help, who needed far more than the physical care she was well-trained in providing. But there was something more, something about those eyes that took her back to a place and time that she tried to block from memory, knowing full well that memories could never truly be blocked.

Somehow, through Chris's eyes, even in the cold rain, Gemi felt lost in the bright heat of the Ethiopian sun of her childhood. She was no longer walking on wet Seattle asphalt but instead playing in a dusty, dry street in Addis Ababa not far from the open-air market where her mother was shopping for their afternoon meal of lentils and vegetables. She was playing *kare* with her older brother, the game of sidewalk squares and tossed stones being as international as the happy laughter of healthy children. She was still young, too young for the *shash*, the Muslim headscarf required of all young women, still young enough to play in the street with her older brother and his friends. Soon those games would end, to be replaced by the community of women.

She remembered the day of her first menstrual period: the day her mother bound her head in a tight scarf for the first time before she was allowed to leave the house. She remembered the excitement of becoming a young woman. In Ethiopia, as a young Muslim woman, she became part of a whole. She had a sense of place, of belonging, of being loved. Feelings she was certain the young woman at Rainier Rehab had never experienced. Not because she wasn't Muslim – Gemi's beliefs were not so strong as to lead her to exclusionism – but because Chris was so very alone.

"Where is the child's mother?" Gemi wondered aloud as she opened the door of her parked car and relieved her arm of the weight of her heavy woven basket. She walked to the driver's seat and slid out of the rain, lost in thought.

The room felt more quiet and empty than ever after Gemi left. But not as lonely, Chris realized, for a bit of Gemi remained when the door closed behind her. A bit of hope. A bit of curiosity.

She stretched out on the sofa where they had just shared tea and conversation. Twisting her mother's blue silk scarf around her fingers, she replayed the visit scene by scene. The tea reminded her of something, a long-ago memory, but still she couldn't grasp it. She pushed it away, instead remembering her first glimpse of Gemi standing in the doorway. And then she began to laugh, a loud raucous laugh this time, as she toyed with her mother's blunder. She knew her mother would never have hired this African woman with a Muslim headscarf and the clothes of a cleaning woman, worse than the cleaning women she hired and fired on a regular basis. It was the accent that had fooled her into thinking she was hiring a proper British nursemaid.

Chris wondered about Gemi's accent. Her voice was warm and melodic, but her accent was hard to define. The top layer was formal, precise, almost British. But beneath that façade, there seemed to be a layer of pain and struggle Chris couldn't identify and didn't understand.

Perhaps her mother had found her the perfect companion in Gemi, Chris thought. During the entire visit they never spoke of the physical or medical assistance she would need when she moved home. Or even of Chris's injuries and their cause. Instead Gemi asked her questions about her life, her hopes, her dreams. Gemi asked the questions of a friend or a mother, the questions that her own mother never asked.

Chris realized that for the first time in years she had thought about, had even talked about, the creative writing degree at the University of Washington that she had abandoned when she joined the airlines. She remembered her long-abandoned dream of becoming a writer.

My very own Mary Poppins, she thought. I'll have to rent the movie and show it to her sometime.

In that split second it took for the thought to form, Chris became aware she was thinking about the future, actually planning and looking forward to the future. She smiled with the gentle joy of knowing that Gemi would return the next day, that she would drink another cup of warm, sweet tea in beautiful floral china and share more quiet conversation.

ELEVEN

"IT WAS THE ALONENESS THAT STRUCK ME," Gemi said. "I know aloneness. Without my dear British nurse, I likely would never have survived."

"But from what you've told me, this is different," Carolyn said. They were having burritos at their favorite taqueria on Broadway, walking distance from their shared house. Over the years of friendship, Gemi had shared her story with Carolyn. It was told in bits and pieces, like a puzzle that had to be assembled to see the whole. In many ways, Gemi knew, it was Carolyn who had helped her assemble the puzzle of her own life. For that alone, if nothing more, Gemi would always cherish the woman's friendship.

"You were alone, completely alone. You'd lost everyone you loved. This young woman has parents, right?" her friend said, interrupting her thoughts.

"Yes, but what kind of parents vacation in Hawaii while their daughter is in the hospital?"

Again silence fell over their small table as they sat engulfed in the clatter and conversation of the noisy restaurant. Gemi was in a faraway hospital ward surrounded by the pain of others, lost in her own agony. It was a nurse, a gentle nurse old enough to be her own mother, but who could never replace the love of the woman who had given Gemi life and lost her own; this nurse had helped her find reason to live.

"We all must choose," the pale nurse had told her.

"Choose?" Gemi had asked.

"Choose the life we will live. Choose if we will live."

Over time, Gemi had chosen life despite the despair of her many losses.

"Maybe you can be that nurse for Chris," Carolyn said, interrupting her friend's thoughts.

"Perhaps, but she still has her own mother," Gemi said, pulling herself back into the present.

"And you didn't, Gemi. It still breaks my heart to think of all you lost."

They had been shopping together at the open market in Addis Ababa. A weekly ritual. Mother, daughter and granddaughter, for Gemi had her own daughter wrapped tightly on her back with a colorful shawl. Three generations of women, connected, laughing, sharing. Three generations, still young. Her mother had yet to reach forty. Her daughter was less than a year. And then, in that horrible hospital ward, a gentle nurse with a pale face told her that she was alone, totally and completely alone.

"So what has Chris lost?" Gemi asked, more to herself than to Carolyn.

"What is it that causes such pain and loneliness in the lap of luxury, you mean?"

"Indeed," Gemi said.

"I suppose not just anyone stays at Rainier Rehabilitation Center."

"No, it is quite posh. Still, something happened in that girl's life. I'm sure of it. Why would she drop out of the UW in her junior year?"

"Why would she even be at the UW?" Carolyn said, completing her friend's thought. "Sounds like she could have gone to any Ivy League school she chose with that kind of money backing her. But you know what, you'll figure it out. If anyone can reach her, it's you."

"Thank you for that vote of confidence," Gemi said. "It is odd. When I made tea for her today, she said she had no memory of ever having tea, and yet I had this distinct impression that she had indeed a memory, perhaps a fleeting memory, that she could not grasp."

For Gemi, the memories had returned slowly in that far away hospital bed, the images blocked by pain and morphine. The explosion had come first. Then the screams, the blood, the pain. She'd felt herself thrown through the air, her baby torn from her back by a force, a heat too powerful to describe. That was all. She remembered nothing more. It was much later, after her body had healed, that she was able to piece together the events in that market in Addis Ababa during the Red Terror of the seventies, when a military coup took over the country and systematically murdered all political opponents. And it was then that she knew she was indeed alone in the world, for the violence of civil war had taken her entire family, picking them off one-by-one like pop-ups in a hideous carnival sharp-shooting gallery.

Carolyn must have read the look on Gemi's face. Such was the nature of their long friendship. "If I remember right, it's been about thirty years, hasn't it?" she asked.

"Yes," Gemi said, wiping a tear from the corner of her eye.

"And almost twenty of those years you've been a nurse, dedicating your life to helping others, right?"

Gemi only nodded.

"So, I repeat – if anyone can reach this girl, it's you," Carolyn said. Her voice had a tone of finality that made Gemi smile.

"Thank you once again for your vote of confidence, my dear friend."

"Always a pleasure," Carolyn said as she raised her lemonade in a mock toast.

Gemi was reminded of why she cherished this woman's friendship. It wasn't just that she was a wonderful listener or that her positive attitude was infectious, but it was the understanding she'd gleaned from decades of working with immigrants and refugees. Because of her experiences, Carolyn understood the life that had brought Gemi to Seattle in a way that few Americans could fully comprehend.

TWELVE

CHRIS WAS SURPRISED when the package arrived. It had no return name or street address, only a postal box number with a Seattle zip code. For a moment, a very brief moment, she felt a glimmer of excitement that it might be a Christmas gift. But almost as fast as the thought formed, she dismissed it. Her parents didn't send Christmas presents. And there was no one else.

Tearing open the package, she gasped in recognition. A notebook. A bit warped and worn, but she knew immediately that it was hers, and it felt a bit like an old friend had stopped in for a visit. As she flipped through the familiar pages, a small piece of paper floated to her lap. With slow, deliberate movements, she unfolded and read the contents of the brief letter.

Dear Chris,

I know you asked me to leave you alone, and I'll do my best to honor your request. But first, I need to give you this journal that I'm certain is yours. I found it at the site of your accident, and I read only the date and the final entry - just enough to know what I already suspected. There was no accident, was there?

Chris, you're in good hands at Rainier Rehab. I hope with all my heart that you seek the help you need. If you change your mind about seeing me again, please give me a call.

All the Best,

Jake Bowmer

The letter was handwritten in tight, blue script with Jake's address and phone number included after his name.

"Damn him," Chris tore the note into tiny pieces and crumpled the fragments in her angry fist. "Damn, damn, damn. How dare he read my private journal!"

Then she sat in silence, wondering about the legality of suicide and about Jake's decision to mail her the journal instead of turning it over to the police or to her doctor, or even just dropping it in the trash. She fingered the thin spine, grateful to have the physical reminder of her own identity.

THIRTEEN

CHRISTMAS HAD COME AND GONE at Rainier Rehab, but Chris barely noted the festivities. It was only Gemi's visit that she looked forward to each day. Now, it was ten o'clock on a late December morning, and when Gemi pushed open the door to Chris's room, her colorful basket wasn't on her arm. Chris rose from her customary spot on the sofa, steadied herself with the metal walker that stood sentry beside her, and hobbled towards the door.

"Now, look at you, child."

"Isn't it great? The doctor removed my casts yesterday. I'm supposed to be able to walk without this thing pretty soon, but I haven't found my balance yet. Or, maybe they're only walking casts when you just have one."

Chris's spirits soared. For the first time in over a month, she was able to get around on her own without a wheelchair. And, for the first time in longer than she could remember, she had someone with whom she wanted to share her joy. "I'm all set, Gemi. I signed the release papers about an hour ago. I'm ready to go home."

"Okay, child. Now let me see. What do we have to take with us?"

"Only this bag. But I don't think I can carry it. Would you mind?"

Gemi picked up the small bag from the bed. "Let's go, child. My car is right out front. Shall I get you a wheelchair?"

"Not a chance. I'm walking out of this place on my own two feet. Or, to be precise, on my own two casts."

The music of Gemi's melodic laugh filled Chris with joy as she put on the new coat she'd worn only once – the day her mother put her in a cab in front of Harborview Medical Center. Then, Gemi helped her steady herself as she began the long walk to the front exit of Rainier Rehab. As they left the building, Chris paused to drink the air deep into her parched lungs like a desert animal at a rare oasis. A weak sun break in a month of cold rain welcomed Chris back into the world. She smelled the sweet fragrance of damp earth and rain-clean air.

It wasn't a long drive, only long enough for Chris's excitement to melt away. When they crossed the West Seattle Bridge and exited onto Harbor Avenue, she felt the familiar darkness closing in on her. She opened the window and gulped the salt air, remembering the phone conversation she'd had with her mother a few days earlier.

She'd called midmorning hoping to catch her mother as she read the morning paper, before going out for the day. She knew they'd be on Maui. They were always on Maui at Christmas. When she heard her mother's voice, she spoke rapidly, rushing to get the words out. Certain she'd be cut off.

"Thank you for hiring the home healthcare nurse for me, Mother. I'm checking out of Rainier Rehab and going home in a few days."

"Well, you do have a perfectly good condo that your father and I paid for. It's a ridiculous waste of money for you to stay at Rainier. I assume the arrangements with the nurse will be satisfactory. We also took care of your condo fees for the year. We thought that would be a suitable Christmas gift. I hope you appreciate all your father and I do for you, Christine."

"Of course I do, Mother. Thank you. For everything," Chris stammered. Only later would she remind herself that it was her mother that moved her to Rainier Rehab in the first place.

"Your father and I will be here until after the New Year should you find it necessary to contact me again," her mother continued. "Is there anything else, Christine? I have things to do."

"No, Mother. Nothing at all. I just wanted to wish you and Dad a Merry Christmas." Silence. Her mother ended the call without another word.

Now, Chris stared out the car window at the panoramic view of Elliott Bay against the magnificent backdrop of skyscrapers. She looked further to the south where tall orange cranes dotted the skyline as they moved endless shipping containers from cargo trains to freighters and back again. The Port of Seattle never slept.

The sky was a deep Seattle blue, and the water was dotted with tiny whitecaps. The wind was strong and cold, but still the afternoon runners and cyclists were out in their tights and vests. Chris stared at them, her eyes glued to the Alki Beach running path as Gemi drove towards her condo. She brushed the tears from the corners of her eyes.

"You will be back out there, child. Do not give up hope," Gemi said, and she reached over to give Chris's arm a gentle pat.

"I don't know, Gemi. Will I ever be able to run again? Really?" Chris asked as she pushed the memory of the brief phone call into the darkest corners of her mind.

"Of course you will."

Chris turned and rewarded her with a weak, upside down smile. The kind of smile that wasn't really a smile at all.

"That's my building. Right there next to Starbuck's."

Gemi stopped in front of a three-story, cedar-shake building with white window trim and balconies facing Elliott Bay and the downtown Seattle waterfront.

"Wait," Chris said, before Gemi turned off the ignition. "You know what? I don't have a car now." It was as though the realization just hit her. "Why don't you take my spot in the garage? That way you won't be searching for parking every day."

Following Chris's directions, Gemi circled the block, entered a driveway and punched in the code Chris dictated. The heavy metal garage door rolled open, and a few minutes later they came to a stop in Chris's parking space.

"Rest here for a moment, child. Let me get your walker."

Chris watched as Gemi emptied the trunk, placing the metal walker and the new overnight bag as well as her own basket and a few bags of groceries on the pavement next to the passenger door. Then, Gemi opened the door and helped her out of the car.

"Okay, child, lean on me. Steady now."

"What's all this?" Chris asked, as soon as she found her balance.

"Well, child, you haven't been home for some time now, so I assumed we might need to restock your refrigerator. If I'm going to help you get back on that running path, we need to make certain that you eat well."

"Anything will be better than hospital food." Chris grimaced, and they both laughed at the old cliché.

Chris dug in her purse to find the keys she hadn't used since the accident, and they rode the elevator to the top floor in silence. She slow turned the key and pushed open the door, exposing a large living room, dining room and kitchen area. The air was stale, the space dark and cold. Chris hesitated, standing in the doorway, supporting herself with her walker, reluctant to cross back into a life she had tried to end.

"Come along, child, let's open this place up a bit," Gemi said, her voice full of goodwill. "It's been empty for a while, right? It just needs some freshening up."

Chris made her way into the living room, and Gemi breezed past her with the grocery bags in one hand and her woven basket along with Chris's overnight bag in the other. Chris watched her set everything on the kitchen floor and cross the room to open the front drapes. A flood of sunlight brightened the room. Gemi opened the sliding glass door that led to a balcony facing Elliott Bay and within moments a salty, ocean breeze filled the condo.

"Sit down and put your legs up for a few minutes, child. With your permission, I will poke around a bit. Shall I make us a pot of tea?"

"Sure, make yourself at home."

Home was a large, white front room. White walls. White carpeted floors. A simple maple dining table with four matching chairs stood in the dining area. The only living room furniture was a nondescript sofa and coffee table in front of a gas fireplace and a chair – Ikea wood and canvas with a matching ottoman – in the opposite corner with a tiny table to one side. The chair faced the front wall of windows with a panoramic view of downtown Seattle, the water and the running path.

The Alki Beach running path had convinced Chris this was home. A place to watch other runners, the water, the city. A place to lose herself in novels or to write in her journal. The wall behind the chair, on both sides of the fireplace, was lined with built-in maple bookshelves and loaded with books. There were a few black-and-white framed landscapes on the walls, and a couple of runner magazines on the coffee table.

A hall led to the back of the condo—the dark end. There was a bathroom and small bedroom to the left that Chris called a TV/guest room, but no guests ever used it. To the right were the master bedroom and bath. Stark, neat, and clean, the place resembled a high-end hotel suite.

Dazed and tired, Chris sat down in the chair by the front window and stretched her legs out on the ottoman while Gemi opened doors, curtains and windows in every room to get light and air flowing through the stuffy condo.

"That's a lot of cold air. Do you need a sweater, child?"

"I'm fine, thanks. The air feels wonderful." After so much sterile, recirculated institutional air, the saltwater breeze was like a balm to her soul. The view of the sun on the water and the Olympic Mountains in the distance gently soothed her. She must have dozed off.

"Here we are, child. Let's have a treat. I've made a nice pot of tea."

Chris opened her eyes and looked over at the tray set on the coffee table in front of the sofa. It held the small floral teapot and cups that she had come to look forward to every afternoon at Rainier Rehab. There was a plate of cookies and another of sliced fruit and cheese. And there in the corner was a small vase with a single, deep orange Gerbera daisy. Tears overflowed.

"It's so beautiful, Gemi. Thank you."

"Never mind, child. Here let me help you come a bit closer."

Settled together on the sofa, they sat in comfortable silence and watched the gulls over Alki Beach. A buzz sounded in the back of the condo. "That must be the washer. I will be right back." Gemi headed to the laundry area in the back hall to put the bedding and towels into the dryer.

A few hours later there were fresh linens on the bed, towels in the bathroom, and food in the refrigerator. Together they walked through the condo, Gemi making certain that everything Chris might need was within easy reach and reminding her to keep her cell phone close at hand at all times. Before Gemi left for the day, they went to the lobby to get Chris's accumulated mail from the on-site building manager.

"It's good to have you home again, Chris. The wife and I were worried about you. Oh my goodness, but just look at you now. Your mother sent in the association payment. Just a note, nothin' more, sayin' you were in the hospital. You're all paid up for twelve months."

"Thank you, Fred. I'm okay now. This is Gemi. She's going to be coming by to help me out for a while. Please let her into my condo any time," Chris said.

"Nice to meet you, ma'am. We're glad to have Chris back. We were so worried. Every day she was in town, we'd see her go running. Never could understand it, but there she'd go. Then one day, one week, she just wasn't around. Didn't know what to do. Thought about calling the cops, you know. Then the check came with the note from Mrs. Stevens, and we figured it was okay."

"I'm sorry I troubled you," Chris told the stooped old man in workman's overalls, a baseball cap hiding his balding head. "I should've called."

"No problem. Just glad to have you back."

FOURTEEN

PALE LIGHT CREPT INTO THE BEDROOM around the edges of the heavy curtains. Chris opened her eyes and lay for a long time watching the play of shadows on the walls in the silence and solitude. It was the silence she noticed first. The hollow, pervasive silence. For close to six weeks she'd been surrounded by doctors, nurses, physical therapists, and other patients. The solitude was new and strange, but familiar all the same. A blessing and a burden all wrapped up in one neat package. The solitude allowed the loneliness to seep back into Chris's fragile being.

"No," she whispered to the shadows on the walls as she threw her comforter to one side. With a force of will, she swung her walking casts over the side of the bed and sat up. She stood, supporting herself with a hand on a sturdy bedside table. Unwilling to admit she needed her walker, she used the walls to steady herself as she made her way to the bathroom with slow, measured steps.

A brown plastic pharmacy bottle stood on the vanity next to the sink. She fingered the container. Shook it and listened to the rattle of pills inside. The temptation was strong, strong like a bottle of Thunderbird to a drunk, strong like heroin to an addict.

... She sees herself jerk the white plastic top off the brown bottle and dump the pills into her open fist. With her free hand, she fills a water glass. Then, with one big gulp, she downs the fistful of small blue pills.

She wants to go back to bed, climb into her big soft clean bed and go to sleep forever. But it's too much trouble, too much pain. Instead, she throws a pile of fluffy white bath towels onto the bright tile, lowers herself to the floor, and drifts off on a wave of drug-induced euphoria.

Several hours later, Gemi rings the doorbell. After several attempts, she presses another button on the panel.

"Fred? This is Gemi Kemmal speaking. We met just yesterday."

"Sure, I remember you. You're helping our Chris. What can I do for you?"

"Chris is not answering."

Without waiting for her to finish, Fred buzzes Gemi into the building and together they take the elevator to the third floor. Fred unlocks Chris's front door. Calling her name, they search her condo.

It's Gemi who finds Chris's dead body on the bathroom floor ...

Chris stood for several minutes in front of the vanity mirror turning the pill container over and over in her hands, listening to the sound, a bit like that of a baby's rattle. When she glanced up, it was Gemi's face instead of her own in the mirror before her. In the flash of a runner's second, Chris remembered that Gemi would be ringing the doorbell at ten o'clock.

The pill bottle fell to the floor, and Chris dropped to the toilet seat, her face in her hands, sobs shaking her slender shoulders. She heard the plastic bottle roll across the tile floor, the pills clicking against each other in the hollow silence of her empty condo. Again the face appeared in her troubled mind. A broad, smiling, dark face with gentle, loving eyes.

"Gemi," Chris whispered.

Using the protruding toe of one heavy, casted leg, she inched the pill bottle close enough to reach down and grab it. Then she stood, and with careful, deliberate movements, she opened the bottle, dumped the pills into the toilet and flushed away temptation.

She made her way back to the bedroom to claim her walker, then hobbled to the living room and opened the curtains that Gemi had closed before leaving the night before. The sky, the water, the city – all were a soft, Seattle gray. She found the fresh ground coffee that Gemi had brought and made a small pot. A paper filter, a scoop of grounds, water in the container, push the button. Every movement measured, controlled. Nothing wasted.

She leaned against the kitchen counter. Nowhere to go. Nothing to do. Walking hurt more than standing still, so she stood and waited, enjoying the strong, heady aroma as her coffee brewed. "God, I missed this," she murmured to no one.

She filled a large, commuter mug and tightened the lid, thoughts of pills bombarding the recesses of her memory. She stuffed the sealed cup into her bathrobe pocket and shuffled her walker towards the sofa. Her legs propped up on the coffee table, she drew the shopping bag full of accumulated mail close, but she couldn't focus. She stared at the bookshelf in front of her, but it was Beth she saw, Beth and pills. There, stuck among her books, she noticed a collection of old notebooks – her journals. They seemed to call to her, taunting her. Unable to resist, she pulled herself to her feet again.

She made the slow journey back to the bedroom and retrieved the notebook from her bedside table where Gemi had left it the night before when she unpacked the small overnight bag Chris brought home from Rainier Rehab. "Lord, I need a new journal," she said, as she fingered the water-warped pages.

As she hobbled back to the living room, she grabbed a pen from the kitchen counter. Then she collapsed on the sofa, her mind a blank, her eyes full. She saw it all like a movie playing on the backs of her closed eyelids, and she began to write.

It was late fall and already dark enough outside to let you forget that it had been dark, drizzly, gray since the day began. I was sitting on my bed doing homework. Quadratic equations, I remember. God how I hated algebra. Geometry wasn't so bad, but algebra was killing me. Beth poked her head through the door of the bathroom that connected our bedrooms.

Chris stopped and took a deep drink of coffee. As she twirled a dark curl around her index finger, a rare smile played on her lips, a smile of a happier time. She saw her sister's face before her, the smiling face of the older sister she adored. She heard their young voices play in her memory and wrote.

"Hey, Chris, I've got a secret."

"Yeah?"

I'd learned not to show too much enthusiasm. Beth loved to tease me. Whenever I made the mistake of letting her know how badly I wanted in on her secrets, she'd taunt me for hours. I had homework to finish, and I didn't want to play the teasing-pleading game, so I feigned disinterest.

"Hey, this is a good one."

"Yeah?"

I looked up from the meaningless numbers on the page.

"Sorry Beth, I wasn't listening."

I always called her Beth instead of Elizabeth. It drove Mom crazy, but I did it anyway. "I'm buried in old man Patterson's math assignment. The guy's some kind of sadist or something."

"I've got a secret."

"So...?"

I was a model of disinterest, bordering on annoyance.

"Okay, listen. I've decided what to give Damien for his birthday."

She climbed onto my bed. She was carrying a small paper bag, half hidden behind her back. My ears perked up. I was no longer half listening, half pretending, half doing homework. Damien was Beth's boyfriend, had been since he took her to his senior prom. He'd already graduated and was at the University of Washington, but they were still together, still in love. I thought it was great. Mom and Dad didn't think he was good enough for her. How typical. Nothing was ever good enough for them. Not even me.

The pain caused Chris to pause, her pen sliding from her hand. "Not even me," she whispered into the empty room. The pain gripped at her heart. Made her gasp for air. She tried to take deep, calming breaths, but when that didn't work, she reached for her coffee and stared at nothing but the image of her beautiful, older sister forever imprinted on her memory. She had no pictures of Beth on her walls, no frames in her bookcase, unable to face the daily reminder of all she'd lost. She reached for her pen and continued writing.

"Well, finally. What'd you settle on?"

Beth flopped on the bed beside me, the small paper bag clutched in her hand. She unfolded the top of the bag and pulled out a small, rectangular, plastic case. With a dramatic wave of her hand, she snapped open the case to reveal twenty-eight tiny blue pills in neat rows of plastic-coated aluminum foil.

"So you decided he's the one?"

"Yeah. I'm going to do it with him."

"Well, it's about time."

I was full of sixteen-year-old bravado. My birthday wasn't for another month or so, but like most teenagers I was trying to grow up as fast as I could.

"I wanted to be sure. Wanted it to be right. I love him, Chris, and I didn't want to screw it up, you know what I mean"?

"Worried he'll find some college sorority girl, aren't you?"

"I know I can't use sex to keep him, or any guy for that matter, not ever. I'm just ready. God, I'm almost eighteen and still a virgin. I must be a one percenter or something."

"Naw, you're about a fifty-two percenter. I looked it up. It's not like everybody out there is sleeping with somebody. But who cares anyway?"

"Yeah, when it's right, it's right."

"Are you excited?"

"Yeah. And scared too."

"When are you going to tell Damien?"

"His birthday's on Saturday."

"Oh, you naughty, naughty girl."

I shook my finger and did my best Mom mimic. We started giggling. Giggling and tickling and rolling around the bed like we were kids again, little carefree kids.

The buzz of the intercom startled Chris. She staggered to her feet and made her way to the panel by the door to give Gemi access to the building. Then she unlocked the condo door and left it ajar, before she shuffled back to the sofa. There she stuffed her journal and pen into the crack between the sofa cushions.

Fifteen

CHRIS THREW HER JOURNAL across the living room and watched it hit the bookshelves and flutter to the floor. She'd been home for almost a week. Gemi came daily to take care of the shopping and household chores, to make sure she exercised and ate properly, and to take her to physical therapy. Best of all, she made tea and they talked. But today was Sunday. Gemi's day off.

Chris stood and hobbled to the front balcony. She felt like a caged animal desperate for escape. Caged in her own body, unable to move with the graceful ease she'd always known.

"Monday," Gemi had promised. "Monday will be a good day to take your first walk outside."

But Sunday morning Chris was up at seven pacing the living room. Pacing with short, painful steps, pacing with a walker, but pacing just the same. She'd had enough of sitting around watching dust bunnies collect in the corners of her living room. Tired of writing in her journal, of flipping through daytime television, of surfing the web and paging the books and magazines that Gemi brought for her.

She hadn't slept much the night before, and now she couldn't relax, couldn't take her eyes off Elliott Bay. Cold winter sun sparkled on tiny whitecaps. But despite a strong westerly wind, groups of runners assembled, earlier groups already returning. She watched the new arrivals as they got out of their cars and headed towards the miniature Statue of Liberty – the standard meeting place. She watched from her living room as they slapped each other on the back in greeting, as they stretched and waited for others to arrive. Their small group assembled, they were off. A parade of tight bodies clad in vivid Lycra. In an instant, her imagination took her where her body could not.

... She feels the cold wind in her hair and the power in her legs. She fills her lungs and feels the drumming of her heartbeat. She is unstoppable, euphoric, passing one group of runners and then another and another. Weekend warriors. Not serious runners. Not daily distance runners with strength and stamina. Not runners who run for survival, for life itself.

For a brief second, she sees Jake. She feels the pull of his tall, lean body. But she looks away and keeps running. She regulates her breathing. Slow, deep, steady. Air in. Air out. She runs and runs until she runs out of trail to run, and still she runs. She heads south along the coastline leaving the city of Seattle far behind her. She crosses the Columbia River without getting her feet wet and barely notices the rock formations along Cannon Beach. Her feet fly over the sand dunes of the Oregon coast. The vineyards of northern California stain her shoes purple. She runs through the streets of LA, passes the San Diego zoo. The Mexican border looms before her and still she runs, her breathing steady, her legs powerful ...

"I can't stand this," Chris moaned to the suffocating condo walls. "I can't take it a day longer." She headed back to her bedroom, opened her closet doors, and dug around for a pair of Lycra running pants and her favorite Asics. With a bitter laugh, she threw the shoes back in the closet. "Won't be needing those."

She tugged a fleece pullover off a hanger. Pulling on the top was as easy as ever, but it was harder than she expected to put on the pants. She'd been living in T-shirts and loose, cotton boxer shorts. Getting dressed hadn't been an issue.

She opened the ankle zippers, but still she had to tug. The right leg hurt at the femur, the left at the ankle, and neither wanted to bend and push into a pair of long pants no matter how stretchy the fabric. After several unsuccessful struggles, she threw the pants across the room in frustration. She hobbled back to her open closet and dug around until she found a pair of faded, baggy cotton sweats with elastic at the ankles. Opening the drawer of her bedside table, she grabbed a pair of large sewing scissors and cut about six inches off each pant leg. Then she sat on the edge of the bed, bent to the floor, and pushed each walking cast through the proper leg opening. Standing, she pulled up the baggy sweats. It all felt strange, foreign, like someone else's body or someone else's clothes. She wasn't sure which.

She zipped up a fleece-lined windbreaker, grabbed her walker and headed out the door. After a moment's hesitation, she returned to the living room, picked up the journal and pen from the floor and crammed them into an oversized pocket with her wallet. Keys in hand, she left the condo.

Her determination was steadier than her balance. She made her way to the elevator and exited into the empty lobby, pausing for a brief glance at her mailbox. C. Stevens in neat handwritten lettering. She knew it was empty. Gemi picked up her mail every day, and she was still digging through the pile of junk Fred had saved for her. Still, it felt good to see her name there. Proof of existence.

She pushed open the front door of the building like a curious young child venturing into unfamiliar territory. The three front steps were a challenge, but she held tight to the handrail with her right hand and dragged the walker behind her with her left. She stood still and felt the cold, ocean breeze caressing her senses, and the bright sunshine warming her upturned face. Gemi would be upset, she knew it, but she couldn't stop herself. She decided she'd only go as far as Alki Bakery, only one block, certain she could handle that much. Starbuck's, Alki Bakery, Tully's – all in a row with restaurants, fish and chip stands, rollerblade and bicycle rentals and bars stashed between them. In rainy, gray Seattle, there were never too many coffee shops.

She made her way to Alki Bakery wanting desperately to cross the street to the beach side, the running path side. Instead, she tugged the heavy coffee shop door. It had never been heavy before. Now was different, now everything was a struggle, even the simplest task was difficult. The coffee shop was a small place filled by an active Sunday morning crowd. An assortment of tiny café tables lined the sidewalk window with a long view of the water and the downtown skyline. Chris made her way to the counter at the back of the room, her movements measured and painful. The barista looked up as she approached.

"What can I get for you?"

"A cup of English Breakfast tea with cream and sugar, please. And a blueberry scone."

She took Chris's money and said, "Hey, why don't you just get yourself a table, and I'll bring this to you when it's ready."

Chris gave her a grateful smile and made her way through the crowded coffee shop, shuffling her walker in front of her. A man at a window table stood to leave, gesturing Chris to take his place. She collapsed, exhausted, into the chair. She looked at the newspapers scattered around the room, but was too tired to get up and grab one. Instead she sat and stared out the window.

"Here's your tea and scone. I brought some cream, and the sugar packets are right there on the table. Can I get you anything else?"

"Would you mind passing me that newspaper?" she said, pointing to an abandoned *Seattle Times* on an adjacent table.

She sat and read, losing track of time until it caught up with her. She needed to move. She couldn't bear being on the inside looking out a second longer. She got up, steadying herself with a hand on the table. Pain shot through her legs. Determination gripped her with a force that denied all logic. She headed out the door toward the crosswalk. An elderly couple stood waiting to cross. Eyeing the old woman's walker, Chris made a split-second decision.

She took one painful step off the curb and then another, bracing herself on her own walker. She followed the elderly couple across the street and made her way to the first of numerous benches that lined the beach. The sun warmed her cheeks, her heart, her soul. The breeze tousled her curls. She watched the gulls swoop and soar, the children dig in the sand, the runners and walkers pass in front of her. She was home. This was her place. She belonged. But not sitting. She needed to be moving, walking, running. Anything but sitting. She felt wired, desperate to stretch, to run. Impatient anger seized her. She set her watch for five minutes. Five in one direction, five back. She was a runner. Timing herself was something she knew. Then she stood and began a slow, painful walk heading south, away from her building.

Ten minutes later she again sank back onto the same hard, wooden bench. For a long time, she just sat and watched the beach scene unfold in front of her. Then, she took out her journal and tried to scribble her thoughts, her memories, but she couldn't focus. Instead, she just sat and absorbed the beauty around her. She had no idea how long she'd been sitting there when a chill set in, forcing her to her feet despite the pain. She struggled back to her condo and collapsed on the sofa.

Sixteen

CHRIS AWOKE TO THE INSISTENT BUZZING of the intercom. She looked around her, disoriented. She was still on the sofa. Still in the chopped off sweats and polar fleece from the day before. She sat up, but when she tried to stand, red hot fire shot through her legs. She collapsed back onto the sofa. The intercom continued to buzz. In frustration, Chris buried her head in a pillow in a feeble attempt to ignore it. In a few moments, the intercom was followed by the ring of her cell phone. With a sigh of relief, Chris peeked out from under the pillow, grateful that she'd kept her cell close at hand.

"Gemi?" Chris asked.

"Good morning, child."

"Can you buzz Fred to let you in? I can't get up."

"Don't move, child. I will be right there," said Gemi.

A few minutes later there was a rap on the door as the key turned in the lock. Gemi rushed into the room.

"Fred says he saw you leaving the building yesterday morning, but he didn't see you come back. Where did you go, child?"

"Just for a walk," Chris said, her voice that of a disobedient child.

"How much of a walk? Let me look at those legs." Gemi bent over Chris's extended legs. The inflammation above the casts was obvious at first glance. "It was too much, too soon, child. Why did you not wait? I told you we would go out today."

"I was going crazy. I had to get out of here."

"Call me next time."

"It was Sunday."

"Call me, child. Do you hear me?" She turned to the entrance where Fred still stood by the open door, waiting. "Fred, can you help me get her to the bedroom?"

Supported by Gemi on one side and Fred on the other, Chris hobbled into her bedroom and stretched out on the bed.

"Thank you, Fred. We'll be all right now."

"Okay. Let me know if I can help."

"I will," Gemi said, and she walked him to the door.

Relief and gratitude flowed over Chris as she lay on her bed waiting for Gemi to return. She felt safe.

"Now, let's get you out of this interesting pair of pants and see what we can do about all this inflammation. Some massage should get your blood circulating. Then we will get some food into you. When did you last eat, child?"

Chris only shrugged.

It wasn't a comfortable massage. Gemi's expert hands worked the knots in Chris's leg muscles above the casts until they relaxed and her body felt fluid again, unfrozen, unlocked.

"How long were you on that sofa?" Gemi asked.

"It must've been around noon when I went out. I only walked for ten minutes, really. But I sat at Alki Bakery for a while first, and then on one of the benches for a long time. I don't know how long. It was probably early evening when I got back. I must've fallen asleep on the sofa and stayed there all night."

"You gave me quite a scare, child, but you will be fine. Sore for a few days perhaps, but no damage done," Gemi assured her. "I know you want to be out there walking again, and running, too. And you will be. But you must take it slow. Now let's elevate these legs and get some ice on them. "

By the time Gemi left hours later, Chris was again able to hobble around the condo. She was freshly bathed, well fed, and ready to go to bed for the night. Before leaving, Gemi went back into the bedroom.

"I am off now, child. I think you're all set."

"Gemi, thank you. Thanks for all you do. It means so much to me. I'm sorry I scared you today. Here, take this." She handed her a single key.

"I know it is none of my business," Gemi said, as she took the key. "Your mother hired me to care for you. We have never spoken about that. Maybe we should. Is there no one else? Friends or family you can call?" She saw the tears form in Chris's eyes, and she stopped.

"I've always been alone," Chris stammered. "There's nobody." She closed her eyes and turned away.

"Okay, child, good night then. Sleep now. I will see you in the morning. And thank you for trusting me with your key."

"Could you do me one more favor before you leave?"

"Of course, child. What do you need?"

"In the pocket of the jacket I was wearing yesterday, there's a small notebook. Could you get it for me, please? And the pen?"

A moment later, Gemi returned with the journal and a pen. Handing them to Chris, she asked, "And what is this, child?"

"Just a journal."

"Do you write every day?"

"Almost. Sometimes more than once a day. Lately, I've had lots of time to write."

After Gemi left, Chris lay wide awake, remembering a time when running was her life, a time when she had someone to share her pain and her joy. Finally, unable to sleep, she switched on the light and sat up in bed. Relaxing into her pillows, she began to write the memories that had flooded her as she sat at the beach the day before.

> *School was out on a warm, spring afternoon. Let me see. It must've been 1996. I was still at Madison Middle School. I promised Beth I'd meet her on the street in front of the school as soon as the last bell rang. She was already there as I ran down the front steps, sitting behind the wheel of her brand new Jetta – a sixteenth birthday gift from Mom and Dad. The stereo was cranked, the windows low. It felt great to climb into that car with the whole school standing and gawking at us.*

> *Beth's long brown hair was smoothed back and fastened in a loose ponytail. She was wearing running shorts and running shoes.*

> *"How'd you get changed so fast?"*

I was still fastening my safety belt when she pulled from the curb.

"I get out earlier, remember? One of the few perks of high school."

"Lucky you. Where am I going to change?"

"Right here, I guess."

"No way."

"Yes way. I'll drive down the Indian Trail. There's never anybody there. At least not at this time of the day. Just slip off your jeans and put on your shorts."

And I did. I always did what Beth told me to do. She was zany and crazy and fun, but she was also smart and cautious when she needed to be. I knew she'd never steer me wrong.

Chris stopped, the wave of memories too intense to keep writing. She put the pen and journal aside, took a drink of water and turned off the light. Settling into the comfort of her bed, she willed herself to sleep. But it didn't work. The memories had surfaced and were demanding attention. She could no more stop them than she could stop the tides on Alki Beach. She turned the light back on, grabbed the notebook, and continued to pour her soul onto paper.

By the time we reached Alki, I was ready. Beth was on the high school track team. She wasn't that great and didn't even like it that much, but she was always worried about putting on a few pounds and figured running was an easy way to control her weight. Besides it was another extra-curricular to add to her college applications. And then there was the lure of Alki Beach – teen heaven with beach volleyball in the afternoons and fire pits in the evenings. It was the place to see and be seen.

After circling a few blocks to find a spot, Beth parallel parked like a pro. Then she turned and looked me in the eye, the serious-Beth look.

"Okay, we'll start at a slow, steady pace and go for thirty minutes. I'll set my watch. If I'm going too fast, if you're having trouble

breathing or keeping up, just tell me, and we'll slow down or cut it short. Sound okay?"

"Sure, I guess."

It was the first time I'd ever gone running, with or without Beth, and I was excited. We took off along the Alki running path without bothering with any warm-up stretches. As the salt air filled my lungs, I felt an exhilaration I'd never experienced before. The air ruffled my hair and tickled my skin. I felt the muscles in my thighs and calves warm and relax into a steady rhythm. It was wonderful.

After a while, I noticed Beth's labored breathing as she pounded the pavement beside me, and I realized that I was having no trouble keeping up with her. She realized it, too, and gave me a thumbs-up and a huge Beth grin, too winded to say anything. She was never one of those sisters who had to be better at everything.

When her watch buzzed, we slowed to a walk.

"You're amazing. You're not even winded."

I remember gushing about how fantastic it was. I bragged I could just keep going and going. That's when she started calling me the Energizer bunny and told me she'd ask Coach James if I could join the track team the following year.

SEVENTEEN

EXHAUSTED AFTER A RESTLESS NIGHT, Chris struggled awake, reluctant to start her day. It was an early surgery. Gemi would arrive at half past six to take her to Harborview. Pushing her legs to the edge of her bed, she stood.

She was scheduled for an early morning procedure to remove the heavy white walking casts as well as the hardware that Dr. Anderson had inserted into her legs to stabilize the bones and insure proper healing. Hardware. It sounded a bit too much like building supplies.

She pulled on the pair of old sweats that she'd cut off just below the knees and hobbled to the bathroom. When she heard the doorbell a half hour later, she was ready to go.

The drive to Harborview was silent. The staging area, that's how she thought of it, like a staging area before a marathon, was full of gurneys and patients, fear painted on their faces and needles stuck in their arms. No upbeat, Lycra-clad athletes here. Like her, each of them was waiting for a surgeon, an anesthesiologist, the blessed escape. It was pain that Chris feared most. She remembered the pain that gripped her body when she awoke from surgery, the pain that returned when she went off the morphine drip, and the pain of putting weight on her legs, of learning to walk again.

Pre-op smelled of fear and antiseptics, dimly lit in a feeble attempt to help patients relax. Chris lay on a wheeled gurney, dressed in a pale green hospital gown with her head in a surgical shower cap. She was cold. Even the second blanket a nurse put over her couldn't stop her teeth from chattering. Nurses came and went, busy with their pre-surgical activities, the latest leaving an IV needle taped in Chris's left arm.

"Good morning, Chris. Are you set to go?" It was Dr. Anderson with his friendly smile, his air of calm and confidence.

"I'm scared," Chris whispered.

"You've been through a lot, but this is nothing. We'll have you in and out before you know it, and you'll be walking home."

"Walking?"

"Absolutely. The doctor here is going to give you something to sleep now," he said, his hand on the shoulder of the anesthesiologist. "You'll only be asleep for about twenty minutes. I'll cut off those casts, remove the hardware, and you'll be walking out of here."

"Walking?" Chris asked again.

"Yes, walking," Dr. Anderson assured her. "On your own two feet. No casts, no walker, no crutches."

"But how are you taking the hardware out?"

"I'll just make a tiny incision. Probably won't even need stitches. Just a couple of butterfly bandages."

Tears of panic filled her eyes. "Will it hurt when I wake up like it did last time?"

"No," the surgeon said. "After the accident, you were in pretty bad shape. Now you're healed. You'll be fine. This is going to be a breeze. The easiest thing you've done since the accident." With a slight nod towards the anesthesiologist, he turned back to Chris. "Dr. Quintana is giving you something to relax now. I'll see you later, okay?"

"But there was no accident," she whispered as she drifted off into an oblivion of Pacific clouds, of Alki fog, of beautiful Seattle gray. Again, no one heard her.

Gemi sat on a hard, straight-backed chair positioned between the pea green wall and what looked like a minimalist recliner. Cocooned by a floral curtain hanging from a semi-circle metal rod overhead, Gemi and Chris were separated from the other patients in post-op. Chris half-sat, half-reclined with her legs stretched out in front of her, her eyes closed, her breathing slow and gentle. Gemi knew she would feel no pain when she awoke, only a raw scratchiness in her throat. She'd also come to suspect that Chris suffered a greater malady that no surgeon could alleviate, a secret that was eating her up inside.

Gemi didn't know the whole story, didn't understand why her employer wasn't at the hospital that morning with her daughter. But she knew there was a story. She reminded herself to be patient, knowing Chris would speak, would open to her, only when ready.

As she sat and watched Chris stir under the fading influence of anesthesia, she remembered her own return to the world, awakening to the clear blue eyes of that kind British nurse so very long ago. The gentle face so close to her own, she thought she was seeing an angel in the afterlife. Such a clash of memories: loss, pain, loneliness, love, hope, joy. How could she help this young woman find and understand her own mess of feelings?

Gemi saw Chris opened her eyes, saw the flash of confusion, then panic. "Here, child, suck on this," she said, slipping a tiny ice chip between her lips. "There, now. The worst is over."

"Really? Over?" Chris said, her voice hoarse.

"Yes, child," Gemi assured her. "It's over."

"Are they gone?"

"The casts and hardware? Take a look for yourself. All you have now is pale, wrinkly skin that needs some good sunshine." She reached down and lifted the soft blanket to reveal Chris's bare legs. A tiny gasp escaped Chris's lips. "The scars? Do not worry about those, child. With a little sun and exercise, they will disappear in time."

Chris closed her eyes with a small sigh and sucked on the ice chip. A hint of the upside-down smile that Gemi had come to know formed on her lips.

"Are you thinking of Alki, child?"

"Yes," she whispered.

"You will be there soon. Very soon." But Gemi saw the shadow pass over Chris's face, and she knew that it would not be so easy. She suspected that Chris's thoughts had already shifted. They were already someplace else, someplace Chris would rather not be.

Chris walked out of the hospital on her own two feet, just as Dr. Anderson had promised her she would. It was a slow walk, but a walk without casts or crutches, and she was thrilled. Still, when she got back to her condo, when Gemi had left and she was alone, the memories hit her full force.

They never wanted me. They still don't want me. Mom didn't even bother to come to the hospital today. Sure they're in Hawaii, but how convenient. Beth was the only one who cared about me, who really wanted me. Lord, I'm pathetic. Always a disappointment, a mistake, a blot in Mom and Dad's perfect world. I was just in the way, extra, superfluous.

I think they probably tried to love me. But love can't be forced. It can't be created where it doesn't naturally exist, and it doesn't grow where it isn't nurtured. Love is like cooking, I suppose. Some people are just born good cooks. They love food, love to cook, and have an innate sense about what works and what doesn't. Others can read a dozen cookbooks, take cooking classes, and maybe learn to put together a few good meals, but they're never at home in the kitchen. Their hearts are elsewhere. That's how it's always been with Mom and Dad's love. But why? Why couldn't they love me like they loved Beth? What was wrong, what is so very wrong with me?

Chris stood and got herself a tall glass of water, so lost in memory she wasn't aware of what she was doing. As if in a dream, she returned to her chair and continued writing.

I must have been about four. I was coming in the back door. It was springtime and the back garden was bright with sunlight and vibrant with new color. I hid under the bushes and played quiet games every chance I got. But I was hungry. Dinnertime was approaching, so I headed into the kitchen to see what I could find. That's when I heard them talking in the dining room.

"Look, I'm sorry, really sorry, you didn't get what you wanted. But you know what, she's your kid too, so you could at least try to be a decent father. You don't even look at her."

"Don't give me that shit again, Ellen. You're just as damn disappointed as I am. Neither one of us thought we'd have to deal with a constant reminder."

I slipped back outside and hid behind the bushes. I can see that little girl in the shadows of the rhododendrons trembling with arms wrapped tightly around knees. I willed myself not to cry and waited until I heard Mother call Beth for dinner before I went inside.

But what? A constant reminder of what? What did I remind them of that was so very terrible that they couldn't love me. Oh hell, maybe I'm just remembering it all wrong.

Awakening

EIGHTEEN

"WAIT FOR ME, CHILD. You're getting so fast, I'm having trouble keeping up with you these days." Gemi followed Chris down the hall to the elevator wondering why the girl was in such a hurry.

"Come on, Gemi. These walks are good for both of us."

"You're absolutely right. Since your accident, I've lost five pounds. It's as though I'm in training. I should be paying your mother instead of the other way around." She chattered her way out of the elevator and through the lobby, so busy zipping her jacket and putting on gloves, she didn't notice the wash of tears in Chris's eyes.

They crossed Alki Avenue to the sidewalk and began their walk along Elliott Bay. Chris was unusually quiet, even for her. They walked in silence until Gemi said, "That's probably far enough, child. It's the farthest we've come since the accident."

Chris turned and began to walk back the way they had come without a word.

"Why so quiet?" Gemi said. "I expect some teasing. Or, at the very least, some encouragement for this chubby, old body."

Still Chris remained silent.

"What is it, child?" Gemi insisted. "Don't worry, your strength will return. I just don't want you to overdo it again and end up back in bed."

"No, that's not it. I'm sorry, Gemi. You've been so good to me, and I'm such a liar."

"Liar?"

"Yeah, I'm a liar. I'm worse than that. I don't deserve you. I don't deserve to be alive."

"Wait one moment, child. Nobody *deserves* that kind of talk. Come over here and sit down." She put a hand on Chris's arm and pulled her to one of the wooden benches lining the sidewalk. "Now tell me what's on your mind."

There was a long, painful pause before Chris spoke again. Then, as though her frustration got the better of her, she blurted out, "The accident, the so-called accident."

"What about it? It was horrible. You're lucky to be alive. You'll probably have nightmares about it for a very long time." Gemi paused. Then she turned to face Chris sitting beside her and looked into her eyes. "Wait just a moment, child. I'm not listening to you. What did you mean by 'so-called accident'?"

Again Chris remained silent, lost in thought. Gemi waited. On the sidewalk in front of them a little girl with wild, black curls and hot pink rubber boots squealed in delight as gulls flocked around her, greedy for the breadcrumbs her young, curly-headed mother scattered on the pavement in front of them. The mother and daughter held hands and laughed. Then, the mother whispered something in the child's ear and together they walked away.

"Come on, child," Gemi urged in a gentle whisper. "Talk to me."

"It was a horrible night, a horrible time, a horrible life. I don't know where to begin."

"Begin with the accident."

"That's just it, Gemi. There was no accident. I did it on purpose. I accelerated. I turned the wheel. I wanted to die. It was my birthday. I wanted to die on my birthday like Beth. Why didn't I just die?"

The sobs came in an uncontrollable torrent. Gemi slid closer and wrapped Chris in her arms. She held her tight and, again, she waited. When Chris's shoulders stopped trembling and her ragged sobs turned to sniffles, Gemi reached in her coat pocket and pulled out a plastic packet of tissues.

"Here you go, child."

Chris took one, as compliant as the young girl feeding the gulls. She wiped her red eyes and blew her nose. "I'm sorry. You're not being paid enough for this. If I know my mother as well as I think I do, you're not getting paid enough at all."

"Forget that, you hear. Forget that and talk to me, child."

"I don't know what to tell you."

"Can you tell me what happened that night?"

"There's nothing to tell. It wasn't an accident. I did it on purpose."

"Okay, but something mighty awful must have happened that night for you to want to end your life."

"Nothing any different from any other day," Chris said. "All the days just ran together. All the same. That day was no different. It was just an accumulation of loneliness and bad memories, I guess." She stopped and sat silent, lost in thought, a shadow over her beautiful, young face. Gemi longed to be able to make her feel better, to take away her pain.

"The accident was during rush hour, wasn't it?" Gemi asked. She winced at the sharp look Chris shot at her, but to her relief, Chris responded with what seemed to be new-found calm.

"Yes," she said in a voice so soft it was lost in the call of the gulls swarming overhead. Gemi leaned closer to listen. "I was driving home from the airport. I was a flight attendant, you know." Gemi only nodded. "I remember the rain. The lights and the rain. And I remember thinking about my condo. I dreaded going back to that empty condo and the weekend ahead. It was so depressing. I'd thought about doing it before, you know, about ending it all. It had become almost a game. A sort of what-if game. What if I stepped in front of that bus? What if I jumped off the Aurora Bridge? But it wasn't a game, not really, and it was driving me crazy. There was always somebody else to think about, to worry about. I didn't want to hurt anybody. I didn't even want to involve anybody else. As I came over that big hill on 35th Avenue, I saw the totem pole, and I knew the golf course spread out below even though I couldn't really see it in the dark. You know the spot, don't you Gemi?" she asked, her voice anxious with the need to be understood.

"Yes, child, I know the place," Gemi said, her voice soft and reassuring.

"I remember thinking about my father, about all the weekends he spent on the golf course. All the weekends I was left alone after Beth's death; my mother off to who knows where. I never knew where she was. And then, I don't know what happened. Not really. I guess I just pulled the wheel to the right. That's all I remember."

Her confession made, Chris sank into Gemi's gentle arms. They sat in silence for a long time as Gemi stroked Chris's back remembering that long-ago feeling of stroking the tiny back of her own infant daughter. "Why were you so alone, child? Had you no friends?"

"Beth was my best friend."

"Can you tell me about her?"

"She was my only sister."

The echo of pain in Chris's voice stopped Gemi cold. They sat in silence as gentle waves lapped the shore and gulls cried overhead. They huddled together as though Gemi were sheltering Chris from a storm. Chris leaned tight into Gemi's embrace. For a brief moment, Gemi wondered what they must look like to the many strangers walking, jogging, biking and boarding past them – a middle-aged African woman wearing a traditional Muslim headscarf, her arms wrapped tightly around a slender white American woman half her age. They both faced the gray sky that hung low over Elliott Bay.

It was Gemi who, again, spoke first. She began in a voice of cream and honey, remaining motionless and speaking without shifting her embrace. "I know someone who might be able to help you sort this out, child. He's a mental health therapist I've worked with in the past, and he's very good."

"A therapist?" Chris asked, sitting up abruptly, pulling away to turn and face Gemi. "Do you think I'm crazy?"

"No, child, I do not think you're crazy. But you were suicidal and possibly depressed. You said so yourself, didn't you?" Chris only nodded. "You might benefit from talking with someone."

"But I can talk with you, Gemi."

"You know I love talking with you, child, and I will always be available when you need me. But I am not a trained therapist and, frankly, I'm too emotionally involved to give you the right kind of guidance. You might also want to see a professional. It sounds like maybe there are some issues from your childhood that need some attention, don't you think?"

"I suppose," Chris said.

"Don't worry. You'll like Peter Bentley. He's a good man. Now, let's start back before we catch a chill sitting here, and I'll get the phone number you need."

Slowly they stood and stretched before beginning their slow walk home. After a few minutes, Chris spoke. "But Gemi, where's his office? How will I get there?"

"Well, child, I may just have to be your chauffer for a bit longer. What do you say to that?" Gemi watched as a smile spread across Chris's face, and she knew she said the words Chris needed to hear.

When they arrived back at the condo, Gemi dug in the large basket that was always on her arm when she arrived at Chris's condo. She extracted a business card and handed it to Chris. "Shall we call now and set up an appointment, child?"

"Now?" Chris hesitated.

"Now." Gemi handed her the phone and watched as Chris punched in Peter Bentley's numbers with trembling fingers.

Twilight settled like a soft blanket over the city as Gemi left the home of her final patient of the day. An elderly widow in her late eighties, Mrs. Anderson was determined to stay in the home she'd shared with her husband of fifty-three years, despite her children's preference that she be moved into an assisted-living facility. It was that fortitude that endeared her to Gemi and fed her own decision to do all she could to help her stay in the home she loved. As on most evenings, she made certain that Mrs. Anderson ate a healthy dinner while she took care of a bit of light housework. Then she helped her bathe and prepare for bed before wishing her a good evening.

Her work for the day complete, Gemi climbed into her car, ready to head home. Before turning the ignition key, she remembered the call she'd wanted to make since leaving Chris's condo earlier in the busy day. She found Peter Bentley's number on her speed-dial, smiling with the memory of their first meeting years before when she signed up for a workshop he was offering on geriatric mental health through the University of Washington. She was already a registered nurse and didn't need any more continuing education credits, but the description fascinated her, so she went ahead and signed up for the workshop. It was a decision she never regretted. Since that first day, she and Peter had formed a close working relationship, sharing patients and comfort through the years.

After only a few rings, Gemi responded to her friend's warm greeting. "Hello, Peter. It's Gemi."

"Hi, Gemi. I was expecting a call from you this evening. Another referral for me today, huh? What's that all about?"

"That's why I called, Peter, to thank you for working Chris into your schedule for tomorrow. I know you're usually booked quite tight."

"No problem, Gemi. I assumed it was important or you wouldn't have been hovering in the background coaxing her when she called."

Gemi could hear the smile in her friend's voice and laughed. Then in a more serious tone, she said, "It is important, Peter. And she's a very special young woman." Gemi wanted to tell him more. Wanted to tell about Chris's confession that afternoon and her own concerns about a possible repeat attempt. Wanted to tell him about the empty pill containers she'd found the day after Chris returned to her condo and the suspicions that had stemmed from that discovery, but she said nothing. They both respected the confidentiality of their shared patients.

"Okay, Gemi. Thanks for the referral and the heads up. I'll do my best."

"No doubt," Gemi laughed softly. "I would expect nothing less."

That same evening, Chris slumped in her chair by the front window, exhausted more from emotion than exercise. Her soul relieved of its secret, a glimmer of hope began to form in her heart. She had an appointment with a therapist, someone Gemi knew and recommended. For the first time in years, Chris allowed herself to sink into the memories of her sixteenth birthday, that horrible, horrific day she tried so hard to forget.

She was sixteen years old again, and all the pain, so carefully locked away, flooded over her like a tidal wave. She gave herself to the pain. Sliding from the chair, she dropped to the floor and rolled into a fetal position, hugging herself, and letting the tears flow.

With time, calm returned. As if in a dream, she crawled to her feet and took her rain warped journal and pen from the coffee table and began to write.

I should've gone with her. But she wouldn't give me a ride after school that day. She told me to go running without her, said she had a special errand to run. I knew from the twinkle in her eye that it had something to do with my birthday. Usually I'd beg her to take me with her, but not that day. I wanted a birthday surprise, so I let her go alone. I should've gone with her. I would've died with her and not be sitting here crying on to paper.

Chris paused, lost in memory and pain. Then, she began again, facing the horror of the day she wanted to forget. The day she would never forget, etched as it was in minute detail on the fabric of her brain.

It was a dreary, drizzly gray afternoon that had turned pitch dark by five. It was about six o'clock. I was wet and tired from a long run and wanted to jump into a hot shower before getting something to eat. I figured I had about an hour before Beth would get home. She told me she'd be late, so I just assumed I'd have the place to myself until she got there. Our parents wouldn't be around. They never were. It was my sixteenth birthday. I knew they wouldn't remember, but Beth already had. I couldn't wait to see her, to tell her about my run, to see what kind of birthday surprise she had in store for me.

As I approached the house, I stopped in my tracks. Cars filled the driveway. Mom's, Dad's, and two others. Cars I didn't recognize. I knew something was wrong. I felt it, a shiver climbing my spine. Something was horribly wrong.

Chris shook the shiver from her spine. "What's wrong is me," she moaned to the walls. "I can't do this. Not yet. Not today." As the sun sank late on the horizon, Chris sat in silence, unable to ink another word on paper.

NINETEEN

IT WAS MID-AFTERNOON when Gemi stopped at the curb in front of a large, craftsman home in pale blue with welcoming white shutters. Capitol Hill. An area popular with homeless runaways, drug dealers, community college students, and more recently, a growing community of Ethiopian refugees. Gemi's small apartment was only blocks away, though she'd chosen the location long before.

Chris climbed out of the passenger seat and made her way up the short flight of steps to the panel of doorbells beside the front door, the first indication that this beautiful old house was no longer anyone's home. She found Peter Bentley's name in tiny, neat print and pressed the button next to it. At the click of the front door lock, she turned to give Gemi a quick wave good-bye and pushed her way inside. She found herself in a small entry with two doors to the right and a straight, steep stairway leading to the second floor in front of her. Unsure, she paused for a second wondering which way to go. A door opened at the top of the stairs and a tall, slightly stooped man with Einstein hair, wire-rimmed glasses and running shoes stood above her.

"Chris Stevens, I presume," he said.

"Peter Bentley?" she asked.

"Yes."

"Oh, crap! Stairs. Wouldn't you know it?" she muttered as she began the long, painful climb up to his office. Although she walked daily now, it still took a force of will, especially to climb a steep, narrow stairwell in a converted old house. She grabbed a tight hold on the utilitarian banister and with the help of her upper body strength, she started climbing one step at a time.

"I'm sorry," Peter Bentley said as she neared the top. "I didn't know the stairs would be a challenge."

"Only one of many."

"Still, I should've mentioned them on the phone." He paused as though lost in thought as Chris finished her slow climb. Then, offering his hand for a formal introduction, he said, "I'm Peter Bentley. It's a pleasure to meet you. And I do apologize about the stairs."

"Six months ago it wouldn't have mattered."

"But now it does."

"I suppose," she said. "Bentley? Like the car?"

"Yup."

"My father has one."

"Come in," Peter Bentley said.

As Chris stood in the office doorway, the warmth and comfort seemed to draw her forward. Entering the room at the top of the stairs was a bit like meeting bright sunlight at the end of a long tunnel. The walls were a warm Tuscan yellow, and a bank of windows on the west wall flooded the large, airy room with light. The floor was bare, polished hardwood with a bright Gabbeh rug in the center that anchored a heavy rattan loveseat with soft cushions and matching chairs. At the far end of the room stood a simple desk with an open laptop, a phone and a gooseneck lamp. Several large plants softened the corners of the room, and quiet jazz filled the silence.

Chris walked across the room to stand before the wide windows and stared across Elliot Bay to the West Seattle peninsula on the other side. "Nice view," she said in a quiet whisper.

"It keeps me grounded," Peter agreed. "Would you like to take a seat?"

Chris turned towards the loveseat. "I can't lie down on this."

"Do you want to lie down?"

"I thought that's what people did at a shrink's office."

Bentley only smiled at the old cliché, deep laugh lines creasing his wise face, as Chris sat down facing the windows.

"When we spoke on the phone, you mentioned that Gemi Kemmal suggested you see me. Would you like to start there?"

"I guess," Chris said, shifting in her discomfort. She met the therapist's eyes for the first time. They were the kind of eyes that made it easy to speak, eyes that were free of judgment and full of compassion. "I thought I could just talk to her, but she thought I should see a professional. So here we are."

"Why do you think she suggested a professional therapist?"

Chris was quiet for several long minutes before she trusted her voice to speak again. "I suppose," she whispered. "I suppose, she cares." From her spot on the loveseat, she felt afloat on the heavy rain clouds blowing down from the north, blotting out the fragile winter sun. She wondered how many runners were out at Alki.

"Chris, you're far away. Where are you?"

"Oh, sorry."

"No, it's okay. Tell me. What were you just thinking about?"

"Runners. Running Alki."

"Are you a runner?"

"I was. Before this." She nodded towards her legs.

"Once a runner, always a runner. You'll run again."

Chris looked at this tall man with long, bony legs and rounded shoulders. She looked into his eyes and saw truth.

"So, Chris. Tell me what brought you here and up those horrible stairs."

"Bentley... Can I call you Bentley?"

"Sure. Did you say your father has a Bentley?"

"Yeah. That's one of his cars. He'd have a fit if he knew I were here."

"So your dad doesn't believe in counseling, I take it?"

"Nope, it's like, if you can't handle your problems yourself, you're just too weak."

"Do you agree with that philosophy?"

"Well, I'm here, so I guess not."

"Okay, so now that you're here, what can I do for you?"

"I don't know. Help me sleep at night. Fix my legs. Take away the pain. Convince me life's worth living."

"Tell me about your legs."

"I was in a crash."

"When? How did it happen?"

"Two months ago." Chris paused, then added, "Gemi tells me I need to face the truth."

"So what's the truth?"

"The cops say I lost control of my vehicle. Who knows what my parents are telling people."

"What do you say?"

Chris stared out the window at the remnants of winter sunlight glistening on the waters far below as tears overflowed and rolled down her face. Bentley offered her a tissue box and urged her to continue.

"Tell me about the accident, Chris."

"There was no accident." Bentley arched his left eye brow, but didn't say a word. "I did it on purpose. I turned the wheel."

"Can you tell me why?"

"I was tired."

"Tired?"

"Tired of living, of life, of work. Tired of the pain. I wanted it to stop. I didn't want to live anymore. Sometimes I still don't. Why didn't they just leave me alone and let me die like Beth?"

"Beth?"

"My sister."

"Tell me about her."

"She was a year and a half older than me. My best friend, the only person in the world who loved me. She knew our parents didn't want me even before I knew it. She was my friend, my ally, my protector. She taught me to run. She was everything to me."

"What happened?"

"She was driving home and a drunk in an SUV ran a stop and plowed into her. She was killed instantly."

"I'm so sorry."

"Yeah. Eleven years ago. You'd think I'd be over it by now."

"Not always. These things don't just go away. They take time, and they take work."

"Work? What do you mean?"

"I mean we have to face our pain. Meet it head-on. Shake its hand and introduce ourselves. Once we do that, we can start working through it. Pain never just goes away. Were you thinking of Beth the day of your accident that wasn't an accident? The day you turned the wheel?"

"It was my birthday."

"The day of the accident?"

Chris just nodded.

"Can you tell me what happened?"

"It was dark, early evening. Raining hard. Traffic was horrible. I was driving home from the airport. I'm – well, I was – a flight attendant. I just got in from D.C. I live down on Alki. I was driving north along 35th Avenue. Do you know that steep hill above the totem pole and the golf course?"

Bentley nodded his head. "I know it."

"I accelerated and jerked the wheel to the right. I don't remember much after that. Only the pain. Later. When I woke up and realized I was still alive. That's when the pain was unbearable. They wouldn't leave me alone. They wouldn't let me go." She buried her face in her hands, hunched her shoulders, and pulled inward like a child in the womb.

"Chris, can you remember what was going through your head that night as you were driving home?"

"Why? Why do I have to think about that? I don't want to."

Bentley was silent for a moment, then redirecting the conversation, he said, "You mentioned you're a runner."

"Was," Chris snapped, bitterness contorting her features, the physical bruising all but gone. Only the very short curls a visible reminder of the surgery she endured.

"Did you run a lot before the accident?"

"Every day for at least an hour."

"Wow. I'm impressed."

"Do you run?" She pointed to his worn running shoes.

"Yup. All my life. Now only a mile or so a day. But I still get out there."

"Lucky."

"Why do you run?" Chris gave him a sharp look. "Okay, why did you run?"

"To keep my sanity. I guess I'm screwed now."

"Not necessarily. Did you go running the day your sister died?"

Chris stood and walked to the window, rubbing her hands through her hair as though she were trying to clear the cobwebs from her memory. She stared in silence at the Olympic mountain range in the distance. The movement of the clouds. She turned back to the warm yellow room and spoke with resolve. "It was another cold, wet day in November, just like the day I drove off the hill. I got home wet and tired, ready to strip off my running clothes and jump into a hot shower. I didn't expect anybody to be there. Beth said she'd be late and our folks were never around."

She hesitated as the evening played in her mind as if it had been the week before. "When I got to the house, there were like three or four cars in the driveway. At first I thought maybe it was some kind of birthday surprise for me, but Beth's car wasn't there, so I pushed that idea away as fast as it popped into my head."

"Why?"

"Because I knew they'd never have a party for me."

"They?"

"My parents."

"Okay, go on."

"I went into the house and looked in the living room. It was like I didn't know what to expect, but something told me it wasn't good. There were three strangers with my parents. My dad was standing in front of the fireplace with two men, and another person, a woman, was sitting on the sofa with my mother. She was crying and this stranger was patting her arm. That's what really hit me, you know, that stranger touching my mom. Nobody ever touched my mother."

"What did you do?"

"They didn't see me, so for a while I just stood by the door watching. Then I heard one of the men ask if someone was having a birthday. My parents didn't say a word. They just stared at each other with this dumb, shocked look on their faces. So, I walked into the room and told the man that it was my birthday, and he handed me this crumpled gift with a torn red ribbon on top and said, 'I guess this must be for you.' Then my mom started wailing. I rushed to the sofa and tried to pat her shoulder like I'd seen the woman doing, but she pushed me away and started screaming at me."

Chris stopped. She felt as though she couldn't push the words out of her body.

"What did she say, Chris?" Peter asked, pulling her back. "What were the words you remember?"

"It's all your fault," Chris whispered. "That's what my mother said. She kept repeating it over and over, but I still didn't even know what she was talking about. I asked my dad what was going on, but he just turned away. I started screaming at the other faces, begging them to tell me what was going on. Finally, after what seemed like forever, the man who had given me that pathetic birthday present stepped towards me and asked me my name. I told him who I was and asked him where Beth was. That's when I knew. Even before he said the words, I knew I'd never see Beth again."

For several minutes they sat in silence, listening to the gentle strains of soft jazz that seemed to float through the air.

Peter broke the silence. "Good job, Chris. That's how you begin the work. Unfortunately, we need to stop for today. I've enjoyed meeting you, and I'd like to work with you if that's something you want. What do you think?"

"I guess so."

"And the stairs?"

"I can handle them."

"Okay then. Is this a good day and time for you?"

"Sure."

"Before you go, I have something for you." He stood and walked to the small bookcase next to his desk. Chris watched as he took a small notebook from a stack.

"Here. Take this home with you and try to write as much as you can."

"You mean like this?" Chris asked as she reached into her backpack for her tattered notebook.

"You're a writer?"

"I kept a journal when I was a girl. I used to write short stories and try to illustrate them," she said. "When I graduated from high school, I started the creative writing program at the U, but I dropped out. I sort of stopped writing then, except my journal now and then."

"Are you writing about any of this? Any of what we've talked about today?"

"Only a little. I just started writing more when I was at Rainier Rehab. Nothing else to do, I guess."

"That's good. Keep at it. Write it all. All that you remember. All that hurts." Crossing the room, he handed her the new notebook. "Here, looks like you could use a new one."

"Yeah, I guess so. Thanks. It feels good to write. Kind of a substitute for running, I suppose. Helps keep the sanity," she added, the hint of a grin tickling the corners of her mouth.

"We gotta hold onto it however we can, right?" Bentley said, his smile broad and warm. "Until next week then." He shook her hand and watched as she made her way down the steep staircase, one slow step at a time.

TWENTY

LATE THAT AFTERNOON, after Gemi had dropped Chris off at her condo and left, Chris stashed her old rain-warped journal in that special spot in the bookcase that held her collection and settled into her chair with the new notebook Bentley had given her. She sat deep in her chair and began to write. Her pen flew across the pages. She wrote until her hand was sore, her wrist limp and her tears dry. She wrote her heart, her soul and her blood. She wrote for herself and for Beth. She was sixteen years old. The pain was fresh and raw. She wrote because she had to write.

"What do you think you're doing in here? This isn't your room."

It took me a few minutes to put the pieces together. Beth was dead. It hit me full force in the stomach. I ran to the bathroom that connected our bedrooms and vomited bile from my empty stomach. Stumbling back to Beth's bedroom, I flopped on her bed. Mom was still there, waiting for me.

"Just what do you think you're doing in here? Get off that bed and out of this room right this minute." I tried to argue with her, but she wouldn't listen. She just kept hollering at me. "You heard me. Out. Get out and stay out. This isn't your room and never will be."

As I stumbled to my feet, she caught sight of the crumpled birthday gift lying unopened on the bed. Grabbing it, she tore off the paper. A heavy leather-bound journal fell onto the bed and with it a black leather case. She screamed and threw the wrapping paper in my face.

"This is what she died for. To get you a damn birthday present. I hope you're happy. Now get out of here. I don't want to catch you back in this room, ever."

I grabbed the journal and case from the bed and staggered out of the room. I noticed that it was dark outside. I remember glancing at the hall clock as I made my way to my own room. 7:57. I knew it couldn't be 7:57 p.m. I hadn't even gotten home until about five. No, it was morning. I'd spent the night in Beth's room. No one had come to me all night. No shower. No dinner. It was 7:57 a.m. and Mom and Dad were getting ready to leave the house. I wondered where they were going. I wondered if there would be a funeral. Of course. Mom would want the show. And it would be perfect.

I knew I had to get back into Beth's room before... Before what? I wasn't sure. I just knew I had to get there first. I went into my room and locked the door. I cleared off a special place on the top of my dresser for the journal and case, and then I flopped onto my own bed and waited. Forty-five minutes passed before I heard the front door close and the roar of my father's car as they drove away. I figured I had at least a few hours before they returned.

I tiptoed out of my room through the bathroom and back into Beth's room, still as quiet as a mouse in an empty house. I knew what Beth would want me to do. I also knew what I didn't know – that Beth had one hiding place that she hadn't shared with me. I remembered her complaints.

"It's not that I have some sort of sordid secret life. Why can't Mom just give me some space? Some privacy. But no. And if it's not Mom, it's the housekeeper. Somebody's always poking around in my private stuff. I wish they'd just stay out of my room. I'll clean it myself. I'll even do my own laundry, but no. Mom comes in to snoop, to live vicariously through me. But I've got some really good hiding places now."

"What are you hiding?"

"Oh, the usual. You know, my journals, my reference photos and notes, and my portfolio. I really don't want her looking at my artwork."

"Why not? Mom loves you. She's nice to you. She'd probably arrange a show for you down in one of those Pioneer Square galleries or something."

"My point exactly. She takes over my life and ignores you completely. You don't know how lucky you are."

But I never felt lucky.

"Chris, promise me that if anything ever happens to me, you'll find my hiding places and take my stuff before Mom gets it."

It was odd. I remember thinking it was odd when she said that.

"What's going to happen to you?"

"Oh, I don't know. We never know, do we?"

"Well, okay. But how many hiding places do you have?"

"Three".

"I only know about two. The carpet and the attic."

We were huddled on her bed whispering. Alone in the house, but still whispering as if we were afraid the walls had ears.

"Don't worry, you'll find the third if you ever need to. Just remember, it's the place where we share the most."

At the time, I guess I just thought it was some kind of puzzle we were playing. Keeping secrets. But as I entered my sister's room that morning after my parents left the house, the conversation replayed in my head. How long had it been? Only a few months. I remember thinking it was almost as though Beth knew her end was near.

The place where we share the most.

A movie played in my head, a replay of life in Technicolor and Dolby sound. Lying on Beth's bed together watching videos and eating Ben and Jerry's Chunky Monkey ice cream. Laughing at Beth dragging clothes from her closet and deciding what to wear to school the next day. I knew Beth wouldn't hide anything outside of the house or even outside of her room. Her room was her sanctuary. Her treasures, her secrets, were in that room, and I was determined to find them before Mom did.

I'll be systematic, I told myself. I'll go from one side of the room to the other and cover every single square inch. But I didn't. Instead I went straight to the back corner of the closet. The corner where Beth had loosened the carpet tacks. Gently I turned back the carpet and reached into the hole in the subfloor to lift out a large accordion file secured with twine. Sitting on the floor I opened it. Letters and notes fell to the floor and with them a small condom package. I remembered the day Beth had come home from school and told me about the health class and the condom. I shoved everything back into the file and twisted the twine tight.

One down. Two to go. I walked to the dresser and moved it out from the wall. A small dresser, it wasn't heavy. Behind it was a hinged door that led into the slanted attic crawl space. I opened the hatch and found the metal flashlight that I knew Beth always kept just inside. I switched it on and directed the beam of light into the musty, dark space. I crawled half way inside. I knew exactly what I'd find there. Beth's prized possession – a large, leather portfolio case she'd bought with her Christmas money the year before.

I shined the light on the wall to the left, just inside the opening, and there it was, standing upright tight against the wall where no one poking a head into the attic would ever find it. Gently, reverently, I lifted it out. It just barely fit through the attic door. I knew that was no accident. I set it on the bed, latched the attic door and pushed the dresser back against the wall making certain that nothing was moved, nothing looked disturbed. I knew Mother would notice even the slightest change.

I sat on the carpeted floor and unzipped the portfolio. I reached inside to pull out the artwork I knew I'd find there, but stopped. Later. I'll look later, I told myself. Two down, one to go. The secret spot. Her journals. Where would she put her journals? The place where we share the most. I stretched out on the carpeted floor. The place where we share the most.

Chris set down her pen and put a temporary stop to her frenzied writing. The sun had dropped beyond the horizon, and darkness had settled over the condo. She stood, stretched, and flicked on a few lights. "God, I'm hungry," she told the walls. She found some leftover pasta in the refrigerator and remembered that same hunger years before. She reheated her dinner and took it to the table where she continued writing between bites.

I was hungry then, too. And frustrated with Beth's riddle. I headed downstairs to find something to eat. The kitchen was a mess, the same mess the housekeeper cleaned up every day. Dinner dishes and breakfast dishes. It was the one area of the house that wasn't spotless. We had our meals in the dining room. That was spotless. After every meal we simply cleared the dirty dishes to the kitchen. By dinnertime, food was prepared, the dining room table set, and the kitchen spotless again. The same routine day after day.

I rummaged through the refrigerator and found some leftover lasagna. Funny how I remember these details. I can hardly remember what I ate for dinner yesterday, but I remember that lasagna. Anyway, I zapped the container, grabbed a fork and headed back upstairs. I knew the housekeeper never arrived before noon, but Mom's schedule was a mystery. I didn't want her coming home before I was finished. I took my lasagna back to Beth's room and climbed onto her wide bed. The bed where we watched so many movies together, where we whispered secrets and slept together, where... I stared at the blank TV screen. That's it, I thought. The place where we share the most. This bed. That's the place. But where?

I got up and removed the bedding. The soft blue comforter, the floral print sheets, the Eddie Bauer mattress pad. Nothing. I dragged the bed away from the wall and looked at the brass frame. I pushed the mattress off until all that was left was the box springs and dust ruffle. I pulled that off, too. Still nothing. I collapsed on the floor, sweating.

I remember lying there thinking, it's got to be here. That's when I got up and lifted the edge of the box springs. I heard something slide to the far side. I stood the box springs up on its side and examined the bottom. There it was. On the left side near the head of the bed. A long slit in the fabric. I set the box springs back down on the bed frame, made my way around the bed, climbing over piles of bedding to the other side. Again I lifted and again I heard something slide back to the opposite side. I carefully set the box springs back down on the metal bed frame and stretched out on top of it lying on my belly. I reached down with my left hand and slipped my fingers inside the slit in the fabric and pulled out a plastic case that measured about a foot square and a few inches thick. There was a simple snap closure and a quick peek told me what I already knew. This is where Beth hid her dozens of thin journals. I got up and walked to the corner of the room near Beth's desk where I'd set the accordion file and the leather portfolio. I added the journal case to the pile.

I wasn't worried about where I'd put these things. I had my own hiding places, even though I knew I didn't really need them. Mom was interested in Beth's life, not mine. She never snooped in my room. The only people who ever even came into my room were the housekeeper and Beth, and I never had secrets from Beth. Tears surfaced. Not now. Too much to do, I told myself as I looked around. The room was a mess. I knew I had to put it back together exactly the way it was before. Mom would know I'd been there if I left anything out of place.

Later, when I knew the room was perfect, I took one final look around. Good bye, Beth, I whispered. I kept my promise. Tears tracked my dirty, sweaty face. I knew I'd never set foot in that room again. I gathered my sister's secrets, tiptoed out the door, and closed it silently behind me. When I reached my own room, I opened my secret hiding place. Slipping the accordion file and the journal case inside the large portfolio, I hid them all away. Later, I whispered. I'll look at these later.

I kicked off my running clothes from the day before, a lifetime before, and climbed into my own bed. I sank into darkness and stayed there for days. The sound of the locksmith working on Beth's door finally brought me back.

Exhausted, Chris dropped her dirty dishes into the kitchen sick, turned off the lights, and shuffled to her bedroom, knowing that she would continue her story the next day.

TWENTY-ONE

"TELL ME ABOUT YOUR WEEK," Bentley began.

"I stared at the Alki runners. I walked for thirty minutes twice a day. I went to physical therapy. I ate. I slept. I wrote. Nothing too exciting."

"The Alki runners?"

"Yeah, I live on Alki. I have a view of the water and the running path. I used to be out there every day. Now I only watch."

"What does your doctor say? Or your PT?"

"They say it's only a matter of time. If I want to run again, I probably can."

"Do you want to?"

"Don't know."

"Why?"

"It hurts."

"Where?"

"Where do you think?" she snapped. "My legs, my head, my whole damn body."

"Is that all? What else hurts?"

"I don't know what you mean."

"You mentioned a sister named Beth who died in a car accident. She was a year older than you, right?"

"A year and a half."

"Was she a runner?"

Chris only nodded in response, her face a mask. The room was filled with a silence so deep it made her squirm.

"Do you want to tell me about her?" he finally asked.

"She taught me to run. Helped me get on the varsity track team when I was only a freshman. We started running together when I was about fourteen. She only wanted to lose weight. For me, it became a passion. I couldn't live without it. I couldn't live without her. Then she was gone. She was the only person in the world who ever loved me."

With those words, the tough façade cracked, and Chris slumped forward, wrapping her arms around her torso in a tight hug, tears of pain streaming down her face.

"What happened after Beth's death?" he asked, his tone neutral as he handed her the box of tissues.

"I wrote about it," she said, wiping her eyes. Then, she leaned over and pulled the new notebook from her backpack. "Here, you can read all about it."

"Thanks, but you keep that. I'd rather you told me."

"I wrote about the funeral. I remember the casket was at the front of the church. Set up on some kind of pedestal. It was all white, with white flowers. Virginal white. Mom and Dad thought she was a virgin. It's like, they thought they knew everything, but I knew Beth made love for the first time just before the accident. And I was glad."

"Glad?"

"Yeah, you know, glad that she had one more first, one more experience to take to the grave with her."

"I see. What else do you remember?"

"The air was heavy. Most of the people were strangers, my parents' friends paying their respects, I suppose. But I knew Beth's friends. They were all seniors. Friends she should've been graduating with in June. God, I remember feeling so totally alone. I didn't even go to the service with my parents. They were sitting up in the front somewhere, but I just snuck in at the back."

"What did your parents say about that?"

"Nothing. They'd always pretty much ignored me. It was Beth that made life worth living. I remember one time when I came home from my first track meet. I was a freshman, but I ran on the varsity team, so it was a pretty big deal, you know. I'd run the 3200m and came in second place. My parents didn't bother to come. When Beth bragged about me, all they said was 'Why second place?' and 'Who took first?' Later that night Beth found me crying in my room. When

I complained about them hating me, she told me the same thing that she always told me. She said they didn't really hate me. I just wasn't what they'd wanted. I wasn't the son they wanted to complete their perfect little world."

"Do you really think that having a son was so important to them?"

"I don't know. All I know is that they never wanted me and they still don't. It was the explanation Beth gave me and that was enough for me because I had her. Then she was gone. I remember slumping in the pew and trying to disappear. I wanted to die right along with her."

There was another long silence as Chris gathered the images of that day. "You know, I guess I did sort of die that day. I remember the funeral service droned on, but all I heard in my head was Beth's promise that we'd always have each other."

"What happened after the funeral?"

"There was a reception, is that what you call it, a reception? Anyway, nobody talked to me. It was like I was invisible. I overheard somebody comforting my mother. She was saying something like, 'Rest assured, Ellen, it was instantaneous. It happened so quickly Elizabeth felt nothing.' Like that was supposed to make anybody feel better. Still, at least they were trying. Nobody talked to me about the accident at all. It was like they either didn't know who I was or they blamed me for Beth's death. Either way, I was totally alone."

"Do you blame yourself, Chris?"

"I suppose I did for a long, long time. But not so much anymore. I mean, rationally I know I didn't cause her death. But, you know, I still feel like if she hadn't been getting me that present, it might not have happened, you know?"

"Present?"

"Yeah, she was killed on my sixteenth birthday. She was driving home with my birthday present in the backseat of her car when she was killed."

This time, when Chris stopped talking, she didn't sink into the sea of tears and pain she knew so well. Instead, she sat quietly with her eyes closed and breathed. She felt the air entering her body, filling her lungs with life, and giving her strength to face her pain. As she exhaled, she let go of a bit, just a bit, of the agony that gripped her soul.

TWENTY-TWO

CHRIS TOSSED HER JOURNAL onto the coffee table and stared at the boring white wall in front of her. "God, I've got to paint this place," she moaned. "No, I've got to get out of this place."

Another hour of talking with Bentley, an afternoon of writing about Beth, about loss was enough. Chris was fed up with loss. She was fed up with sitting around her condo alone and fed up with long, boring walks along Alki Beach.

She knew what she needed. She'd put it off long enough. Three months had come and gone. She'd followed the doctor's orders. She'd bought and worn the ugly walking shoes the PT recommended. She'd walked until she was sick and tired of walking. Enough was enough.

Chris walked back to her bedroom, opened her dreary white closet doors and rummaged through her wardrobe until she found what she was looking for – her favorite running shoes. Ultra-light weight, high-performance, distance shoes. The best the world of running technology had to offer. At least to non-professionals. Shoes made to endure no matter how many miles of pavement a runner pounded each week. Some runners bought them for show. Chris bought them for protection. She wasn't a woman who spent money on clothes. Her wardrobe consisted of little more than her work uniforms, a few pairs of jeans and khakis, and some T-shirts and pullovers. It was her running clothes that mattered.

She looked at her shoes as though they were old friends she hadn't seen for a while. Then in a flash, she changed into Lycra, put her friends on her feet and headed outside.

She began slowly, knowing her body was out of shape, her muscles slack. But she also knew she needed the fresh air filling her lungs, the pumping of her heart and the sweat on her brow. She was unaware of the cold wind that tangled her short, dark curls or the cacophony of gulls overhead, the waves lapping the shore as a barge was towed through the harbor or the kids screaming with joy on the winter beach. Chris felt only her body as she ran. She didn't smell the salty air but regulated her breathing and felt her lungs fill. She focused her attention on her right ankle and her left femur, watching for telltale signs that she was pushing too hard, too soon. Finding none, she pushed a bit harder, picked up her speed and felt the joy she hadn't known since long before that horrible night on the 35th Avenue hill. She was running again, and she knew she was truly alive.

When she reached her mile marker, the spot where the endless row of new, high-rise condos began, she slowed to a walk, reversed direction and headed home, her mind at ease, her body relaxed and her heart full.

As she approached the Statue of Liberty, she noticed a group of runners gathering. That's when she saw him. She would have recognized his handsome face anywhere. Shame washed over her. She crossed to the opposite side of the street with her head down and hurried back to her condo.

TWENTY-THREE

THE CONDO SMELLED LIKE FRESH COFFEE and ocean air. The sliding glass door was cracked open and a cool breeze off Elliot Bay drifted inside. The orderly living room was a clutter of newspaper classifieds spread on every flat surface, including the floor. Chris sat cross-legged on the carpet, a large cup of coffee on the coffee table beside her and an open computer on her lap. Her hair was an uncombed mass of curls, her full lips were pursed in concentration, and she was still in her pajamas when the doorbell rang.

Gemi came once a week now, but the doorbell still rang at precisely 10 a.m. on the scheduled day. She got up, walked to the door, and pulled it open. "You could just use your key, you know." The same comment every time. Gemi only smiled.

"What are you looking at?" Chris asked when she saw Gemi take in the disarray that had become her living room.

"This room. What happened here, child?"

"You told me last week that I needed to think about getting a car. Did you say something to my mother?" Without waiting for a response, Chris continued. "I got a check in the mail from her. I wish I could just send it back, but I'm no fool. I need the money."

"Then use it, child. Let's find you a car. You know, I'm pretty good with cars. I grew up with a father and an older brother who taught me all there is to know about keeping them running."

"Great – because I know nothing. I hate cars."

"Understandable."

"I've been looking at Autotrader.com, but I don't even know enough about all the brands to know what to look for."

"Makes."

"Makes what?"

"They're called makes of cars not brands."

"Oh, so now you're correcting my English? That's a bit much."

"Maybe so, but I can help you with this if you will allow me."

"I'm sorry, Gemi. I'm just really on edge. I hate cars."

"I know, child. But that's not going to stop you. Now, what are we looking for? An automatic with two or four doors?"

Chris only shrugged. After hours of reading ads, she still had no idea what she wanted.

With little more than a glance in her direction, Gemi pushed on. "A four door sedan would be a good choice, I think. Let's look for something with sixty thousand miles or less. Something that's never been in an accident and gets good gas mileage. What do you think?"

"Sounds okay to me. You seem to know what you're doing."

"What about color?"

Chris paused for several seconds before responding. "Not blue, dark blue," she finally said, her voice a heavy whisper.

"Okay, nothing blue."

"And not a Jetta. Or a Corolla."

"Okay, child. But remember, cars don't kill. Drivers kill."

After looking at the third car on their list that day, after she had refused to drive for the third time with little more than a glance, Chris saw a new side of Gemi.

They drove back to the condo in silence. There were only a few other cars on Harbor Avenue when Gemi pulled off the road and parked. To Chris's surprise, she got out of the car, walked around to the passenger's side and opened the door.

"What are you doing?"

"I am doing nothing, child. You, on the other hand, are going to drive yourself home."

"I don't want to drive your car."

"You don't want to drive any car, but you must. So let's do it. Now."

Without a word, Chris climbed out, walked around the car and slid into the driver's seat. She clasped the steering wheel so tightly, her knuckles turned white. And the car wasn't even moving yet.

"It's okay, child. You can do this," Gemi whispered.

But Chris wasn't so sure. In her imagination, time turned backwards.

... The streetlights flash in the darkness and the rain pelts the windshield as tears roll down Chris's face. She sees the totem pole. She knows the golf course lies far below.

She drives home from SeaTac airport after working a miserable, overbooked flight from the other Washington. A plane full of overexcited middle schoolers. She's exhausted to the bone, the weariness settling over her with the weight of pregnant gray clouds over Elliott Bay. She drives fast, much too fast, headed north on 35th Avenue. The rain pounds her senseless and the streetlights blind her in the darkness as she approaches the 35th Avenue hill.

Yet as the cityscape spreads before her in glitter and lights, a wide smile spreads across Chris's face. She moves her right foot from accelerator to brake and slows over the crest of the hill, making her way to the right hand turn lane and onto Avalon Way at the base of the hill. She's almost home ...

Chris turned the key in the ignition, and Gemi's small car seemed to roar. With extreme, excessive, absurd caution, Chris pulled back onto the empty street. She started slowly, too slowly, almost crawling along Harbor Avenue, but after a few cars passed her, gesturing their annoyance, she gained speed. Within a mile or so she relaxed. It wasn't much farther to the condo when Gemi spoke.

"Let's keep going a bit more, child."

"Where should we go?"

"Let's see. We could go to the grocery store up at Admiral, or down to Westwood Village to do a bit of shopping, or maybe we should go out for an early dinner. What do you think?"

"Don't you have to be going?"

"I have no other appointments today. I'm at your disposal, child. Come on. This will be fun."

"Okay. Sure."

They did it all. Groceries, shopping and dinner. In the process they crisscrossed most of West Seattle. By the time they returned the parking garage under Chris's building, the spot Gemi had been using for the past couple of months, Chris was driving again without fear.

"I'll help you upstairs with those bags," Gemi said.

Chris stopped her with a hand on her arm. "Thank you," she said. Tears filled her eyes. Gemi leaned over and gave her a tight embrace.

"We all have our fears, child. We only need to learn to face them."

TWENTY-FOUR

THE FOLLOWING MORNING, Chris stood on her balcony, steaming coffee in hand, and watched the cars pass along Beach Drive below her.

... She sees herself sliding behind the wheel of a bright red sports car and emerging from the underground garage beneath her. She turns right out of the building and cruises the beach, windows down, sunshine overhead, the rich aroma of salt water and sand massaging her soul. She drives to work, to the University of Washington, to visit her parents. She crisscrosses the city until she finds herself at SeaTac airport where it all started, and she retraces her drive home so long ago. It is not raining or dark. There are no blinding lights. As she heads north on 35th Avenue, she gasps at the beauty of the city that lies before her. Sun sparkles on the water, on the windows of downtown skyscrapers, and Chris shudders at the thought of ending her life ...

With a shake of her head, Chris turned back into her living room, found her cell phone and called the owner of the third car she'd seen the day before. A bright red something. She didn't remember the make and it really didn't matter at all. The owner was more than willing to drive to Alki and spend some time at the beach while Chris took the car to a mechanic to have it checked out. A few hours later money changed hands, the transaction was closed, and Chris was again a car owner.

As she sat alone in her apartment that evening, she felt the lightness and joy of a child on Christmas morning. She had a gift. In her mind her new car was a gift from Gemi. Not from her mother who had sent the check to pay for it, but from Gemi who showed her the path and gave her the strength to move forward. And it was that thought – the thought of a gift – that pulled Chris to her journal.

Sunlight was filtering into the bedroom around the edges of the curtains when I finally opened my eyes. I hadn't left my room or even opened the windows since Beth's funeral. The air smelled used. My hair, my body, smelled as bad as the room. I still refused to go to school or even talk to anyone. My father was back at work and mother was doing whatever it was she spent so much time doing, both pretending that everything was okay, everything was normal. Life went on.

But not for me.

The beautiful journal and leather case were still in the same spot on my dresser where I'd put them the morning after the accident, the morning after my mother ripped off the shiny red paper and threw it at me. The morning she accused me of causing Beth's death.

I stood in front of the dresser and fingered the elegant case. I carried it to my bed, pushed aside the pile of musty bedding and sat down with the case in my lap. It was my final connection to Beth. Her final gift to me. With trembling fingers, I unlatched the ornate closure and opened the case. Fixed inside the lid was an envelope with my name. I recognized my sister's handwriting and new tears began their slow journey down my cheeks. The case held a sleek wooden stylus and a collection of steel nibs of assorted shapes and sizes. I knew what they were. I'd seen them before in my high school art room. There were also two small bottles of ink, one sepia and the other black. I fingered each item and wondered what my sister had been thinking when she bought me this gift. I didn't know anything about calligraphy, just that I always thought it was beautiful.

All that remained to open was the envelope. Beth's final message to me. I removed it from the lid and opened it with extreme care. I held a homemade card in my hands. A small watercolor of a runner in mid-stride. I remembered the day several months before when Beth had insisted on taking photos of me running. I'd gotten mad at her. I'd told her she was nuts. I complained that she was embarrassing me, but she'd insisted we could use the pictures to improve my form. We'd never looked at them. In fact, I'd completely forgotten about them. But now, here I was in watercolors, running along Alki, the large old poplar trees, the tiny Statue of Liberty and the blue waters of Elliott Bay in the background.

Chris stopped writing and set down her pen. She could see the card – the painting on the front, the words written inside. She could see them as clearly as if they were on the table in front of her. And she knew exactly where they were. In the storage closet in the back hallway. There with Beth's portfolio. But it was too soon. She wasn't ready to open that closet yet. Instead she wrote the memories.

I opened the card and a small rolled paper, squashed from being inside a sealed envelope, fell to my lap. I still remember Beth's exact words on the card...

> *Dear Chris,*
>
> *You're an incredible runner. You're also a writer and artist. Follow your dreams this sixteenth year and always. I hope this gift will give you one more tool for expressing the beauty within.*
>
> *I will always love you,*
>
> *Beth*

I read those words over and over curled in a ball on my bed, rocking myself in pain and longing. I must have fallen asleep, the words etched on my permanent memory. Later I opened my eyes and saw a small rolled piece of paper on the bed beside me. I sat up and unrolled the heavy parchment. The words were penned in beautiful calligraphy:

> *Linda Wong*
> *Beginning Calligraphy Classes*
> *Six Months – Paid in Full*
> *Schedule Negotiable*
> *1345 Jackson Street*
> *Chinatown*

It took a moment for the information to register, for me to realize that Beth had given me calligraphy classes. I looked at the calendar on my wall. Thursday, December 5th. The funeral had been on the 24th. Thanksgiving had come and gone. I had skipped school all week. No, I hadn't been back to school since the accident. Beth wouldn't want that. I knew Beth would want me to go back to school. And I knew Beth would want me to keep writing and keep running. I decided to go back to school the next day, get all my missed assignments and catch up over the weekend. Catch up before winter break. I spent the rest of the afternoon cleaning my room and trying to find new order in my shattered life, but in the back of my mind I heard Beth's message, and I saw Linda Wong's name in beautiful calligraphy, and I tried to make a decision.

Night had fallen over Seattle, and Chris could see the twinkle of the city lights across the water. Although she felt like she was in a dream, she knew she couldn't sleep. She needed to finish the story. As she stared out into the night, a kernel of realization formed. "I'm writing a story," she whispered to the journal in her hands, to the spirit of her sister that she felt in her heart. And she continued to write.

A week later I left school after the last bell and took a bus to Chinatown. I'd MapQuested the address the night before and found the bus route to get there. I'd never taken a bus alone, and I'd only been to Chinatown once with Beth. She had been on another of her crazy diets and was convinced that Uwajima had the best veggies and seafood in the city. Still, I knew I could find the place, and I did. I'll never forget that first conversation. A small, middle-aged Asian-American woman opened the door.

"Yes?"

"Are you Linda Wong?"

"Yes, I am Linda. Who are you?"

"My name's Chris Stevens. I have this." I showed her the small parchment scroll.

"Why didn't you come sooner? I waited a long time. Maybe three, four weeks. You're Beth's little sister?"

"Yes."

"Where's Beth? You came alone?"

"I took a bus from West Seattle."

"Where's Beth? Beth said she'd drive you here. You wouldn't come alone."

"Beth's not here."

"Where's Beth? I made the deal with Beth."

My knees felt like rubber. All I wanted to do was sit down. Melt into the pavement. Leave nothing but a tiny puddle.

"Beth is dead."

It was the first time I said the words aloud. A pause, a flicker of understanding in her dark eyes.

"Come. Come in, please. Sit down."

She led me into a small dark room. There was a large, ink-stained table in the middle with gooseneck lamps on each end.

"I'll make tea for Beth's little sister."

She moved to the side of the room where there was a sink and counter. She filled a metal tea kettle and set it on an electric hot plate. Then she came and sat beside me at the large table.

"Tell me."

"It was my sixteenth birthday. November 20th. She was driving home. Maybe she was coming home from here."

"You wait. I'll check."

She opened a large leather ledger on the table and paged through lists of handwritten names and dates.

"Yes, here. Beth Stevens. November 20. Beth was here that day. Continue, please."

"She was driving home. A drunk driver hit her car and killed her."

"You just now opened the gift, decided to find Linda Wong, yes?"

"Yes."

"You took the bus?"

"Yes."

"You want the gift your sister Beth gave you?"

"Yes."

"Okay. I'll teach you."

"I brought this."

I pulled the leather case from my backpack, but I didn't take out the leather-bound book. I wasn't ready to soil the silky pages.

"Good. This is good. First I'll teach you to hold the pen. Then I'll teach you to make Western letters."

For an hour Linda taught me the fundamentals of loading and holding a stylus. She showed me how to angle the stylus for different line widths. And all too soon it was over.

"We'll stop now. When will you come back?"

"This is a good time for me, at least until school gets out in June."

"Thursday, 3:30 p.m.? Okay. See you next Thursday. Practice every day."

"Yes. Thank you. I will."

"For Beth."

"For Beth."

I repeated the words as I left her tiny shop.

Chris dried her eyes, stood and stretched. Lost in time and space, she walked to the kitchen and plugged in the tea kettle. She was still in Chinatown drinking bitter green tea with Linda Wong. She poured a bit of milk into the bottom of her cup and dropped in a cube of sugar, remembering the day she met Gemi. With a smile she realized she was capturing on paper the memory that had eluded her that day at Rainier Rehab when Gemi offered her that first cup of black tea with milk and sugar. Minutes later, warm tea in hand, she returned to the unfinished memory.

As I left Chinatown that first day, I couldn't go straight home. It was too soon. My head was in a fog. I wandered westward towards the water as though a magnet were pulling me. I wasn't sure where I was until I stood at the foot of the old Smith Tower. I'd been there on a class field trip in fifth grade. I kept walking until I saw the lacy cast-iron pergola still decorated with tiny white lights for the holidays, and I knew I was in Pioneer Square. Turning south on First Avenue, I realized where I was headed, where the invisible magnet was drawing me: Elliott Bay Book Company. A spot Beth took me more than once to browse for books or just for a snack after a day of downtown shopping. Did she stop here for a latte on her way home the day she was killed? I'll never know.

I made my way down the wooden staircase to the basement café as if I were sleepwalking, as if Beth were guiding me. I ordered a hot cocoa and sat at a corner table against the bare, red brick wall. For several hours I practiced the lessons Linda Wong had taught me that day, and in doing so I established a routine that I would repeat with every lesson I took at Linda Wong's tiny shop.

TWENTY-FIVE

"HEY, BENTLEY, COME HERE." Chris walked into her therapist's office and straight to the window overlooking the street below. "Take a look at that!"

"What? What am I looking at? The street? Cars?"

"Right. See that red one there. That cute little Honda Civic. It's mine. I drove here myself today."

"No more Gemi waiting for you?"

"Nope."

"Congratulations. You're back in the saddle again."

"I sure am. And it feels okay. A little scary. Especially at first. But Gemi made me drive her car, and then I was all right. I bought this by myself. Well, I saw it with Gemi the first time, but then I called the woman back and drove it and bought it. I really love it. It's so cute!"

"You love the car?"

"I sure do. And I'm not afraid to say it out loud."

"And you'd never do anything to hurt it?"

"Never."

"What about yourself, Chris? Do you love yourself?"

Chris stopped cold. She felt the smile disappear from her face. "Boy, you sure know how to burst my bubble. Thanks a lot."

"Just a reality check. I don't want you floating around in that bubble you mentioned. You're driving again. That's great. But as your therapist I want to know where your head's at."

"I know. You want to know if I've had any more thoughts of suicide. I'm behind the wheel. Would I do it again? Right?"

"Right." And there again was that arched left eye brow. The question mark on Peter's face that Chris knew so well.

"Not consciously. Not unless depression sets in again."

"Would you see it coming?"

"The depression?"

Peter only nodded his head.

"I think so," she said slowly, deep in thought. "I feel so different now. Happy, upbeat, full of hope. I'm still a bit lonely, but the tunnel has light at the end. Life isn't an endless black hole."

"We've talked before about your parents, about their lack of love for you. Indifference can be a very destructive form of child abuse."

"Abuse?"

"Yes, abuse. If a child feels unloved, she feels unlovable and shuts herself off from the world as well as from the possibility of giving and receiving love. Fortunately you had Beth, at least for those first sixteen years of your life, so you learned to love and be loved. Now we need to help you acknowledge your own self-love so that you can open yourself to others."

"But I already have."

"Tell me about it."

"I love Gemi. She's like a mother or sister to me. It hurts so much not seeing her every day now. I want to get to know her better. She's been so wonderful to me." She was quiet, and then added, "That's what it's all about, right?"

"All about?"

"Yeah, life. That's what life's all about – giving and receiving love. Sharing. Being part of a family even if they're not blood family. Community, friends, love. Creating happiness or well-being. It sounds so hokey, but without it, life has no meaning. I almost killed myself because my life had no meaning, because I had no love. I guess I didn't even love myself."

"Congratulations." Peter smiled as he handed her the tissue box.

Taking a tissue and wiping her eyes, Chris smiled. "There's still so much more I need to figure out, Bentley. I'm feeling a bit overwhelmed."

"Okay, let's take a crack at it. What's bothering you?"

"School or work or both? I need to decide what to do. I'm running out of money and I can't keep living off my parents' handouts."

"You were at the University of Washington for a while, right?"

"Uh-huh. I dropped out fall quarter of my junior year. I was an English major in the creative writing program."

"Tell me about it," Peter urged.

"I was living alone in a studio apartment, walking distance from the U. I was getting ready for class on the morning of September 11. The TV was on and I watched as the planes flew into the Twin Towers. I don't really know how to describe what happened next. It was almost as though a heavy black fog settled over me. I just got lost, I guess.

"My apartment was really small. But it had one of those closets, you know, the kind that used to hold a pull-down Murphy bed. That's where I had a small study area with a makeshift desk. I'd put it together myself with two file cabinets and a board. After 9/11, I just sat at that desk like I was trapped or something."

"Do you remember what was going through your head at the time?" Peter asked.

"Questions. Lots and lots of questions."

"What kinds of questions?"

"Why did Beth die? Why were all those people in the Twin Towers killed? What does it all mean? Why am I here? Questions that didn't really have any answers. So I just kept watching those horrible images on TV and seeing that drunk driver smashing into my sister. All the nightmares I had after Beth's death came back, but now Beth's mangled body was intertwined with the burning bodies of 9/11 victims, or she was jumping, falling, slow-motion on live television from the Twin Towers, or she was thrown from her car as it smashed into the telephone pole at the foot of Charlestown hill. I couldn't sleep, couldn't get up. I stopped going to class. I think that's when I started playing the 'What if?' game in my head."

"The what game?"

"You know, like what if I stepped in front of that truck, what if I jumped off that bridge."

"Suicidal fantasies."

"Yeah, I guess so. Anyway, I dropped out of the U. Didn't return for winter quarter. Instead, I applied for a job with the airlines. I told myself I wanted to fly, see the country, do something different. But I lied. What I really wanted was to die and airplanes just seemed one step closer."

"What was your parents' reaction?"

"Typical. I mean, they didn't really care if I went to school or not. They weren't crazy about me being a flight attendant because it wasn't something they could brag about, but they left me alone. In fact, that's when they gave me the condo on Alki. For my twenty-first birthday."

"They gave you a condo? Nice birthday gift."

"It's not quite as amazing as it sounds. I mean, sure it's pretty cool, but my dad's a developer. He bought the property and renovated the building. Retaining one of the units was some kind of tax deduction or write-off or something for him."

"Okay, so you joined the airlines and that's what you've been doing since early 2002, right? Then, you hit rock bottom. Now what?"

"Now? I suppose, I have some hope now. But I just don't really know what I want to do with my life."

"So what are the options you're looking at?"

"I'm thinking about resigning from the airlines and going back to school. But even with the condo paid for, I'll need money for tuition and food and stuff. I'd have to get some kind of job. And then, the big question is whether I could get back into school, and whether... I don't know..." She stopped, lost in thought.

"What don't you know?"

"Well, like, am I too old? Am I smart enough? Can I really do it?"

Peter broke into a gentle laugh. "How badly do you want that degree?"

"A lot," Chris said, without a moment's hesitation.

"Then go for it, Chris. You're only in your twenties for heaven's sake, and you're bright as a whip. If you want to do it, you will. What about going part-time with the airlines? Maybe a desk job downtown or at the airport?"

"I'm still on a six-month leave," Chris said, thinking aloud. "But I bet I could get a part-time spot somewhere."

"You won't know until you ask," Peter said.

TWENTY-SIX

"HEY, YOU. MOVING A BIT SLOW, aren't you?" Carolyn's cheery voice greeted Gemi from the flower garden as she parked at the curb in front of the old Victorian and climbed out of her car. "Usually you're rushing in and out for a quick lunch. What's up?"

Gemi plopped down on the front steps and watched her friend pull weeds from the fresh turned soil of the flower garden. "She doesn't need me anymore. That's the truth of it."

"Chris?"

"Yes, Chris."

"Isn't that what you wanted? Didn't you say she needed to learn to stand on her own again?"

"Yes, I did," Gemi admitted, more to herself than to Carolyn.

"So, what's the problem?"

"No problem at all. The child is driving again. She drove herself to her appointment with Peter today."

"That's wonderful," Carolyn said.

Gemi watched her friend stand and brush the dirt from her hands before walking over to sit on the step below her.

"So, it's a bit like pushing the chick from the nest, right?"

"Yes, indeed." She heard the weight in her own voice and knew that Carolyn heard it as well.

"So you've become that emotionally attached." It was a statement. Not a question. "Letting go is tough."

"That it is," Gemi said. "Especially when what one wants most is to wrap the child in a tight hug and keep her safe. Ah well. Time to find myself a few new patients. Better get to work." She pushed herself to her feet and started up the steps. Then she turned and said, "What about you? What are you doing home in the middle of the afternoon?"

"Ah, the perks of teaching," Carolyn said. "It's quarter break."

"You certainly don't do it for the salary," Gemi said. "Now, how about a walk? We really should take advantage of this weak excuse for sunshine."

"You've got it," Carolyn said, using the handrail to drag herself to her feet. "A walk would be just the thing to loosen up this old body. Gardening seems like a lot more work than it used to be. Just give me a minute to clean up."

With a laugh, she looped her arm through Gemi's, and they climbed the front steps together.

TWENTY-SEVEN

ONLY A FEW TABLES WERE OCCUPIED when Chris walked into the Alki Bakery lost in clouds of change and memory. Her new job would begin next week. An office job. No more long flights and lonely hotel rooms. When she finally got around to turning in her resignation, a customer service position was available and she grabbed it, more than happy for the part-time hours.

"What can I get you today? Tea?" asked the familiar barista, pulling Chris from her reverie.

"Yup, English Breakfast please," Chris said.

As she made her way to a window table, she realized she was searching the faces of the runners gathering at the statue on the other side of the Alki Avenue. Spring had arrived and over a month had passed since that first run when she saw Jake. Now, she admitted to herself, she watched for him. She had unfinished business. That's what Bentley would call it, she thought. Unfinished business. She knew she'd have to do something about it. In fact, she wanted to do something about it. But not yet. She wasn't ready yet.

Today she had another task at hand. It had been almost a week since she last saw her therapist, and she wanted to get started. She took out her journal and the print-out of the essay guidelines for the UW entrance application. She began to write, lost in the personal essay that she hoped would earn her a place at the U and allow her to finally finish her abandoned degree. She lost track of time and space, scribbling ink on paper, passion and pain, telling the story of why she had dropped out and why she wanted a second chance.

The words mixed with tears as they poured onto her paper. The world around her, the coffee shop, no longer existed. She wrote fast, furious, concentrated words until finally she stopped. She dropped her pen, closed her notebook, and reached for a sip of cold tea.

When she looked up, looked around her, her eyes locked with those of another young woman several tables away. The woman smiled, stood, and walked over to her. She was petite like Chris, but a bit heavier. Her dark eyes were intense and intelligent, her skin was light brown, and straight jet black hair framed her round face.

"You were lost there for a while. Lost to this world anyway."

"Yeah, I suppose I was."

"Are you a writer? Stupid question. Of course you're a writer. You write. I've seen you here before."

"I'm just working on an essay..."

"Must be some essay."

"...and I keep a journal. But I'm not a writer."

"Words on paper. You're a writer. Do you ever write with anyone, take any classes, go to conferences? Sorry, too many questions. I've got a bad habit of throwing too many questions at people. Listen, here's what I wanted to tell you, I've been wanting to tell you for the past month or so... Do you mind if I sit down for a minute?"

"Sure. Sorry. Let me get that out of the way." Chris moved her backpack off the spare chair and set it on the floor.

"My name's Karin. Seems like I see you here almost every day."

"I guess so. I've been laid up for a while."

"That's right. You had casts on both legs the first time I saw you."

"Wow. You sound like some kind of stalker." Chris laughed to assure Karin that she wasn't totally strange.

"No, not a stalker. Just a writer. I come here a lot to write and I'm pretty observant, I guess."

"What do you write?"

"I'm working on a novel that explores the lives of Amerasians after the Vietnam War. It's sort of based on my own life, but not a memoir. I'm not brave enough for that," she added with a laugh. "Anyway, I don't want to interrupt your writing, I just wanted to tell you about a writing practice you might want to try."

"No interruption. I'm done for now. What kind of writing practice?"

"It's a loosely-knit group of writers, from beginners to published authors, who come together twice a week to write and share. We do a thirty-minute timed writing. Then we read what's scribbled on the page in front of us. It's a really supportive atmosphere."

"Sounds interesting, but I'm not a writer."

"Journals can become memoirs," she said with a smile. "And writing can be a very lonely life. This is a great way to meet with a diverse group of like-minded people on a regular basis. Anyway, we start writing at exactly 4:00 p.m. every Tuesday and Thursday with whoever's at the table. Here I wrote it all down for you." She handed Chris a small piece of paper and stood to leave. "Hey, it's not for everyone. My boyfriend's a poet, and he hates the timed-writing aspect of it."

"Thanks," Chris said.

"My pleasure." Karin turned to walk away and stopped. "By the way, what's your name?"

"Chris. Chris Stevens."

"Okay, Chris. I'll be watching for you at 3:45 next Tuesday. I hope you try it out, at least once." With a wave of her hand, she was gone, and Chris was left with the slip of paper Karin had given her.

> *3:45 p.m. Tuesdays and Thursdays*
> *The Last Exit on Brooklyn*
> *NE 42nd Street and Brooklyn Avenue NE*
> *University District*

For a long time, Chris sat and stared at the paper and rehashed Karin's comment: "Words on paper. You're a writer... Journals can become memoirs."

... She sees herself walking down the winding wooden staircase at the Elliott Bay Book Company and into the large room that runs along one side of the basement opposite the café, the room used for author readings. She walks into the room confident and happy, eager to begin the reading and to answer the questions she knows she'll be asked. It isn't her first reading. She's done at least a half dozen since the release of her first book. But this reading is special. This is the Elliott Bay Book Company, her bookstore, the place she's come for as long as she can remember to read or to write in her journal, for a latte or a sandwich after a long afternoon of calligraphy with Linda Wong, for an afternoon of comfort on a rainy gray Seattle day. She feels at home in the red brick room with rustic wood shelves and dusty old hardcovers lining the walls.

She walks into the room full of people sitting on wooden chairs, waiting to hear her speak. As she approaches the podium, her heart sings, a smile lights her face, her eyes glisten with joy. She has come home, and she knows that Beth is with her. "Good evening and thank you for being here on this beautiful Seattle evening," she says ...

A gust of fresh air filled the coffee shop and pulled Chris back to the present, as another afternoon customer pushed through the front door. The slip of paper Karin had given her was still in her hands. With a determined toss of her head, she gathered her things and headed for the front door. She was ready for a long run.

TWENTY-EIGHT

THERE WAS A MIDDLE-OF-THE-NIGHT CALM on Alki. The beach itself had been cleared off hours before by the 11:00 p.m. city parks curfew. Traffic had thinned to the late night locals. The lights in Chris's front room were on and the sliding door to her balcony was open, flooding her condo with a cool breeze.

She couldn't sleep, couldn't sit still. She paced the floor in quiet, stocking steps, aware that the world below her was long asleep. She paced in a steady rhythmic pattern, back and forth, balcony to kitchen counter. Outside, on the balcony she paused, breathed in the heady ocean air, heavy with salt, shells and seaweed. Then back across the soft, white carpet to the kitchen counter in slow, measured steps, lost in thought. How does one make a decision knowing that it will change everything? She remembered an expression she'd learned in Spanish class years before. *Mejor el mal conocido que el bien por conocer.* Was that true? Was the devil we know really better?

Chris shook her head in disagreement. "No," she whispered to the empty room. That's settling. Accepting less than I deserve, less than anyone deserves. I'll never know unless I try.

As she paced the floor, her eyes darted back to the large envelope propped up against a vase of brilliant Skagit Valley tulips from the West Seattle farmers' market – vibrant pink, sunshine yellow, deep violet – the colors of spring. The envelope was stamped, sealed and ready to send. She'd gone to the post office on California Avenue earlier that afternoon to buy postage, but she hadn't been able to let go, to leave the envelope with the big-haired postal worker with a bright smile. No, she hadn't been ready at two in the afternoon. Now it was two in the morning.

Chris fingered the large envelope, picked it up and held it in her hands, staring at it. It had taken her over a week to complete the application, most of the time laboring over the required essay. She turned the large envelope over and over in her trembling hands. Again she heard Bentley's words in her head and repeated them as a silent mantra: I'll never know unless I try.

With the new determination of a decision made, she went to her bedroom, slipped on a pair of running shoes and a lightweight polar fleece. Returning to the front room, she grabbed her keys off the kitchen counter and the envelope from the table. She left the condo, locking the door behind her.

Alki almost never sleeps, not completely. In the winter, it's almost deserted, with only the diehard athletes willing to face the cold wind and rain. But as soon as the sun makes her early spring appearance, the place is swamped. The beach is a state park with a closing time, but that doesn't keep runners or cruisers from haunting the beachfront restaurants and bars late into the night and early morning hours.

Still, by 2:30 a.m. the street was empty as Chris walked out the front door of her building towards the mailbox that stood sentry in front of the Alki Bakery. She could have just left the envelope in the lobby mailbox for pick-up, but she needed a more definitive action to seal her decision. She needed to get outside and walk. She needed one of those big blue mailboxes – the kind that takes your envelope and won't give it back.

"I'll never know unless I try," she told the stars, as she pulled open the heavy handle and after one final pause dropped the envelope into the sealed box. Then, crossing the street, she stood next to the miniature replica of the Statue of Liberty.

She reached both arms to the stars far above her and stretched, arching her back, pulling every muscle, separating every vertebra. Then she doubled forward, bowing to the ground, her palms resting on the asphalt. Straightening, she gave herself a quick shake of the head and shoulders and headed home with a peaceful heart.

TWENTY-NINE

IT WAS A QUARTER PAST THREE when Chris walked into The Last Exit on Brooklyn. In a city dominated by Starbucks and Tully's, it's hard to find independent coffee shops that can still pay their overhead. The Last Exit was holding on by a shoestring and looked it. The small room, filled with rickety chairs and cast-off tables, was warmed with the rich, heady aroma of Italian espresso.

Chris had arrived early and the coffee shop was almost empty. She ordered a cup of tea and sat near an outside window facing the door. By 3:30 p.m. people began to arrive and greet each other. It was a mixed group. Young and old, male and female. They set notebooks and pens on a few of the larger tables in the center of the room and ordered and paid for various coffee and tea drinks. Chris knew she was in the right place, knew these were writers filling this space at a normally slow hour of business. Finally she saw Karin push through the front door and stood to greet her.

"Hey, you made it. I'm glad." Karin spoke before Chris managed to get a word out. "Come on. Let's find a spot together at one of the tables." Crossing the room, she dropped a notebook on a large center table and claimed two chairs. Chris set her backpack on one of the chairs and dug for her own notebook.

"Come on, I'll introduce you to a few people." Within minutes Chris was lost in a sea of names as Karin introduced her around the room, telling everyone of her dedicated writing at the Alki Bakery.

"No, really," Chris protested. "I'm not a writer. I just scribble my thoughts in a journal. That's all."

"Hey, that's what we all do," someone said, and everyone laughed.

"Some of us are working on novels, some on memoirs, and others in journals. Some tables even do short five-, ten- and fifteen-minute writings with start lines. It just depends on what the table wants," another person explained.

"I've already explained to her about the timed writing and reading," said Karin. "It's almost four. Are we ready to begin? Who's got a timer today?"

An older woman, tall and dignified, her graying hair twisted into a soft bun at the nape of her neck, set a small plastic kitchen timer in the middle of the table where Chris and Karin sat side by side. "Okay," she said. "Let's begin. Today I'm writing about ..." She pushed the start button and everyone settled deep into their chairs and began to write. Within thirty minutes the crisp, clean pages were covered, some in tight precise lettering, others in scrawl that even the writer later struggled to decipher. At the end of the thirty minutes three buzzers rang out at three separate tables, and as if on cue, a voice at each table began to read. As each reader ended, there were facial expressions of sadness, pleasure and understanding, but there were no comments, no critiques of the writing. The reading continued from right to left around the table.

When it was Chris's turn, her voice trembled, and she had to set her notebook flat on the table in front of her to hide the shaking of her hands. "Today I'm writing about the day I decided to live ..." There was silence, intense focused silence, at her table. Silence in a noisy coffee shop, but Chris was aware of nothing but the story on her pages. When she finished, she looked up from her writing and into the faces at her table. She saw understanding, support and encouragement in those eyes. She looked back at her own words and joy filled her heart.

THIRTY

A HEAVY SPRING RAIN DRENCHED THE CITY as Gemi sat in a comfortable booth of a Capitol Hill restaurant waiting to meet Chris for lunch and remembering the happy surprise in Chris's voice when she accepted the invitation. It seemed like the best way to break the news.

When Gemi glanced up, she saw Chris talking to the hostess by the front door. She was struck by the changes she saw in her. Across the crowded room she saw a young woman with short black curls and the sleek movements of a trained athlete. She carried her slight body with dignity and grace. With confidence. Gemi felt a sharp stab of pain, the long familiar pain of loss for her own daughter. A daughter who would be only a few years older than Chris.

She was transported by memory to a distant land, an open-air market. A young mother carrying her daughter wrapped in a shawl on her back. There was an explosion. She was thrown. Her baby flew from her back. Killed in the carnage. When Gemi regained consciousness and learned that both her only child and her mother were dead, she wanted to die with them. Her father and brother had long since been killed in the civil war that rocked her homeland for thirty years. Her husband had simply disappeared.

She felt Chris's presence before she heard her cheerful voice. "Hey, Gemi, are you okay?"

Shaking thirty-year-old memories back into the recesses of her soul, she turned to this reincarnation in khakis. "Fine, child, just fine. Come. Sit down with me."

Chris slid into the bench across from her and said, "Gemi, you're a terrible liar. You were far away when I walked in, lost in thought. Where were you?"

"Ethiopia. A market in Addis Ababa."

"How old were you?"

"Seventeen, almost eighteen."

"What were you doing?"

Chris was asking questions. Questions like those Gemi knew Peter asked her. She smiled in pleasure, despite the pain of the memories she was sharing, happy that Chris was beginning to find the confidence and trust needed to ask questions. "Shopping," she said. "I was at the market, an open-air market, a bit like your Sunday farmers' market in the West Seattle junction, but much, much larger, louder and more colorful."

"What happened?" Chris asked softly, as though she were afraid to break the spell that had come over them both.

"There was a horrible explosion, child. A military attack. I was thrown through the air like a sack of rice. My baby came loose from the shawl tied to my back."

"Baby? You had a child?"

"My daughter. She was almost a year old. My mother and I were shopping for food for her first birthday feast on the day she was taken from me."

"Your baby was killed in the explosion?"

"Yes."

"Oh Gemi, I'm so sorry. And your mother? Was she okay?"

"No, I'm afraid I lost them both that day." Gemi watched as tears pooled in Chris's large, dark eyes.

Her young friend paused for a moment, and then she asked, "Were you married?"

"Yes. I was married at sixteen." Then, seeing the surprise on Chris's face, she added, "It was the custom in my country for girls to marry very young."

"And your husband? Where is your husband?"

"I do not know for certain. I believe he too was killed in the war, the endless explosions and fighting, but I do not know, child. That is what I was told when I awoke in a Red Cross field hospital many weeks after the explosion. I followed the long road of immigration until I finally arrived here, with you."

"I am so sorry. I had no idea. I've been so self-centered, so selfish."

"No, child, you stop right there. I was hired to do my job. A job I love. Usually I care for the elderly and shut-ins with no hope of recovery. It has been a great pleasure following your path to health – both physical and mental."

"'Has been?' Gemi, you said 'has been.' What do you mean by 'has been'?"

"Calm yourself," Gemi said in a quiet, gentle voice. "I mean, I no longer work for your mother."

"What? My mother stopped paying you? Damn her. I'll pay you, Gemi. I promise. I'll find the money, or I'll make them pay you or something."

"No, child. I called your mother and told her that my work here is done. You do not need my care. You are healthy and strong. You can care for yourself."

"But, I do. Please, Gemi, don't leave me."

The vulnerability that Gemi heard in Chris's pleading voice touched her heart. She remembered her friend Carolyn's comment and felt very much like that mother bird, pushing her chick from the nest to show her she could indeed fly.

"Child, I said you do not need my care. I did not say you do not need my friendship and my love. And I did not say that I do not need yours. You have become much more than a client, Chris. You are the child I lost."

"You are the sister I lost and the mother I never had," Chris said, her voice calm. A moment passed, and then she added, "Do you think we could meet once a week for lunch? Can I call you whenever?"

"Of course, child. And I will call you as well."

Gemi watched her young friend stand and walk around the table to slide into the booth next to her. They wrapped each other in a tight embrace, sealing a pact of love that neither could fully explain.

THIRTY-ONE

IN THE LATE EVENING Chris sat curled in her favorite chair by the window with her journal, but her thoughts moved away from Gemi and the shift in their relationship. Instead she was thinking about another relationship, one that didn't yet exist. She began to write.

I saw him again today. I pulled out of the garage on my way to see Gemi and there he was. Jake. Jake Brown? Jake Boller? Jake something. I was so awful to him. But then he read my journal, damn it. How dare he read my journal? He knew. He knew, or at least he suspected, that it wasn't an accident, even before he read my journal. Why else would he have gone back there? And if he hadn't gone back, he wouldn't have found my journal. And I wouldn't have gotten it back. So where does that leave me?

All he wanted to do was help me, and I pushed him away. He saved my life, and I told him to leave me alone. What a fool. A nice guy with a hot body. A runner even. How often will I find that combination? I wonder how often he runs. I wonder if he's ever alone. I wonder if I have the nerve.

Chris dropped her pen. Her imagination flowed faster than words onto a page.

... She is alone on the beach wearing only a sports bra and tight Lycra shorts, the sun warm on her sleek, bare skin. She's running in the sand at the water's edge, her feet splashing in the gentle waves. Looking up, she sees a man in the distance. A tall man, lean and muscular. He's running towards her, not veering to the right as runners do, but staying at the water's edge. The distance closes between them. They slow to a gentle jog, then a walk, matching each other's pace. Neither wavers off course, neither moves away from the water's edge. Their eyes lock as their steps shorten. Arms outstretched, they fall into each other's warm, sweaty embrace, the icy cold of Elliott Bay lapping at their ankles.

Chris raises her face to Jake's and sees the desire in his eyes. In that moment, in the warmth of his eyes as the sunlight dances on the varied hues of green and gold, in the passion of his embrace as he wraps his long muscled arms around her, she knows that her eyes reveal the same intense desire that she sees in his. She closes them to the warmth of the sun, the heat of his body against hers, as his hungry lips find her own ...

The sound of the washing machine buzzer startled Chris back to the present. "A whole lot of good that what-if's going to do me," she muttered to herself as she dropped her journal and pen on the coffee table beside her chair. Rubbing her eyes, she stumbled to her feet and made her way to the laundry room to toss her clothes into the dryer.

THIRTY-TWO

THE CONDO SMELLED OF FRESH SALT AIR blowing in off the water. The slider was open to the sounds of the beach floating up to her balcony – children building sand castles and screaming as the cold waters of Elliott Bay tickled their bare toes, teenagers flirting behind blaring hip hop from a multitude of car stereos, and the occasional rumble of a motorcycle or roar of a city bus. The beach sounds that Chris loved.

At 6:00 p.m. sharp, the doorbell rang. Gemi stood outside the door looking much the same as she had the day Chris met her at Rainier Rehab. Her head was wrapped in a scarf. Her dark face was accentuated by deep expressive eyes that smiled at the corners, hiding a half-century of life and innumerable personal tragedies. She was wearing the same non-descript tan pants and loose, long-sleeved, floral-print shirt. Her body covered.

Chris stood on the other side of the threshold in her baggy, blue plaid flannel pants and a pale blue tank top. Her feet were bare. Her head was bare. Her skin was flushed with newfound health. She was running again, and it agreed with her.

The seconds ticked by. It was Gemi who broke the silence. "Are you going to invite me in, child?"

"Oh, I'm sorry." Chris was flustered as she stepped aside to let Gemi pass. Then, regaining her composure, she told Gemi the plans she'd made for their first evening together as friends.

"Okay, so I figured I wouldn't even try to cook cuz we both know that would be a disaster. Do you like Chinese food? I thought we could order Chinese. Then, I've got a special movie for us to watch." She rambled on, not giving Gemi a chance to respond.

"Special?"

"Yup. Do you remember the day we met?"

"Like it was yesterday, child."

"Remember, I started laughing like a crazy person. I think I startled you."

"Yes, I remember, child. You said something about your mother's mistake."

"Yeah, and I called you an African Mary Poppins, but you had no idea what I was talking about."

"And I still do not, child."

"Well, tonight's the night you'll understand. Look what I've got." She grabbed a DVD case off the coffee table and handed it to Gemi. "See, Mary Poppins."

"I see, child. But she looks quite blond to me."

"Exactly. She's what my mother thought she was hiring when she talked to you on the phone. I guess it was those years you spent in England that confused her. You still have an accent, you know." Chris paused in her excitement. "Oh, I'm sorry. That was rude."

"Not rude at all, child. Of course I have an accent. The question is, what kind? Is it Amharic, British or southern? You know, I spent a few years in South Carolina when I first immigrated to America. But that's another story."

"I want to hear all your stories, Gemi. You know so much about me, and I know nothing about you."

"First the movie, child. I'd like to meet this Mary Poppins of yours. And, by the way, I do like Chinese food. Shall we order?"

THIRTY-THREE

"I WAS IN THE TUBE. You know, Bentley, the subway. It was just like every other summer morning in London. I was on my way to work, briefcase in hand."

Peter sat quietly listening to Chris tell of her nightmare, nodding his head, encouraging her to talk through the horror.

"A sharp jolt slammed me into the seat in front of me. A blast so loud my hands flew to my ears. Windows shattered and glass showered me. Screams, smoke, chaos and darkness.

"I was on the floor of the train. People all around me were screaming for help. I found my feet and stood. A shadowy dim light and thick black smoke filled the tunnel. A man next to me began beating the window with his umbrella. Beating his way out of our communal coffin. Desperate for air.

"I heard a voice telling people, telling us, to stay calm, to make our way out through the back of the train. I was disoriented and stumbled in the darkness. 'Which way is back?' I screamed. Someone took my arm. I took another's hand. We worked our way towards the end of the car and out onto the edge of the tracks. We stepped over bodies, body parts, blood."

Chris stopped, her face in her hands sobbing with the memory of a nightmare so real she struggled to convince herself it was only a dream. Handing her the box of tissue, Peter encouraged her to continue.

"I covered my nose and mouth with the silk scarf from my neck to filter the air. To stifle my screams. It was unbearably hot.

"And then I was outside. In an open-air market. Dust, hot sun, bright-colored tents. People were speaking, screaming, in a language

I couldn't understand. Explosions all around me. Beautiful dark-skinned people covered in blood. I was searching for Gemi. Searching for Gemi's baby girl.

"I couldn't find them. I ran from pile to pile of mutilated dead bodies looking for them. I screamed Gemi's name. I screamed for help. But no one understood me. No one saw me. I was invisible. A shadow in the chaos of bombs and blood."

Again, Chris sank her face into her hands and sobbed. "It was so real, Bentley. I woke up at 3:00 a.m. trembling. I told myself it was only a nightmare. But it wasn't, not really. I mean, a nightmare, yes, but a very real nightmare. Especially for those poor people in London. Especially for Gemi and the people of Addis Ababa. For so many people around the world. God, Bentley, it makes me feel so guilty." She paused to catch her breath, to gulp for air, to organize the confusion in her heart.

"Guilty, Chris? Why guilty?" Peter probed, his voice calm, not wanting to push too hard.

"Because I'm so lucky, so fortunate, so spoiled. Because I have so much, and still I was stupid enough to try to kill myself. Because the world is so damned unfair."

"Well, Chris, maybe let's not take on the whole world at once," Peter said, his face a gentle smile. "Maybe let's take on how we live our own lives each day in a meaningful, mindful, loving manner."

"I know, Bentley. I know I can give back in my own way by opening my heart. I'm learning to live a meaningful life, thanks to you. But, sometimes the world events just get to me."

"It took you back, Chris."

"Back?"

"Yes. That terrorist bombing in London took you back to 9/11. Back to Beth's death. Back to your own near-death. Death, meaningless, violent death, regardless of how distant, triggers the personal memories, and we relive the pain. Because of your love for Gemi, because of her horrific loss in that marketplace in Addis Ababa and her years of recovery in London, the bombings there hit you hard."

"So how do I stop this pain?"

"Ah, Chris, you know you can't stop it. You face it. You understand its roots. And you walk, or in your case you run, right through it."

He gave her a wink and a smile. "With time, and a lot of determination facing down the demons, the pain will get weaker and it will hurt less. You feel deeply, Chris. That can be a blessing or a curse. It just depends."

"Depends? On what? No, don't answer that. I know. I already know. It depends on how I face those emotions. How I embrace them instead of denying them, like I used to do until they blew up like Mt. St. Helens."

She relaxed back into the loveseat and looked at Peter. She saw the approval in his eyes and understood her own growth. "Bentley, something's been bothering me," she said.

"What's that?"

"Could I call you Peter? I mean, when I call you Bentley it reminds me of my dad and his pretentious car. And you're not even remotely like my dad."

Peter's laugh was loud and hearty. Before long Chris was laughing as well.

THIRTY-FOUR

A WARM AFTERNOON BREEZE BLEW INLAND off Elliott Bay as Chris crossed Alki Avenue and headed towards the Statue of Liberty. She was wearing a sleeveless blue tank top and running shorts. Black with a narrow stripe, blue sky up the outer thigh. Her running shoes were well-seasoned but still offered the support needed for distance running on asphalt. She moved with determination. Another decision made.

She passed the Statue, headed towards the water and began to stretch as she waited. Arms reaching the ground, vertebrae separating, oxygen entering the spine. A runner's stretch. Right knee bent, left leg extended back, hands on the hips. Hold. The other leg. Hold. Chris was not much of a stretcher. She usually just started with a slow run, waited until her muscles warmed, and then built speed. But today was different. Today she wasn't here for the exercise. She'd already done a morning run.

Runners began to collect at the base of the statue, strangers that Chris had seen, but never met. The regulars. Strangers that she knew gathered just before 5 p.m. Sometimes only four or five, other times as many as a dozen. She watched as they stretched and jostled each other as they waited for the appointed time to set off. A bit like writing practice, Chris thought. If you're there, you're a runner.

There was always a small group that gathered daily, seven days a week. She knew it wasn't for her. She didn't long to join the group. She didn't need the group commitment to keep her inspired to run every day. Running was who she was, her joy and her passion. She knew she was a solo runner. She preferred it that way – her time to sort herself out. A bit like meditation. A bit like writing. At least now that's what it had become. In the past, it was just an escape. Still, she watched the group with curiosity. She'd watched the group since the day she noticed that Jake was a member.

It had been mid-winter when she first saw Jake join the group one Tuesday afternoon. Even then, she knew she had some unfinished business with him. That day at Rainier Rehab played on her mind too often for comfort. She was not only embarrassed for the way she'd spoken to him, but if she was really honest with herself, at least in the privacy of her own heart, she had to admit that she liked remembering his wavy, dark hair and the warmth of his eyes.

She moved away from the group and headed towards the Alki Bathhouse. This sweet little building was once the center section of a large beach pavilion complete with dressing and locker rooms for those hardy enough to swim in the frigid waters of the Pacific Northwest. Constructed in 1911 as a summer vacation destination, it had included a café, clubroom and viewing balcony that overlooked Elliott Bay and the emerging Seattle skyline. The large pavilion was demolished in 1955, and all that remained was a small section of the west wing. Newly remodeled and painted in earthy-yellow with a brown metal roof, it now served as a community arts center and public restroom. She felt a certain fondness for the little old building. They shared a common theme – reconstruction.

Chris smiled to herself at the thought as she moved away from the gathering group of runners. Finding a spot with a good view of the sidewalk, she continued to wait. Stretching and watching and waiting. She felt a tightness in her chest. She couldn't seem to steady her breathing.

"This is nuts," she muttered to no one. "I'm just going to apologize."

But she knew it was more than a simple apology. She knew she was there to see if Jake was still interested in her the way he had been the last time they spoke. The time she told him to leave her alone. That horrible afternoon at Rainier Rehab played in her mind like an endless video. With each replay, she felt more remorse. So, she waited, stretching, breathing. And then she saw him. He was wearing gray running shorts and a dark blue T-shirt.

He was approaching from the north. She moved quickly, determined to intercept him, eager to speak with him alone, anxious to avoid the curiosity of a half dozen strangers, his friends, his running partners. She climbed the short flight of stairs behind the Alki Bathhouse that separated the boardwalk from the sidewalk and running path, taking them by twos, and approached him. When she was almost in front of him, when she saw the flicker of recognition in his eyes, she spoke.

"Hi. You're Jake, aren't you?"

"Jake Bowmer. Hello, Chris. How are you?"

"Good. Running again. I've got hair," she said nervously, her hands making their way to her head before she could stop them. He laughed easily.

"I was wondering if we could talk. I know you're heading out on a run. Would you mind if I tagged along?"

"Uh, no, that'd be great. Just let me introduce you to my friends so they can go on without me, okay?"

As they approached the group of runners stretching at the Lady Liberty's feet, a few friends began to tease him.

"It's about time you got here, Jake."

"Yeah, he's always holding us up."

"Right," Jake said with an easy laugh. "Hey, this is my friend, Chris. She's running with us today, okay? She's recovering from two broken legs, so we might be a bit slow. Don't let us hold you up."

"Sure, Jake. You'll use any excuse you can to slow it down, won't you?" someone said.

"She'll probably beat your lazy ass," said another.

They joked and jostled, and then they were off at a steady pace, a pace Chris would have found too slow even on a bad day. A bright pack of Lycra and nylon beating the pavement, leaving Jake and Chris to pull up the rear.

"Sorry about that," Jake said as soon as the others were out of earshot. "I probably shouldn't have said that about your…, well, you know. I just wanted them to give us some space."

"No problem. It's fine."

"You know, they're probably right. You probably can still beat my lazy ass."

They laughed, both a bit nervous, and then started a slow, silent run for a few minutes, finding their rhythm, matching their strides, like dancers, their bodies moving in unison.

"I've seen you running," Chris began. "And I've been trying to get up the nerve to come and apologize." Jake began to protest, but she stopped him. "No, hear me out. I need to say this. And I've never been good at saying what I need to say."

Jake fell silent at her side, and Chris noticed that he slowed his pace, only a fraction, an almost imperceptible change, a better speaking speed. She knew he was waiting, giving her the time she needed to organize her thoughts.

"I've wanted to apologize for a long time. I was rude and ungrateful. You saved my life, and I treated you badly. Then you found my journal, and I hated you for reading it. But you were absolutely right." She paused, took a deep intake of air and paced her breathing. She'd been looking straight ahead, her eyes on the path in front of her, afraid to look to her right, to look into his eyes. She felt his hand on her arm, a firm but gentle touch, and she turned to look at him.

"It's okay. I understand."

"No, wait Jake. Let me finish. You were right all along. I tried to kill myself. I drove off the 35th Avenue hill with every intention of ending my miserable life. Then you came along and spoiled my plans by saving me. You knew it and tried to help, but I shut you out. I wasn't ready. It's been a long haul. I've been in counseling, and I'm better. Much better."

Again she turned and looked him in the eye as they ran. "I want to live. It'll never happen again. I just wanted you to know. And I wanted to tell you that I hope you'll forgive me."

Again Jake reached and touched her arm. This time he pulled her to a stop and turned to face her. "I'm glad. Really glad that you found the help you needed. I have a confession to make too since we're being honest here. When I came to see you that last time, I came for me. I couldn't get you out of my head."

Chris blushed, the deep crimson almost concealed by her tawny complexion. "I was lost in my own problems, so I pushed you away," she said.

"And now?"

"No," she said as she looked up at him. "I don't think so."

When Jake wrapped her in a quick, tight hug, she felt odd. Not frightened or nervous, just new, different. When he released her, he held her at arm's-length and looked into her eyes. "Good," he told her. "And for the record, I didn't read your journal, only that last page. Now, let's finish this run and maybe you'll let me take you out to dinner? Let's see how good those legs really are."

"Sounds like a great idea." And she sprinted off leaving Jake struggling to keep up with her easy stride.

THIRTY-FIVE

CHRIS STOOD IN THE DOORWAY of the beachfront chowder house, her short curls still damp from the shower. The place was buzzing with activity, every table full. Music blared, but through the noise, she couldn't identify who it was.

She saw him, sitting alone at a window seat, relaxed in a black T-shirt and a pair of faded blue jeans. She wondered how he could be so calm. Butterflies had invaded her stomach. In contrast, he seemed to be idly watching the teens across the street piling wood for a summer beach fire. Not a care in the world. She brushed past the young woman who approached to seat her and walked towards him.

Jake looked up and caught her eye as she neared him. "Hey, I didn't see you come in," he said. Standing abruptly to greet her, he knocked the table so hard the water glasses rattled, sloshing water on the table. "Damn. What a mess!"

"Here, let me help. It's no big deal." She grabbed the white cloth napkin from the place setting opposite his and wiped the table.

"No, no. I'll get it," he said, using the napkin he still held in his hand. "Sorry for the mess."

"No problem," she said. As she wadded the wet napkins into a pile at the table's edge for a passing waitress and settled into the chair opposite his, she realized that he wasn't quite as relaxed as she'd thought when she saw him sitting there gazing out the window. Somehow that comforted her.

"So, what do you like here?" he asked.

"I don't know. I've never eaten here."

"But, you said ..."

She laughed at the confusion in his eyes. "We were standing just across the street, remember? You asked me where we could we meet, so I saw this place and pointed."

He laughed. "Well, I know they've got great beer and chowder. Do you like beer?"

"I don't know. I mean, I've never tried much more than what comes in those awful kegs they used to have at parties, you know. That doesn't really count, does it?"

"Not at all. Let's have a beer sampler to start, okay?" he said, just as the waitress approached their table.

She took their drink order and walked away, leaving them to try to find common ground. That's what first dates are all about, Chris thought, as she struggled to calm her own nerves. Just getting to know each other. But she knew this was different. They had a history together, and yet they didn't even know each other. An odd place to start. Thoughts raced through her head. As she struggled to think of something to say, he drew her back to the present.

"So how's the running? Back to normal now?"

"Almost. I mean, I run daily now, but only about a mile or so. The PT told me to build slowly, so I'm trying not to overdo it."

"That sounds like a lot to me. What was normal? Before?"

"I've run daily since the summer before high school. I used to be a flight attendant, you know, so I was in cities all over the country. I ran about three to five miles a day when I was on the road and about ten when I was home."

"I'm impressed."

"Don't be," she said, already uncomfortable with the direction of the conversation.

"Why not? That takes a lot of dedication and strength."

"Oh it's nothing. Tell me something about yourself."

"Sure. Let's see. What can I tell you? You know I'm an EMT," he said with a wink. "I grew up here in Seattle with my dad."

"What about your mom?"

"She died when I was ten."

"I'm so sorry."

"It was a long time ago. I was practically raised by my Aunt Maggie. She's great."

"Aunt Maggie? I remember."

"She and my dad both wanted me to go to med school, but that seemed like a bit too much. Maybe someday. Let me tell you, they were not too happy when I told them I wanted to be a medic."

"What's with parents anyway?" she asked, realizing that she didn't want to go any farther down that path before the words were even out of her mouth.

As if on cue, the waitress approached with an oversized platter containing a dozen small glasses of beer in varying hues balanced on her right hand. "Here you are. One beer sampler. Your placemat here tells you the names and characteristics of each brew. Starting from left to right ..."

Chris stopped listening as the waitress explained the names and qualities of each brew. She watched as Jake listened with the patience of a saint and waited for the woman to leave. "That was a bit more than we needed to know," he said with a low laugh as soon as the waitress was out of earshot. "Here, do you want to try? Do you mind sharing? I'm sorry. I should've asked." Concern clouded his handsome face.

"It's fine, really. Here let me try that one first. From light to dark, right?"

"Now this one."

"Oh, yuck! It tastes like bitter mud."

They tasted, laughed and relaxed in each other's company.

"This is nice," Jake said, slouching in his chair and looking out towards the beach, his long legs extended next to her own under the table.

"Ummmm, maybe we could order some food," she said, changing the subject. "I'm starving. Did you say the chowder's good here?"

"The best. Do you want to try the chowder sampler?"

"Can we share it?" she asked with a sly grin.

"Of course."

Again, the waitress returned to their table. "Are you ready to order some dinner?"

"Yeah, we'll take a chowder sampler to share."

"And a couple of dinner salads," Chris added to the order. "Is that okay with you?"

"Sure," he said.

Turning to the waitress, Chris said, "Oil and vinegar for me, please."

"And for you, sir?"

"The same."

"Okay," the waitress said, jotting down their order. "I'll be right out with that."

"I've seen you run with the weekend warriors," Chris said, watching a pair of evening runners on the running path across the street.

"They're not so bad. And I try to get out three or four times a week when I'm not at the station."

"You must live close by."

"On Avalon. I work out of Fire Station 32, right there on Alaska and 35th. West Seattle's great, isn't it?"

"Yeah, I grew up here. I love the beach."

"And you live close by, too?"

Saved by the bell again, she thought as the waitress approached with another large platter balanced on her right hand. She didn't know why she was so edgy, so private. Habit?

Later, as the plates were cleared, Jake leaned back and relaxed. "This is nice," he said again. "Really nice."

"Yeah," Chris agreed, drawing out the word, her lips forming a shy smile.

"Nice enough to try again?" he asked.

"Maybe," she said. "We both have to eat, right?"

"Right." He laughed. "I waited a long time for this," he said. An afterthought, more to himself than to her, it seemed.

"Waited?" Chris felt the confusion, hesitation bubbling up inside of her, but if Jake noticed, he didn't show it.

"I hoped that maybe someday you'd call me or something."

"I threw away your note."

"No problem. You found me." Leaning into the table, he reached across and stroked her arm as though he were trying to draw her towards him. His touch sent sparks through her body. "All this time I kept thinking someday I'd see you again, and here we are, eating dinner together. I'd really like to see you again, Chris." His eyes blazed with desire. Reaching for her other hand, he clasped both of her hands in his own and brought them to his lips.

Pulling her hands from his grasp, she whispered, "I'm sorry, Jake. I'm so sorry. I shouldn't have come here tonight. I'm not ready for this." And before he had a chance to say another word, she was on her feet and out the door.

"Wait, Chris. Wait. I'm sorry!" Jumping to his feet, he headed after her, but the waitress blocked his path.

"Sir, your check."

THIRTY-SIX

CHRIS CLOSED HER CONDO DOOR and leaned against it allowing herself to slide to a sitting position on the floor. Desire surged through her body in a way she'd never known before. Sure, she'd had affairs. And she'd even been a bit promiscuous during those awful years right after Beth's death. She'd tried so hard to find comfort, even love, in the fumbling arms of hormone-driven college boys, but the sex always seemed to leave her feeling worse instead of better. More lonely than ever. With each affair, she felt less loved and less lovable, until she no longer loved or even respected herself. When she left the university and joined the airlines, she left sex and any hope of love behind. It had been a long, long time since she'd felt a man's touch.

The memory of Jake's hand on her arm, and his sweet, soft lips brushing her fingertips made her weak with desire. And with fear. She had thought she wasn't afraid anymore. She'd told him she wasn't afraid just this afternoon.

"What a fool. What a stupid fool. Why'd I have to go and run out on him?" she moaned to the empty walls. "He must think I'm a total basket case. Damn, damn, damn."

She remembered the green and golden hues in his eyes as the sunset fell over Elliott Bay, and the longing for his touch grew inside of her. Pulling herself to her feet, she paced the living room floor, afraid to go out on the balcony for fear he might still be down below at the beach. She knew she was being ridiculous, knew he would have gone home by now, but still she couldn't open the door to her balcony.

Finally she grabbed her phone and punched in Gemi's number. She heard the sleep in her friend's greeting and immediately regretted the call. "Oh, Gemi. I'm sorry. I didn't realize how late it was. Go back to sleep. I'll call you in the morning."

"No, no child. It's all right. I'm awake now. What's got you calling an old lady in the middle of the night?"

"Oh Gemi, I had dinner with him tonight and I totally blew it."

"Dinner with whom?"

"With Jake. Remember Jake? The paramedic I told you about. The one who found my journal."

"Yes, yes, I remember now. The runner with the great biceps," she laughed softly, remembering Chris's blush as she described the young man who had saved her life. "So you had dinner with him, child? And how was that?"

Chris could hear Gemi moving in her bed, settling into a good listening position. She began the story. She told Gemi about the apology, the run and the dinner. "God, Gemi, he was so handsome and so nice."

"Wonderful. You need a bit of romance in your life."

"But I ruined it all, Gemi. He held my hands and kissed my fingers. It was so sweet, and I ran away."

"You ran away?"

Chris heard Gemi move in her bed, imagined her sitting up, attentive. "Yeah. I jumped up and ran out of the restaurant like a total idiot."

"And why did you do such a thing?" Gemi asked with another soft chuckle.

"I don't know. I guess I was scared. And stop laughing at me."

"What are you afraid of, child?"

"I don't know, letting go, losing control, I suppose. I finally have a handle on this life of mine. I'm finally healthy and happy again. I guess I'm afraid of losing that."

"Understandable, but love and romance and sex are all wonderful parts of life. They are nothing to be afraid of."

"I know, I know. I really blew it tonight. What am I going to do now?"

"Well, child, you found this Jake of yours once to apologize, didn't you? I don't imagine that boy will turn his back if you approach him again."

"I suppose I could try again," Chris said.

"Child, I do not know this young man. But I do know that if you are attracted to him, you're making a mistake by trying to deny those feelings."

"What about you?" Chris asked. "Why isn't there a special man in your life?"

"Now that's a conversation for a whole new day. Let's get some sleep now, all right? Tomorrow you can decide when and how you want to approach this Jake of yours."

"Okay. I'm sorry I woke you. Good night," Chris said, already so lost in her memories of Jake's touch that she was unaware of Gemi's careful deflection of her question.

Across town, Gemi couldn't get back to sleep. She got up and went to the kitchen to fix herself a cup of tea. Who am I to give love advice to that girl, she scolded herself. Look at me. Almost fifty years old and still alone. No man in such a long time I'd be a nun if I were Catholic.

She chuckled at herself, her soft, warm laughter filling the emptiness of her comfortable apartment. But Chris had touched on the question that Gemi had been running from for years. Now it was out in the open. Now Gemi had to examine the question. Why wasn't there a special man in her life? And more important, did she want one?

She combed her fingers through her mass of long, tangled curls and knew at least part of the answer. She loved her independence, living life on her own terms. She could not live a life governed by the norms of a traditional Muslim marriage. At the same time, she felt certain that she would never meet a non-Muslim man, or even a non-traditional Muslim man, hidden as she was under her *shash* and the ill-fitting, ugly clothes she wore every time she left the privacy of her apartment. Clothes that seemed to be getting baggier with each passing week as Gemi continued the routine of a brisk daily walk that she'd begun months before with Chris. After so many years of celibacy, Gemi had simply put men out of her mind and dedicated her life to her work, cherishing the memories of the husband and child she'd lost so long ago. Perhaps even inflating those memories, if she were completely honest with herself.

But in the darkness of night, Chris's innocent question rang in Gemi's ears: "Why isn't there a special man in your life?" For the first time in a very long time, Gemi wondered if she might be ready to make some changes.

THIRTY-SEVEN

THE AFTERNOON FOLLOWING HER DISASTROUS DINNER with Jake, Chris pulled on her running shoes and headed south. By following the coastline for several miles, first along the Alki running path, and then on the Beach Drive sidewalk, she reached the lower, neighborhood entrance, to Lincoln Park. She set a brisk, steady pace and regulated her breathing to match the demands of a long run. As she reached the park entrance, she smiled to herself, knowing that she could loop the park and hit the sunset on her return.

As Chris entered at the north end of the beach, she remembered studying about the park years before: over a hundred acres of urban beach front property. She could still identify the Douglas Fir, Red Alder and Pacific Madrone that forested the upper areas of park land that was crisscrossed with an extensive network of trails. But what she loved most about the park was how the cliffs dropped from the upper park to a narrow strip of land that hugged the base of the hill. The beach path along the shore of Elliott Bay had always pulled Chris into the park. The running path and the heated saltwater swimming pool set on the small jetty of land that reached out into the bay midway along the trail.

Rather than following the coastline, Chris veered off onto a steep, switch-backed trail that led to the upper level of the park. She knew the path well. Could do it blindfolded, she thought, remembering the summer before Beth's death when the two of them would wear their shorts over their bikinis and run the park until they reached Coleman Pool. There they would swim and sunbathe for hours before continuing their run, damp swimsuits keeping them cool in the summer heat.

As Chris mounted the top of the hill, she eased onto the gentle path along the bluff, a trail with a panoramic view of Puget Sound and the islands beyond. A good run, she thought, a better workout than the flat of Alki Beach. But it was a run that always made her uneasy; a run that was a bit too close to her parents' home for comfort; a run that carried too many memories of all she lost when Beth was killed.

After looping the upper park, she circled to the south end, near the Vashon Island Ferry dock and headed back down to the waterfront. The first half of the trail was busy with people. Chris caught whiffs of barbecue from the covered picnic shelters as she headed towards Coleman Pool and beyond. This was the part of the run she'd been anticipating. She loved how the waves lapped the shore, falling forward and retreating. She loved how the sparkling golden path of sunlight across the water seemed to follow her like a Mona Lisa smile as she ran the gentle curve of the beach. And now, after so many long months of recovery, the kiss of the setting sun infused Chris with intense joy and trust that life was truly worth living.

In an uncharacteristic move, Chris slowed to a walk. As if in a trance, she left the running path and found her way down to the sandy beach, her eyes never leaving the magnificent sunset glowing across the dark saltwater. Gulls called overhead announcing the end of the day as Chris settled on a comfortable pile of bleached white driftwood to watch the sun disappear. They had a staring contest, she and the sun, and Chris remembered the way she and Beth sat opposite each other on Beth's bed and stared into each other's eyes, a contest of wills, to see who could avoid blinking the longest. Chris smiled sadly, remembering how she always beat Beth at this game, just as she now beat the sun. If there was one thing Jake was right about, it was her determination. She smiled again, shivers coursing her spine, as she felt the whisper of his fingers on her forearm, his soft, moist lips on her fingertips.

"What an idiot," she screamed into the descending dusk. She threw a smooth beach stone at the gentle waves that stroked the sandy shore a few feet in front of her. What an idiot. Now what am I going to do? How many times is he going to listen to my lame apologies. Damn, damn, damn.

For what Chris realized as she sat and stared down the sun was that she was ready to let a man into her life, and she wanted that man to be Jake.

As the last sliver of golden sunlight slipped below the horizon, Chris stood, stretched and returned to the running path, retracing her steps towards home.

THIRTY-EIGHT

THE DOWNSIDE OF MOST ALKI BEACH CONDOS was the room layout dictated by the hillside behind the buildings. Most were built with all the windows in the front to take in the magnificence of Elliott Bay with the cityscape as a backdrop. They crowded the narrow strip of land that lay at the shores of Elliott Bay with Admiral Hill rising like a wall behind them. In recent years the tiny resort homes, 1930s and 1940s bungalows and cabins, had all but disappeared, replaced by high-rise condos.

Chris's building, located towards the southwestern end of the Alki Peninsula where it juts into Puget Sound marking the southern entrance to Elliot Bay, had no hillside behind it. This tiny western tip of West Seattle, crowned by the Alki Point Lighthouse, is flat. Nature had not created a barrier behind her building, but man had. In the form of more buildings. So, like most beach condos, hers was well-lit in the front with an expansive view of the water, but dark towards the back bedrooms. In those dark corners there was more storage space than many small houses could claim.

On the morning of her half-birthday, May 20, six months after the suicide attempt, Chris was determined to take one more step towards facing the pain of her past. She was ready to look at Beth's portfolio, the portfolio she'd taken from her sister's bedroom the morning after she was killed. It seemed like a different lifetime. It felt like yesterday. The pain was always there.

What would Beth have been like in her late twenties? What would she be doing with her life? Would she have married her first love? There were no answers. Chris knew there never would be, so the pain ran deep. Still, she had a bit of Beth that she'd been afraid to look at all these years.

Chris was not a pack rat. She bought little and kept less. Coffee cup in hand she headed to the storage closet tucked under the eaves at the back of the condo. She opened the musty closet, switched on the light and walked in. There were a few boxes of holiday decorations and file boxes of once-important papers. Someone had told her to save everything for five years, so she had. Bank statements, cancelled checks and paid bills. She set her cup on the top of a sealed box and rummaged around until she found what she was searching for: the large black leather artist's portfolio. She knew the portfolio contained not only Beth's artwork, but also her poetry journals and an accordion file full of notes and photos. She knew because she'd put it all together and hid it in her bedroom that day before her mother changed the locks on Beth's room and sealed her memory.

Five years after the accident that took Beth's life, Chris moved into the condo. As she packed her belongings, as she emptied the bedroom of her childhood, she had carefully packed Beth's portfolio among her things, never telling her parents of its existence. Never looking at it herself.

Now, she lifted the heavy black portfolio from storage, and with the gentle touch of a pediatric nurse, she carried it toward the daylight at the front of the condo. Setting it on the large coffee table in the center of the living room, she pulled the long metal zipper with trembling fingers. She felt the resistance of the zipper. As long as Beth's secrets remained hidden in the storage closet, Chris had been able to cling to a bit of denial. She would never have even considered snooping into her sister's secrets when Beth was alive. To do so now, to open Beth's portfolio, was to accept that her sister was truly gone from her life forever.

With slow, tentative fingers, she pulled the zipper that held her sister's young secrets. She folded the sides of the large portfolio case open flat on the coffee table and lifted out the accordion file and plastic case full of journals, setting them on the edge of the coffee table. A pile of artwork lay before her, the artwork of a teenaged girl, her life in pen and ink, charcoal, oils and watercolors. She knew some of Beth's work. She knew the journals were full of her sister's poetry. They had been close. But still, Chris knew there were secrets here, and she wasn't sure how to proceed, how to invade her sister's privacy now so long after her death. She stood and paced the room, hesitating until she knew, until she felt certain in her heart that it was right, until Beth was with her.

When she was ready, she sat on the sofa staring at the work before her: Beth's work, Beth's life, all eighteen years of it, in artwork and poetry. She breathed in the musty scent of paper, ink and charcoal. Scents locked away in that heavy portfolio for so long. She breathed slowly, deeply. She focused her breathing as if in preparation for a long run as she lifted drawing, painting, sketch.

Scenes of their shared childhood lay before her. Studies of their house, inside and out. A Christmas tree the night before, the colorful gifts untouched by excited, greedy fingers. An angle of Beth's bedroom. The family of four in front of the living room fireplace. A group of friends laughing around a beach fire with the Seattle skyline at sunset in the background. She saw herself in full stride, racing across the blue intensity of Elliot Bay, the Statue of Liberty in the background.

Chris wiped her eyes. She remembered the image in watercolors – the card Beth included with her sixteenth birthday gift. But she didn't know her sister had done a charcoal as well.

As Chris turned the pieces one by one, as though she were turning the large pages of an oversized picture book, she realized that each had a reference photograph and neatly printed label taped to the back stating title, date and medium. There was no specific organization and not all of the pieces were finished, but all were labeled in Beth's precise print.

She stood and walked to the bedroom, returning moments later with a box of tissue. Determined not to stain her sister's work with tears, she continued to turn the artwork, large and small, reliving the memories of her childhood.

About midway through the pile, Chris froze. Her hands dropped to her lap as she locked eyes with those of a solitary woman staring back at her. The eyes were black, even darker than the face of the woman before her. There was no smile. Only the creases around the woman's eyes gave her the gentleness that Chris felt as she held the small painting in her trembling hands. There was a familiarity here that Chris didn't understand. A sense of knowing.

Puzzled, Chris turned the painting and looked at the reference photo taped to the back. It was an old black-and-white family photograph of a white man with his arm around the shoulders of a black woman. A small boy of six or seven with light skin and dark curly hair stood in front of them both. The painting portrayed only the face of the woman. She was the subject Beth had chosen.

Chris stared at the photo, understanding crawling her spine even before she read the label. This child she knew. The eyes, the grin, the curly black hair. She saw them in the mirror each morning. She'd seen them at the dinner table of her youth.

"Grandmother Stevens 1920 to 1967" it read in Beth's careful lettering. "Grandmother Stevens?" Chris asked aloud in the empty condo. "Grandmother?"

Turning the canvas, she looked again into the dark, smiling eyes and remembered. It was during the Christmas break, not long after Beth had shown her the packet of birth control pills. She'd gone into Beth's room. She'd knocked first, like she always did, but she hadn't waited for her sister to give her the okay to come in. Beth was furious. "Get out of here and never, ever come in until I say it's okay," she screamed as she stood in front of her uncovered easel, shielding it from view.

"What's the big deal? I've seen your work before. Why not this time?"

"It's a surprise, okay? I'll show you. Just not yet. When I'm done, all right? Now get out of here and knock next time."

Chris sat on her living room floor, her knees held tight to her chest. She'd never seen the painting Beth had hidden from her that day so long ago. Not until now. The painting was never finished: the hair, the face, the eyes, were all rendered to perfection in thick dark brush strokes, but not the body, not the background. As Chris stared at Beth's unfinished painting, she sensed the secret her sister planned to tell her. She felt the truth in her bones. She raked her fingers through her own dark curls and remembered Beth's soft brown waves of silk. Was it possible? She tried to remember those boring high school science classes. How did all that genetics stuff work?

She glanced at her watch: 6 p.m. She hurried to her spare bedroom and used her computer printer to make a copy of the photograph, stuffed it into her handbag and ran out the door. Ten minutes later she pulled into her parents' driveway. There were no cars out front, but that meant nothing. Her mom parked in the garage. She turned off the engine and dug in the glove compartment for the set of house keys she always kept there. Her hands shook.

Keying open the front door to a childhood she still struggled to escape, she called into the foyer, "Mom, are you here?"

"What are you doing here? And why didn't you call first? You know I hate it when people just stop by."

She wanted to say something about not being "people." Instead she ignored both the attitude and the question and followed her mother's voice into the living room. "I needed to see you, Mom. Is Dad home?"

"He works until late every day. You know that as well." Her mother turned back to the magazine she was flipping through as though her daughter being there was a daily, even weekly occurrence, as though it hadn't been more than a year, maybe two, since Chris had set foot in the house.

"There's something I want to ask you about, Mom."

"Is that why you popped in?" her mother said with a sneer.

Again, Chris ignored the dig. "Mom, will you look at this photo? Is this Dad and his parents?"

As Chris placed the copy of the photo in her mother's lap, she jumped to her feet, her face a mask of anger and disbelief.

"Where did you get this?" Her voice was tight and cold.

"That's not the point, Mom. I want to know the truth. Are these my grandparents?"

Her mother balled the paper in her fist and threw it across the room. "Get out of my house."

"I guess that's a yes then, isn't it? What's the big deal? I want to understand."

"I told you to get out. Don't you know when to just leave things alone?" She turned and fled the room.

THIRTY-NINE

"YOU'RE NOT GOING TO BELIEVE THIS," Chris said as she flopped into the loveseat in Peter's office the following afternoon.

"Try me," Peter said.

Chris opened her backpack and took out another copy of the photograph she'd discovered the day before. "I did what you suggested. I opened Beth's portfolio yesterday, but I didn't get very far."

"What happened?"

"I found this," she said, handing him the photocopy. "My sister was super-organized. Each piece of artwork has a reference photo like this taped to the back. This photo is on the back of a painting titled "Grandmother Stevens 1920 to 1967."

Peter looked at the photo, and then turned his gaze on Chris. "Tell me what this means to you."

"I think it means my father's mother was African American. You know, they always led us to believe he was an orphan. So I figure, if that's really him and his folks, I could finally understand why they hate me so much. So I had to find out."

"I'm not sure I'm following. What did you do?"

"I visited my mother. I asked her if this woman was my grandmother."

"How'd that go?"

"Not so good. She crumpled up the picture into a ball and sent it flying right before she told me to get out of her house. So, I figure it's true. I wish I knew how Beth found the photo, but I guess I never will, not for sure. I know she loved to snoop through our parents' closets and the attic and stuff when they were out of the house. She was a whole lot more rebellious than I ever was. Maybe she just found it."

"What does this mean to you now, Chris? What does it tell you?"

"Well, Beth had light skin, brown hair and blue eyes. Then I came along with black curly hair, dark eyes and skin that looked tan year round. Beth used to get so jealous of my skin, and I was jealous of her silky, smooth hair. Anyway, we always figured she took after Mom and I looked more like Dad. But I never realized I looked like my grandmother. Dad was pretending to be white. What's that called?"

"Passing?"

"Right. Dad was passing. Then I came along, a visual reminder of everything he wanted to hide. But I don't get why. What was the big deal?"

"I don't know what it meant to him, but I do know that this is a different time and place than the world your father or his parents lived in. If your grandparents were an openly bi-racial couple, they were very progressive in their day. Who knows the consequences your dad had to pay because of his parents' decision. Depending on where they lived and how they dealt with it, it could've been pretty tough on him."

"Tough enough to lie about his mother and reject his own daughter?"

"I'm not justifying his actions, Chris. I'm only trying to walk through this with you, okay?"

"Yeah, okay, sorry. I didn't mean to bite your head off. So what do I do now?"

"What do you want to do?"

"What I want would be to talk to my parents, but I tried that yesterday and got kicked out of the house."

"Which, by the way, was a big step. You faced your fears and went home to talk to your mother. Good for you."

"Thanks, but a whole lot of good it did me."

"Well now, let's look at that. You learned the truth, didn't you?"

Chris was quiet, and she knew, with deep certainty she knew that those deep dark eyes that stared out from Beth's canvas were her grandmother's eyes, her own eyes, the same but different.

"I know it's true," she said. "And I know they hate me because I am a reminder of their secret. I know they don't even know me, don't want to know me, and never have because I'm a reminder of everything that they've denied. They've built a life based on that denial. I suppose I also know that they will never change. They'll never love me or accept me. Not with this," she said, raking her fingers through her soft black curls.

"And how does that make you feel?"

"Like crap, of course," she snapped.

"Is that all?"

"I guess I'm glad I finally understand why they've always rejected me. You know, I thought there was something wrong with me, that in some way I was at fault. But, you know, there's nothing wrong with me at all. They're just a couple of posing, racist bigots. I'm done with trying to be something they can accept. Maybe I'll go tanning and get really, really dark and go totally Rasta. Then I'll show up at their annual Christmas party."

"Is that what you want? To get even?"

"Not really. I just want to figure out how to get on with my life. But now I'm not even sure who I am."

"You're the same person you were before you peeked into your sister's portfolio, Chris. You just have a lot more information to work with."

FORTY

THE DOOR SWUNG OPEN before Gemi had a chance to knock. She jumped back in surprise.

"Hey, Gemi. Thanks for coming so soon. I really need to talk to you," Chris said in a rush.

Gemi smiled as her young friend's words tumbled one over the other like a cascade of fresh spring water. "My pleasure, child. I was close by when you called."

"Yeah? New client?"

"An elderly woman up the hill. She's confined to a wheelchair, dear thing. Just wants to stay in her own home, but her children want to move her into a retirement home."

"Make life easier for themselves, right?" Chris said.

"Perhaps. But she's a determined soul, she is."

"Well, if anybody can help her, it's you. Take it from me," Chris said as she made her way across the living room. Gemi could see the agitation in the girl and the disarray in the condo. A large portfolio lay open on the living room floor, an accordion file next to it.

"Thank you, child, for your vote of confidence. Now tell me, what's the big secret that brought me running on this beautiful afternoon?"

Chris held an unfinished oil painting, about a foot square, in front of her. "Take a look at this, okay? What do you see? Gut reaction."

Without hesitation, Gemi said, "I see your eyes, child. Your eyes and your expression on a black face."

"That's what I thought," Chris said in a flat tone that made it impossible for Gemi to decipher the emotion.

"So tell me, who is this beautiful woman? Is this one of Beth's paintings? Is this all your sister's work?" she asked with a sweep of her arm that encompassed the portfolio on the floor.

"Yup. I finally opened her portfolio," Chris said.

Gemi noticed that she answered only the latter questions, but not the first. She watched Chris turn the painting over.

"Check this out."

"Grandmother Stevens, 1920 to 1967," Gemi read aloud from a small, handwritten index card attached to the back of the canvas. Then she studied a small, black-and-white photograph taped next to the index card. "So, if this is your grandmother, then this would be your grandfather and your father. Is that correct, child?"

"Apparently so. Bizarre, huh?"

"Certainly a surprise, child, but not as unusual as you might imagine. I have found that things are seldom what they first appear to be," Gemi said. She turned the painting again to look at the painted image of Grandmother Stevens. "When you look at me, you see my dark skin and eyes. You see the curls in my black hair. Therefore, I am a black African to you. But appearances can be deceiving. Let me tell you a bit about Ethiopian history. From 1936 to 1941 my native country was occupied by Italy. And Eritrea, where my mother was born, was under Italian rule from 1886 until 1941."

"Okay, so what's the point?"

Gemi chose to ignore the impatience in Chris's voice and continued. "The point is that like you, I am not what I appear to be. You see, child, my maternal grandfather was Italian with skin lighter than your own. Only my maternal grandmother, like your paternal grandmother here in the photo, was black-skinned."

"You gotta be kidding."

"Not at all, child. It seems that your father, like my grandfather, was not happy with what he saw in the face of his own child."

"You mean when your mother was born? What happened?"

"He abandoned my grandmother shortly after my mother's birth. That was at about the same time as the collapse of Italian rule. He returned to Italy leaving my grandmother to fend for herself with a nursing baby."

"Your mother looked African, like her mother, and your grandfather couldn't take it?" Chris asked, incredulous.

"So it would seem, child."

"Unreal. I'm so sorry."

"It's past history, child. The point is that we are rarely what appearances dictate. I do not recall the exact statistic, but most people who consider themselves white, have a small percentage of black blood running in their veins."

"Sounds like it works both ways."

"I suppose it does, child. But tell me, what does this discovery mean to you?"

"If it's true, and I'm sure it must be because when I showed the photo to my mom, she kicked me out of the house."

"You visited your mother?" Now it was Gemi's turn to be surprised.

"I sure did. Impressed?" Chris said. A wide grin spread across her face.

"Very much so, child. Tell me, what happened?"

"Thanks. Well, I drove right over there and dropped a photocopy of the photograph in my mom's lap. You should've seen her. She acted like it was a spider or a snake or something. I've never seen her move so fast." Chris was laughing, and Gemi only watched in silent amazement. "Anyway, she yelled at me to get out of her house."

"I'm sorry, child. No mother should act in such a manner."

"No, I guess not. But at least I know that it's gotta be true. I mean, why else would she react like that? So, I finally understand why they hate me so much."

"Explain," Gemi said, her voice gentle with emotion and interest, encouraging her young friend to continue.

"I guess I was just one big disappointment to my parents. It's like, they have this big secret, you know. Dad's mom was black, but Dad could pass for white, so he did. You know, I did the math. Dad was born in 1944, so his mom died when he was only twenty-three."

"My word, she died young, didn't she?"

"Yeah, she was only forty-seven."

"My age," Gemi said. It was almost a whisper, air escaping, nothing more. "1967. She missed the March on Washington. She died without enjoying the fruits of the civil rights movement in America. What a pity, poor thing. Do you have any idea how she died, child?"

"No. This is all I have," she said, her hand on the painting. "This and my mom's reaction."

"I'm sorry for interrupting. Finish your story, child."

"Okay, so I figure, he just reinvented himself after his mom's death. I have no idea what happened to his father, but I'm guessing Dad just moved someplace where nobody knew him and passed as white. He made a bundle of money and married my mother who had her own bundle. Their first child – Beth – was a beauty with fair skin, smooth light brown hair and bright blue eyes. The secret was safe. Then I came along, a walking, talking reminder of the racial heritage they were determined to hide. Kinda sucks, doesn't it?"

"It certainly does, child."

"You know, as a little kid, I remember my mom was always smothering me in sunscreen. As Beth and I got older, she harped at both of us to stay out of the sun. That's probably why she hated it when we started running. And, oh crap this is a good one, I remember once, I must've been about ten or twelve, she took me to a salon to have my hair straightened. At the time it just seemed like a rare, special time with Mom. But now I get it. She hated the way I looked. Both her and Dad. My black curls, my full lips, my perpetual tan. It must have driven them nuts."

Gemi listened in silence, feeling the gentle, salt-air breeze off the Sound through the open door and watching as Chris paced the floor, raking her fingers through her curls.

"At least now I get it. They couldn't love me. And they never will."

"I'm so sorry, child."

"You know, I'm okay now, Gemi. At least I finally understand."

For a brief moment, Gemi hoped that it would really be that easy for Chris. That understanding would make the pain go away. But she knew better. She knew that the story wasn't over yet.

Rebirth

FORTY-ONE

THE RING SHATTERED THE DARKENED SILENCE at just after three in the morning. Chris startled awake and grabbed for the phone on her bedside table.

"Hello?" There was silence on the line. Then heavy breathing.

"Hello. Who is this?"

"Your father, god damn it."

"Dad? Is everything okay? Mom?"

"As if you care, you ungrateful bitch. How dare you? How dare you start snooping around where you don't belong? Just who do you think you are anyway? I'm in the car right now, and I'm of half a mind to come over there right now and teach you a thing or two."

Chris could hear the slur in his voice. That familiar slur, the slur of late night arguments between her parents. Arguments that would wake her from a deep sleep and keep her awake for hours.

"Dad, where are you?" She tried not to panic. "Are you driving?"

"Yeah, coming home late from the office. A late night at the office. Your mother still buys that one, the stupid bitch. I'm on the bridge. I think I'll just take your exit."

"Go home, Dad. We can talk tomorrow."

"I don't want to talk to you, you ungrateful bitch. I want to beat the …"

"No. I'm not going to listen to you. I'm not going to talk to you when you're drunk. I'm going to hang up the phone now. Go home."

She snapped the phone closed and sat on the edge of the bed, her head in her hands sobbing. She figured she'd get a reaction of some sort from her visit with her mother, but not this. He was drunk and furious and now he was threatening her. She didn't know how real those threats were, but she knew she was afraid.

She sat in the darkness shaking, not knowing what to do, what to think. In her twenty-six years she could count the number of phone calls she'd received from her father on one hand. Communication never existed between them. She hardly knew the man. But she did remember the loud drunken voice that escaped her parents' bedroom when she still lived at home.

After Beth's death, during those horrible years between sixteen and eighteen, before she could finally get away using a university education as her ticket to freedom, she'd heard her father come in at all hours of the night, heard the drunken insults he spewed at her mother. But never, ever had she heard or seen any physical violence. Her mother kept quiet, stayed silent, maybe in a corner, maybe in the bathroom behind a locked door. For the first time, Chris realized that her mother knew self-preservation. Maybe she felt the same fear. Chris didn't know, and she didn't trust her mother enough to call her for advice.

She pulled a gray fleece over her tank top and headed to the living room through the dark hallway, switching on every light in the condo along the way. The front curtains were open and the lights of the downtown skyline flooded her living room. The lights Chris loved. The lights that used to be her only reminder that she wasn't alone in the world. Before Gemi. Before Peter Bentley. Before Karin and the writers at The Last Exit. Before Jake.

It was raining hard. A heavy spring rain. The kind of rain Seattleites laugh about, claiming it always rains on the Fourth of July. This year it was early. Chris comforted herself thinking about her run the next morning, about how great the air would be after the rain. She made a cup of tea, going through the motions as if programmed for the task. The routine was a comfort. Fresh water in the tea kettle. Turn on the gas. Wait for it to boil. Heat the porcelain teapot with hot water from the faucet. Empty it. A scoop of tea leaves in the bottom. Pour in the boiling water and cover the pot. No single-cup-in-the-microwave for her. She'd learned to make tea from Gemi.

Just as she was pouring the boiling water into the teapot, the intercom buzzer echoed through the condo. Chris froze. Stone-still, she was afraid to move, afraid to pick up the receiver, afraid to hear the voice she knew would be on the line. "It's okay," she whispered to herself. "He can't get in."

The buzzer continued its insistent ring. Ten, eleven, twelve. Chris didn't realize she was counting the rings. She picked up the receiver and pushed Talk.

"Dad?"

"It's about time, god damn it. Open up this fucking door before I break it down."

"No, Dad. You're drunk, and you're acting crazy. Go home."

"I told you to open this god damn door, or I'll break the fucking thing down."

"No, I won't. Go home."

"God damn it, you ungrateful bitch. I built a life for us from nothing and now you start digging around in the past. Open this door so I can teach you a thing or two about the past."

She heard the door handle rattle. She heard something banging against the heavy glass doors. She heard her father's curses.

"Come on, Chris. Let your dad in for a little visit. Come on, honey."

That was too much. The seductive slime in his drunken voice made her feel nauseous. With trembling hands, Chris pushed End and disconnected the intercom. She couldn't see the front door of the building from her condo windows, not without going out on the balcony, and she was afraid to unlock the door. Still, she could hear the pounding of fists on glass. She stood staring out the glass doors, searching for solace in the dark waters of Elliott Bay and the skyline she loved. She knew he couldn't get in. She knew she was safe. But she also knew her own father wanted to hurt her.

The pounding stopped.

"Thank goodness," she murmured.

Then, as she watched with horror from her third floor condo, she saw her father stumble across the street and down to the beach in the rain and darkness. She saw him return to the sidewalk a few moments later, a thick piece of driftwood in the arms of his Versace suit. He stumbled back across the empty street and out of her range of vision. The pounding began again. Louder, heavier. She couldn't hear her father's vile curses or the crash of shattered glass. But she could hear the sirens and see the flashing police lights.

FORTY-TWO

"**GET YOUR FUCKING HANDS OFF ME,** god damn it."

"Look, buddy. You come with us peacefully or we cuff you. Your choice."

"Go right ahead, you little shit head. Just try to cuff me. You'll be sorry."

"Buddy, you might be somebody powerful and important in your world, but right now you're in our world." With those words, the two officers moved in, flattened a well-dressed, middle-aged man to the ground and cuffed him.

"Ah hell, this guy's bleeding like a stuck pig." Standing and turning to the paramedics who had pulled up right behind the squad cars, one of the officers nodded towards the cuffed man and said, "Can you wrap him up enough so we can take him in and book him?"

Jake had been listening to the entire exchange through the open window of the Medic One vehicle. At the officer's request, he jumped from the cab and rushed over, medical bag in hand.

"Looks like you'll need to get those cuffs off him so I can take a look at his arms," Jake said as he knelt next to the man on the ground, now little more than a puddle of drunken humanity, his anger drained, replaced by self-pity.

"How could she do this to me?" the man whined.

"Looks like you might have hit something important when you stuck your hand through that door, buddy," the officer said as he uncuffed him.

"Why would she do this? It's all her fault. She should've opened the damn door."

As Jake worked on the man's arms and listened, the officer moved in closer. "Who?" he demanded. "Who should've opened the door?" "My god damned daughter. Christine. It's all her fault. I bought this place, god damn it."

"What's her name?"

"Christine. I already told you that. You deaf or something? Christine Stevens. The ungrateful little bitch. I'll get her yet."

Jake paused as he wrapped the man's bleeding arms, listening to the conversation.

"Look, buddy. Right now we got you on disturbing the peace and attempted breaking and entering. Don't make it worse on yourself." Then he turned to the second officer and said, "You want to get in there and make sure this Christine Stevens is okay. I'll get this joker down to King County lock up."

"Right," the second officer said.

Just then, Jake saw a wizened old man appear on the inside of the shattered glass door. "I called the police when I heard this guy banging down our front door. You might've gotten here a bit faster and saved the door. Fred's the name. Building manager."

"Do you know a Christine Stevens?" the officer asked, ignoring the old man's complaint.

"Of course. I know everybody in this building."

"Tell me about Christine Stevens."

"Sweet young woman. Lives alone on the third floor."

"Okay, open the door."

The officer headed to the third floor with Fred trailing behind, and Jake finished up his work on the man he now knew was Chris's father.

"He's all yours, officer. Nothing serious, but stitches might not be a bad idea."

"Thanks, I'll have him evaluated." With that, the officer dragged Chris's father to his feet, pushed him into the back of his patrol car and drove off.

Jake was still packing his supplies when the second officer reappeared. "So what the hell was that all about?" he asked.

"The daughter said something about a family secret. A bit shaken up, but okay. Quite a looker that one." Then he climbed into the other squad car and left.

As soon as the taillights faded in the distance, Fred stuck his head out the front door. "Is that crazy drunk gone?" he asked Jake.

"Yeah, he's gone," Jake said. Then he turned to his partner who stood jingling his keys next to their Medic One vehicle and said, "Listen, Dave, I know this girl. I gotta make sure she's okay."

"They'll have your ass for this, Jake."

"Then, let's not tell them. Just give me a minute, okay?"

"You owe me," Dave hollered out the window as he climbed into the cab to wait.

"Your partner don't seem any too happy there," Fred said.

"Oh, he'll be fine. Listen, did you say Chris Stevens lives on the third floor? Is that the C. Stevens here?" he asked pointing to the list of names next to the doorbells.

"Might be. You know her?"

"I know her. And if I know her as well as I think I do, she's up there pacing the floor, worried sick. You think we could check on her?"

"That cop just checked on her," Fred said.

Jake noticed the old man stiffen and said, "We both know that's not the same. No comfort there."

"Suppose you're right. Might not be a bad idea. Go ahead. Intercom's right there."

"You know, she doesn't know me as well as she knows you. Might be best if you called her. Just tell her Jake Bowmer is down here."

"Well, I guess that would be okay." Fred pushed the intercom to Chris's condo. They both heard the faint click as Chris responded on her end. Jake gave Fred a nudge.

"Hello? Hello are you there, Chris? This is Fred."

"Fred?"

"Yes, Fred. The crazy man is gone, but there's a paramedic here. Says his name is Jake Bowmer. Says he knows you. Wants to know if you're okay."

"Jake?"

"Yes, Chris. It's me. My partner and I answered the aid call."

"Again?"

"Yeah, small town, isn't it? Are you okay?"

"Is my dad okay?"

"He'll be fine. Drunk out of his mind, but just bleeding from minor cuts and abrasions. I bandaged him up and the police took him downtown to book him."

"Crap. What have I done now?"

"Sounds to me like you didn't do a thing wrong."

"He's my father. Maybe I should've just let him in."

"Listen, Chris, do you want someone to talk to?"

"Talk?"

Jake heard the hesitation in her voice and remembered their disastrous dinner a few weeks earlier. "Wait a sec, don't misunderstand," he quickly added. "I'm not asking to come up or anything. Why don't you come down? I see a nice sofa here in the lobby. And Fred's right here cleaning up the broken glass."

Jake waited, hoping that the calm assurance in his voice would convince her to come down and let him comfort her.

"No, I don't think so," he heard her say. "I think I just need to sleep."

"Okay, but let me give you my phone number, all right?" he said, hiding the disappointment in his voice and keeping her on the line a bit longer.

"Just a sec." Chris found a scrap of paper and wrote the number Jake gave her.

"Now, call me if you need anything or whatever, okay?"

"Sure, thanks. Good night."

Jake heard the click that signaled the end of the connection. He thanked Fred and headed to join his waiting partner, wondering if he'd ever get a call.

FORTY-THREE

CHRIS STUMBLED BACK TO HER BEDROOM and collapsed. She lay in a tight ball on top of her bed, her knees drawn to her chest, locked in place by her arms. She floated in and out of sleep, losing track of time, no longer able to judge the passing of hours. She couldn't stop the echoing of her father's hateful words in her head. Slowly, lulled by the night calm, she sank into a state of nothingness, dull quiet nothingness.

Darkness. It wasn't a thought, not really. For thought, the word thought, denotes a sense of conscious awareness, and Chris was not yet aware. She felt the darkness. She sensed it as a dog senses an intruder's presence even without sight or sound.

Darkness. This is darkness. I know this darkness. The ideas surfaced as floating fragments. They appeared with growing intensity, insistent, demanding a response. Chris was speaking to herself. Her inner being was speaking to her through the darkness, urging her awareness and her reaction. Urging her to take control of her own destiny, her own survival. She felt the darkness, and slowly she also became aware of it. Aware that this was what she needed to learn to recognize if she were to survive.

Darkness and pain. What had Bentley said about pain? The thought formed as fragments pulling themselves together to create a logical whole like wild geese assembling a perfect flight formation. And then, only then, was Chris able to recognize what was happening to her. For the first time in her life, she recognized the curtain of darkness descending around her, engulfing her, suffocating her. For the first time, she recognized the telltale signs of depression.

He told me to recognize the pain, feel the pain, let it wash over me, and then let it go. What is this sharp, ripping pain? Dad? Dad. Sobs rocked her body. She held herself tighter, her knees to her chest, in a desperate attempt to keep herself together, to prevent her body from shattering into a million tiny fragments. My father wanted to hurt me. That realization, the recognition of the meaning behind those words, ripped through her like a gun shot, like a bullet tearing the tender tissue around her heart.

"Face the pain. Face the pain," she murmured. Releasing the tight arm lock on her knees, she extended her legs, one at a time. She wiggled her toes and reached her arms straight out above her head, stretching her body as long as she could across her bed. Then, she sat up, dropped her bare feet over the side of her bed and reached for her cell phone.

"Bentley, I need to see you. Please," she told the machine. She paced the bedroom floor. What would he tell me? What should I do? I've been through an ordeal. That's what he'd call it. An ordeal. Face the pain. Face the truth. Dad attacked the front door. Dad wanted to hurt me. No more excuses.

Tears of grief streamed down her face. She embraced herself and sank to the floor, again clutching her knees to her chest in a fetal position. She was still on the floor hours later when the phone rang. Fear gripped her as she grabbed the phone from her bedside table. When she saw Peter Bentley's name on the caller ID, she took the call.

"Hi, Chris. You called?"

"Yes. I need to see you." She struggled to keep the desperation from her voice, but Bentley's trained ear caught it.

"Did something happen, Chris?"

"The curtain is falling."

"Okay. Chris, are you suicidal?"

"No, I don't think so. No."

"Okay then. Can you come to my office at eleven?"

"Sure. I guess. What time is it now?"

"It's just after 9:00. Have you gone for a run today?"

"No."

"That's part of facing the pain, Chris. Put your shoes on and go for a long run. You have plenty of time. Go for a run and then I'll see you at 11:00."

"Okay. I can do that." She hung up the phone and opened her closet door. She coaxed herself into her running clothes, tied her shoes, and headed out the door.

When Chris arrived at the top of the steep stairs two hours later, the curtain had lifted. She was invigorated from her run and fresh from a warm shower when she met Peter at his office door.

"Looks like the run did you some good," he said.

"Yeah, you're always right."

"So come on in and tell me what happened."

"I was a wreck when I called you. I hadn't slept most of the night. I could feel the depression coming like a black tidal wave, and I just couldn't stop it. I was paralyzed, lying in a ball, paralyzed."

"But you called," he told her.

"Yeah, and I remembered what you told me about facing the pain. I let it roll over me. I was buried in the pain when I called you."

"Good. Now tell me. What brought this on?"

"My dad."

For the next hour Chris relived the horror of her father's threatening attack on the condo door. As she told the story, she faced the wrong, accepted the pain, and then let go. A heavy burden dropped from her shoulders.

As her story came to a close, Peter redirected. "So, Chris, what can you take from this experience?"

"I suppose I know that Dad's responsible for Dad. I'm not."

"Okay, but how do you deal with these things when they happen?"

"I call you," she laughed.

Smiling, Peter continued, "Sounds to me like your run cleared things up for you before you ever got here. Tell me, what else could you have done? What would you have done if I hadn't been free?"

"I'm afraid I would have stayed in a ball on my bedroom floor a whole lot longer."

"Well, that's one possibility. Are there others?"

"Running." She paused for a moment and then added, "And writing. Writing. Why didn't I think to write? That would've helped."

"Good," Peter smiled. "So that's what you need to take with you today, Chris. Running and writing are your tools. Remember them. Always."

There was silence in the gentle room at the top of the stairs. A comfortable, understanding silence. A peaceful silence after a night of raging hell.

"There's one more thing you might want to think about, Chris." She looked into his wise blue eyes, a question mark in her own. "You might want to consider giving your mother a call."

"My mother? Why would I want to call my mother? She's always been on his side. Always. Besides last time I tried to talk to her, she kicked me out of the house."

"True. But if I understand you correctly, she has also been a victim of your father's abusive behavior. She might not want or accept the hand you extend to her, but you have the right to let her know what happened last night. Your version of what happened."

"Lord, I don't know if I can handle any more rejection right now. My relationship with my father is shot to hell. What if I lose what little I have left with my mother?"

"You're right. It could be tough. But there's always the off chance that you could gain the mother you've never had, the kind of relationship you've always wanted." With a smile, he added, "You'll never know until you try."

FORTY-FOUR

HOME ALONE IN HER CONDO that evening, Chris couldn't sit still. She paced the floor, had been pacing the floor for hours. Daylight faded and the city lights twinkled across the dark water, but the shadows didn't bother Chris. No, it was Peter's words that kept her pacing the floor.

... Again Chris is asleep when the phone shatters the night calm. But this time she is not alone in her bedroom in her lonely Alki condo. Instead she feels the familiar walls of her childhood bedroom safe and solid around her. The phone is silent. Then, she hears the bedroom door open. Her mother's scent fills the room. "Was it Dad?" she asks.

Her mother sits on the edge of her bed, her cool soft hand strokes the side of her face, brushing her dark curls from her sleepy eyes. "Yes, darling," her mother whispers. "Sleep now. I'll never let him come near you. I'll never let him hurt you. I promise." ...

"Fat chance. Like that's ever going to happen," Chris muttered, angry and frustrated with her own flights of fancy. Still, she knew Peter was right, knew it was unfair to judge her mother without giving it at least one final shot, knew she had little to lose.

Her relationship with her mother had always been paper thin. Rice paper thin. It couldn't get any worse. Could it get better? She didn't know. She didn't know her own mother well enough to predict.

"I've got nothing to lose," she whispered to the walls. With a shake of her shoulders and a deep breath, she reached for the phone.

"Ellen Stevens speaking." Her mother's voice was stern and brisk, but not cold, not laced with the ice that Chris remembered.

"Hello, Mother. It's Chris. How are you?" There was silence. No response at all. "Mother, are you there?"

"What do you want?" The old voice returned. The voice Chris knew.

"I was hoping we could meet for lunch sometime this week."

"I'm busy."

"Well, how about next week then?"

"Christine, what are you after? What more do you want to hurl at me after your last little visit?"

Chris waited. Why did I call? Did I really expect anything different? But she had to try, had to give it one last try. "A mother," she heard herself say, her voice almost a whisper. "I want a mother. A mother who loves me, who shows some interest in my life, who shares a lunch now and again. I want a mother I can talk to. A mother who's there for me when I need her. I want the mother Beth had." She heard the heavy silence and felt herself getting stronger, her voice more confident. Like Popeye eating his spinach, she forged forward. "Mom, I want to sit down and talk with you. I want to know the truth about my heritage. And, I want to tell you about Dad's attack last night. Did he tell you about his three a.m. drunken visit? Did he tell you what he said to me? What he said about you? Did he tell you that he was arrested?"

"Lies. All lies. I want no more of you or your lies."

The phone clicked silent.

Chris had expected little more, but she was stunned nonetheless. Standing very still, she felt the shock waves pass through her body. Slowly, she set her phone on the kitchen counter and walked to the front windows. She stared at the rain spattering on the pavement below. Time stood still. Again she allowed herself to feel the pain, to know the pain. Only by accepting the pain could she move forward. At least I gave it a shot, she thought.

Standing before the wall of glass, Seattle rain falling like tears on the other side, Chris wrapped her arms around her own chest and cradled her body, mothering herself because she had no mother to do it for her. Then she turned from the rain, picked up her journal and settled into the sofa to write away her pain.

Well, I gave it my best shot. I can't change her. I can only change myself and how I react to her. Peter taught me that much, right? So why does it hurt so much? And what if he comes again? What if he catches me going in or out of the place? Or running, what if he follows me, stops me, attacks me when I'm running? Can I run or even go out at night alone? What if he does it again? Okay, cool it. Get a grip. It won't happen. At least it won't happen unless I provoke him, right? He's never done it before – no threats, no violence – at least not towards me. He's always just ignored me. I caused this. I brought it on by going over there, by showing Mom that picture. If I hadn't done that, if I hadn't been in his face, he would've just continued to ignore me. So that's what I'll do. Invisible Chris. It's worked all these years, it'll work again. I just can't provoke him. Can't give him reason to lose control.

FORTY-FIVE

"SO, I CALLED HER, YOU KNOW," Chris said. "God, it was awful."

"What'd she do?" Karin asked.

"Called me a liar and hung up on me."

"That's harsh."

It was late afternoon, the quiet time at The Last Exit. The tables had emptied after writing practice. Only two old men sat in the corner playing chess. They looked like they'd been in that exact spot since 1968. A young mother, child in tow, grabbed an afternoon latte to get her through the evening.

Chris had gotten into the habit of staying after the others left. She'd grown to love the place, the fragrance of coffee and tea, the click of the chess pieces as they moved through the silence. She would write or read, or sometimes, like today, Karin would join her, and they'd talk.

"You mentioned two phone calls. What was the other one?" Karin asked.

"I called Jake. You know, that EMT I told you about."

"Yeah, I remember. You wrote about him, too. About how he found your journal."

"Right, he's the guy. Well, I finally met up with him at Alki. We ran and had dinner. Then, like a total moron, I freaked out and practically ran out of the restaurant without him."

"You mean you just left him there?"

"Yeah," Chris said, with a laugh. "Real smooth, right? But then he shows up at my place when they arrest my dad."

"That's weird. Same guy?"

"Yeah. I guess the West Seattle EMT crew must not be all that big. Or maybe he just gets stuck with a lot of the late night shifts because he's young and single. I don't know. It was weird though. Anyway, I'd already found Beth's painting of my grandmother and all that, so I figured I had to call him and tell him."

"Sounds like a good excuse, right?"

"Yeah, maybe."

"So how'd that go?"

"I told him I was multi-racial, and he basically said so what."

"He sounds like a good catch, girl. And he's right, you know, what's the big deal?"

"I don't know. I'm just sorta surprised by it all, you know. And I don't know if I'm ready."

"Sure you are. Just go for it. Hey, I got an idea. Come on," she said standing up and grabbing their backpacks. Then pushing Chris's backpack into her arms, she said, "What you need is some serious retail therapy."

Chris stood in silence, aware that she'd never, ever, felt this sense of belonging, of friendship that flowed over her, through her, like a gentle current of love and acceptance.

"Hey, come on. This'll be great. Let's take my car. I'll drop you back here to get yours later, okay?"

"Sure, I guess. Where are we going?"

"Wait and see," Karin said, a smile wide across her face.

As she headed north on I-5, Chris remained quiet, lost in a sea of thoughts and fears. Karin's voice startled her. "Why so quiet?"

"Can I ask you something?" Chris said. "Maybe it's crazy, but I need to ask."

"Sure."

"Does it make a difference to you?"

"What?" Karin asked.

With a sweep of a hand, Chris indicated her face, tugged on her black curls.

"That your grandma's African American? You've got to be kidding, Chris. Just cuz your parents are messed up doesn't mean the rest of the world is. You just got to let it go. Oh, and by the way, have you looked at my face lately?"

"What do you mean?"

Karin was stopped by the traffic light at the foot of the I-5 exit to Northgate Mall. She turned and looked into Chris's eyes. "You look at my face and what do you see?"

Chris hesitated. She didn't know what to say, what Karin wanted.

"Come on, Chris. What do you see?"

"Okay, I see light brown skin, dark brown eyes, straight black hair with long bangs."

"You see a young Asian woman, right? But you have no idea about my heritage, where I was born, where my parents or grandparents were born. Even my name Karin Mathews tells you nothing. Was I adopted? Was I born in America? These are the questions that go through your head, through everybody's head, right? Come on, be honest." Karin accelerated when the light turned green and entered the large mall parking lot.

"Yeah, okay. I see a young Asian woman," Chris said, almost in a whisper.

"Well guess what, my father was whiter than yours."

Chris felt like she'd been slapped across the face.

"A shock, isn't it?" Karin continued as she maneuvered into an empty parking spot. She turned off the engine and turned to face Chris again. "My dad was a U.S. Marine in Saigon. My mother's Vietnamese. I'm just as mixed as you, so let's just get over it, okay? Multiracial, biracial, mixed, whatever you want to call it, we're still the same people, aren't we?"

"I guess so," Chris said. A smile grew across her face. "Your dad's really white?"

"Yup, whiter than yours, apparently. I can even introduce you to him, but that wouldn't prove a thing, would it?"

"I guess not," Chris agreed. "But I don't even know what box to check now."

"Box? Oh, you mean those stupid ethnicity questions like on registration forms and stuff."

"Yeah."

"I can't tell you what to do, but I just check 'other' and keep them guessing."

"I suppose you're right. It doesn't really matter, does it? It's just so strange, you know. I'm not who I thought I was."

They sat in silence for a moment. Then Karin pulled the keys from the ignition and opened her door. "Okay, now that we've got that settled. Let's go shopping."

"What are we shopping for?" Chris asked as they got out of the car and headed into the mall. But Karin wouldn't answer her. She dragged Chris into Macy's and just kept walking, weaving her way through the large department store and out the opposite doors into the center of the mall. A few minutes later, she came to a dead stop in front of the large pink awning that hung over the front door of Victoria's Secret.

"Here we are," she said. "Let's get you ready for Jake. I'm guessing you don't own anything but jogging bras, right?"

"Right," Chris laughed. "But I'm not much of a shopper, Karin."

"Well, that's why I'm here. I'm a pro," Karin said, and she walked into the store as if she owned it.

Chris had never been a lingerie girl, but with thoughts of Jake churning in her head, she followed her friend into the brightly lit store. At first it was all too overwhelming. The sexy mannequins wearing almost nothing at all, the walls and walls of lace and silk in so many colors and styles Chris felt her head spin. And that was only the bras. The world of panties was just plain crazy. Sure she'd seen the Victoria's Secret ads, but she'd always ignored them, never moving beyond basic cottons.

She stumbled around the store, tagging along behind Karin, totally overwhelmed and with absolutely no idea of what she was doing when a salesclerk approached her with the customary, "Can I help you find something?"

Chris was relieved that the woman appeared older than she was, even a bit big-sisterly, but still she had trouble controlling her natural shyness. "I'm not really sure," she mumbled. "I need a few new bras and panties, but I'm not even sure of the size or style I want." She saw Karin across the bright display of panties, a huge grin on her face.

"It might be best to start out with a fitting," the sales clerk said. "Then I can bring you a variety of styles and you can choose what fits and feels best to you. Does that sound okay?"

With a nod from Chris, the clerk led the way back to the fitting room, and once Chris got past her initial embarrassment of a bra fitting, the fun began. Within a few minutes Karin and the sales clerk were on a first name basis and working in tandem to bring a seemingly endless variety of bras and panties to the fitting room for Chris to try.

"Come on, Karin," Chris said from behind the closed fitting room door. "You've gotta get something new, too."

"Not a chance, girlfriend. If I put one more thing on my card, they'll take it away from me. Besides," she added with a hearty laugh, "I don't have a Jake drooling over me."

An hour or two later, when they left the store still giggling like school girls, Chris was swinging a large pink striped bag containing a selection of sexy new bras and matching panties in a variety of colors and feeling absolutely wonderful.

FORTY-SIX

"YOU REALLY MUST DO SOMETHING about those clothes, Gemila. I'm serious now. Mrs. McPherson came over just last week asking about the new house cleaner I hired. House cleaner, mind you. Is that what you want people to think you are? A house cleaner?"

They were sitting at the old oak kitchen table in Mrs. James Newbury's elegant Genesee Hill home, an expansive view of Puget Sound and the Olympic Mountains spread before them from every westward window. Her newest client, Mrs. Newbury, a retired Boeing engineer now in her eighties, was confined to a wheelchair. A woman accustomed to getting what she wanted, she was relentless in her assessment of Gemi's appearance.

"And please explain to me why you insist on wearing that hideous scarf over your beautiful hair every time you enter or leave my home. It's religious, isn't it?" Then more to herself than to Gemi, she added, "Always the limitations of belief systems constructed by men."

Gemi only smiled as she got up to prepare Mrs. Newbury's midday meal before beginning the exercise and massage routine designed to maintain proper blood circulation throughout the elderly woman's body.

"I'm waiting, Gemila."

"Yes, Mrs. Newbury. It is a religious belief to maintain the head covered in the presence of men not of one's family, but it is also tradition."

"Are you a practicing Muslim?"

"Practicing?" Gemi said. She knew the conversation wasn't over, so she sat back down at the table, across from her client. "No, I am not a practicing Muslim."

"Do you consider yourself Muslim?"

Gemi paused, unable to answer, unsure what the answer was. It was a question she seldom allowed herself to consider. And yet, here she was listening to the demanding questions of a determined old white woman and becoming uncomfortably aware of her inability to find an answer. "I suppose," she heard herself saying, "I suppose the headscarf is my connection to all I lost so long ago."

The kitchen was peaceful, quiet. The ticking of the wall clock a reminder of time drifting through their fingers as the women sat and stared into each other's tired eyes.

"My dear, Gemila, we mustn't live our losses all the days of our lives." Mrs. Newbury said in an uncharacteristically gentle voice. "Now come here with me, my dear." She rolled herself into the living room where she swung around in front of a large antique wall mirror in a gilded frame. "Stand beside me, here. Now take a good look at yourself."

Gemi stared at her reflection in the mirror, as docile as a young child. Her head was uncovered, as it always was when she was indoors in the presence of only women, her long black curls pulled into a single loose braid. Then she allowed her eyes to drop to her body. Her pants were baggy and worn, the nursing tunic hung almost to her knees. Yes, she admitted to herself, she looked worse, far worse than Mrs. Newbury's cleaning woman, worse even than the gardener. Is this what she wanted for herself as she edged towards fifty?

As if reading her thoughts, Mrs. Newbury broke the silence. "You're still young, Gemila. You have another life yet before you. You must embrace it."

Mrs. Newbury was the only person that Gemi had met since childhood who insisted on using her full name. It touched her heart. She leaned forward and kissed the old woman on the cheek just as she had once kissed her own mother.

"Thank you, Mrs. Newbury. You have given me much to consider."

"Consider nothing," the old woman spat back, the glimpse of gentleness gone. "You need to go shopping. Push me back into the kitchen, and I'll give you the number of my personal shopper. A wonder of a woman. How do you expect to ever get a man in your life if you don't fix yourself up a bit? A pretty thing like you should have lots of beaux."

For the hundredth time, Gemi regretted having ever told Mrs. Newbury that she was unmarried. Married, divorced, remarried and now widowed, Mrs. Newbury simply couldn't understand or accept the notion of choosing to live alone.

But was it a choice? Or a choice by default? Even neglect? Gemi wasn't certain. She did know, however, with absolute certainty that there was no point in arguing with the elderly woman, just as she knew that she'd never use the number on the business card that Mrs. Newbury pushed into her hand. Still she listened.

"Now just give Jeannie a call. She'll know exactly what you need. How can I possibly recommend you to my friends without a decent wardrobe and makeover? And about that headscarf of yours. I can't tell you what to believe, young lady, but think long and hard about it because it seems to me that you're not so sure yourself."

Her work for the day finished. Mrs. Newbury's words continued to echo in Gemi's ears. Was she choosing to hide behind her ill-fitting clothes and dedicating her life to patient care because she was afraid to expose herself to the possibility of love and the potential loss that love carries?

Without volition, Gemi found herself taking a downtown exit off the freeway. She drove into the Macy's garage and sat for a moment in silence. Then, with newfound determination, she headed into the store and took the escalator to the women's department. After wandering aimlessly for ten or fifteen minutes pulling and replacing pants, blouses and sweaters from the racks surrounding her, she realized she needed some help and began sizing up the sales people. She spotted a woman that she judged to be about her own age and approached.

"Excuse me," she said. "I'm hoping you might be able to assist me."

"Of course. My name's Sheri. What are you looking for today?"

"Everything," Gemi said as she made a broad vertical sweep of her arm. "I need a new wardrobe."

"Well, you're in the right place. What kind of look are you interested in?"

"Look?" Gemi repeated, puzzled by the question.

"Yes. Or, what kind of work do you do? What kind of clothes do you want?"

"I'm a home healthcare provider. So, I guess I need comfortable, casual clothes that fit me and look much better than what I am wearing at present. Maybe something along those lines," she said, pointing to a mannequin in khakis and a fitted sweater. And then she added, "But perhaps not quite so fitted. And maybe some jeans if they are not too tight."

"Okay," said the saleswoman. "That gives us a place to begin. Now what size do you wear?"

"I'm afraid I really have no idea," Gemi said with a laugh. Then, she pulled the elastic waistband of her pants and her baggy tunic around her body and asked, "What do you think?"

"Let's start with tens and see how close we are, okay?"

After about fifteen minutes of what seemed to Gemi a bit like traditional hunting and gathering practices, Sheri led her to a fitting room, arms loaded with garments. Gemi hesitated. She'd never tried on clothes in a public place.

"Here you go," said Sheri. "Now start with these, and if you need more sizes or styles, just let me know."

Gemi heard the frightened child in her own voice when she asked, "Do men come in here?"

"Oh no," Sheri assured her. "This is a women's only area."

"All right then," she said and entered the small fitting room. With slow, deliberate movements, she removed her scarf and her clothes. She pulled on a pair of trouser-fit khakis and a dark brown sweater. She was smoothing her hair from her face when she heard a gentle knock at the door.

"How's it going in there, Gemi?"

"I think we're off to a good start. What do you think about these?" As she opened the fitting room door, she heard a tiny gasp escape from Sheri's lips.

"Are they too small? Too tight? All wrong?" Gemi asked, her voice full of concern and embarrassment.

"Oh, no. You look absolutely stunning. It's just that… I'm sorry. I just had no idea such a beautiful woman was hiding under those clothes."

Gemi left the store hours later with a new wardrobe, far from complete, but for now, the bags in the backseat of the car were plenty. She thought about calling Chris to tell her all about it, but then she decided against it, knowing that this was a change she needed a bit of time to grow into.

She drove home, humming softly to herself. She parked, unloaded her bags and headed up the stairs to her apartment.

"Looks like you've been busy."

Hearing her friend's voice, Gemi groaned with the realization that in the bustle of her day and the newness of shopping, she'd totally forgotten their weekly walk. "Oh Carolyn, I'm so sorry. I was very distracted."

"I can see that. What've you got in all those bags?"

Gemi stuttered with sudden and unexpected shyness. "Oh nothing. Here, let me just set these down and we can go."

"Hold it right there," Carolyn said with a laugh. "Do I detect a secret here? Come on. Share. That's what friends are for, right?"

"All right, then. Come on up and I'll show you," Gemi said.

She dropped her bags on the living room floor and began pulling outfits from the bags and laying them out across the sofa, grouping coordinated pants and tops together. She even set out two new pairs of shoes. Carolyn watched in silence until all the outfits were assembled and the bags lay empty on the floor.

"There you have it," Gemi said.

"What does this mean? A make-over? A new Gemi?"

"Mrs. Newbury, you recall?"

"Opinionated old engineer in a wheelchair? I think you said that someday I'd be just like her."

"Yes, that's the one. She told me that I looked worse than her gardener and that she couldn't recommend me to her friends until I did something about my appearance."

"Ouch."

"Yes, ouch. But the worst part is that she is correct. I had a look at myself in one of her gilded mirrors, and I had to admit that I looked dreadful. So, I stopped at Macy's on my way home. I'm very sorry that I kept you waiting. Shall we go?"

"Not so fast," Carolyn said. "What's your plan here? When does the world see the new Gemi?"

"I haven't decided." And in the silence that followed, Gemi knew the question that her friend wanted to ask. "And the headscarf?"

"Yes," Carolyn said. "I know you've been thinking about that for years. Are you ready?"

"Not today. Soon. Baby steps, okay?" Again Gemi heard the child in her own voice. Heard the layers of tradition and restraint controlling the child, but slipping from the adult. She knew the day would come when she'd leave the sanctity of her apartment in her new clothes with her head uncovered. But not yet, not today.

FORTY-SEVEN

CHRIS CLIMBED OUT OF HER CAR in the N2 lot on the University of Washington campus as a cold rain, more mist than rain, settled over the campus. She walked through the large campus carrying a backpack full of required textbooks and notebooks, paper and pens – the necessities of any college student. Looking around her at the young faces of her fellow students, she felt old. These kids were only five or six years younger than she, but only a few months shy of twenty-seven, she felt old beyond her years.

She climbed the worn steps of Denny Hall, the round sandstone and brick turrets towering on each side like sentinels guarding the entrance into the sacred sanctity of a university education. Denny Hall, the first building on the University of Washington campus, opened its doors, and the towers began their sentry duty, in 1895 as the first two hundred students began their university education.

Now it was Chris's turn, not to begin, but to complete the education she had begun years before. As she climbed the stairway of the imposing French Renaissance building, she knew she was in the right place, knew she'd made the right decision. She was finally ready to finish a degree in creative writing.

She found the still-empty classroom and chose a desk, not too far back, but not front row, center either. A bit off to one side where she could see the treetops through the tall windows that reached to the high ceiling. A modern white board and individual tab-arm desks were the only semblances of modernization in the room. She sat dreaming of chalk dust and old oak tables. Or would they have been individual desks? She didn't know. When she closed her eyes, she could hear the ghosts of the first two hundred students who graced this room over a hundred years before.

She was deep in a world of voices from the past when she heard the door open. She watched as other students began to trickle into the classroom. There were scattered greetings. The beginnings of new alliances and study partners forming, or the reinforcement of old friendships from prior quarters and classes. They found desks, the same desks they were likely to claim throughout the quarter. Not because it was required. Just because that was the way it always worked. You chose your seat and you kept it. Chris smiled, remembering earlier years of being a student. As she watched, she also realized that age wasn't something she should worry about. There were a couple of other students her age and even older. She began to relax. She smiled, chatted, became a part of this new group.

Professor Mackintosh walked into the room in a flowing cashmere skirt the color of warm oatmeal drizzled with maple syrup, chocolate brown leather boots and a soft sweater. Her long brown hair was smoothed into a clasp at the nape of her neck. Her bright blue eyes scanned the room as silence fell like winter snowflakes. Chris's first creative writing class had begun.

As each student was asked to introduce him- or herself and share what they were working on, Chris sank lower into her desk chair. She had visions of a trapdoor opening at her feet, allowing her an easy escape.

"... my third short story," a woman said. She looks half my age, Chris cringed. "I had one published last year in The Sun."

"A novel," said a young jock who looked like he belonged out on the football field. "About two hundred pages written."

The number of pages, the accomplishments were rattled off around her. When it was her turn, Chris struggled to speak. "I'm Chris Stevens. I'm not working on anything specific yet. Only journal writing. Maybe the beginning of a memoir."

"Personal writing is writing," Professor Mackintosh smiled. "It's where we find our inner source and how we develop our personal voice. Thank you, Chris."

Chris's lips formed a weak, grateful smile, and she sat a tiny bit straighter in her desk chair. We all have to start somewhere, she assured herself in silence.

Fifty minutes later, as the room emptied, students heading off in different directions, rushing to other classes, lunch, jobs, Chris remained glued to her chair. It felt so right, she didn't want it to end. Professor Mackintosh gathered her felt-tipped pens, snapping the tops tight, shuffling her lecture notes and collecting her books. She wiped the whiteboard, picked up her bag and was headed for the door when she noticed Chris still sitting in a silent, trance-like daydream.

"See you tomorrow, then." Chris didn't respond. "Chris? It's Chris Stevens, right?"

"Yes. Oh, sorry. I suppose I should be going," Chris stammered, as she looked into her professor's questioning eyes. "I was just thinking about how great it is to be back."

"Back?"

"Back in school." She twisted a curl at her ear and stared at the floor in front of her desk.

"How long has it been?"

"A lifetime," Chris whispered. Then she looked up and said, "About seven years."

"A lifetime," Professor Mackintosh agreed.

Chris didn't know if she'd heard her whisper or not. It didn't matter. The woman understood. There was a connection. Another human connection.

"Well, welcome back," Professor Mackintosh said, interrupting her thoughts. "What brought you to this class?"

"I want to develop my writing skills. I want to write. Like I mentioned before, I have a lifetime of journals and the start of a memoir, but I really don't know what I'm doing."

"Do you enjoy writing?"

"It saved my life," Chris said with simple honesty.

"Then you will write that memoir. You might want to look into the Creative Writing Program. It's competitive, but worth the extra effort."

"Thank you, I will."

"Do your research and then make an appointment to see me in my office. Maybe you'll show me a bit of that memoir."

"Thank you. That'd be great." Chris felt like she was ten years old, in awe of this older, articulate, educated woman. As she followed her professor from the room, she felt like a child trailing the mother she never had, the mother she'd always wanted.

She had an hour break before her next class. Too excited to eat or write, she walked. As she circled the large campus, reintroducing herself to buildings, pathways and gardens lost in the far reaches of memory, she was content. She could see the next few years strung out before her and was eager to get on with the journey.

FORTY-EIGHT

THE RICH AROMA OF CLAM CHOWDER greeted Chris as she entered the restaurant and saw Jake waiting for her at the same window table they'd shared the last time they'd had dinner together. Summer had come and gone and a number of long runs together had passed since the night he'd bandaged up her father, since the day she told him she was biracial. Running together was something she could handle. There was distance and distraction. Dinner together she wasn't so sure about, especially in the same restaurant, at the same table.

She saw him watching her as she approached the small table. She knew she looked good in her khakis and a fitted black fleece jacket. She even felt a bit sexy, armed as she was with her secret, super-powered bra and panties hidden under her clothes. Sexy despite the fact that it had taken her a couple of months and a whole lot of Karin's teasing to get used to wearing them.

"Hi, Chris," he said as he stood to greet her. "Thanks for agreeing to try this again."

Her eyes dropped. "I'm sorry about that. About running out like that last time we were here."

"No," he stopped her. "No, it was my fault. My timing's not so great sometimes. I was moving too fast. I wanted …" His voice trailed off and there was silence at their table amidst the hum of the busy beachfront restaurant. She busied herself with the menu until a waitress approached and took their drink order.

"Why, Jake?" Chris asked, as soon as the waitress was out of earshot. "From the very beginning when I was at Harborview. Why have you been there for me?"

He took a deep breath. "Listen, I need to tell you something. I've got my own secrets, you know. I suppose we all do. Some worse than others."

Their eyes met, and Chris waited, giving him the time he needed to sort his thoughts as he played with the miniature pumpkin arrangement that decorated the table.

"I told you before, I watched you running Alki long before your accident."

Chris winced at the word.

"Accident? That word bothers you. What should I call it, Chris?"

"Call it by its real name. Call it a suicide attempt."

"Okay then, even before your suicide attempt, I saw you run. And I liked what I saw. But it wasn't just that body of yours." He smiled, and Chris felt a soft blush spread across her face. "It was your determination and dedication that really struck me. But I didn't know how to meet you. So when I saw you on that gurney, I saw my chance, and I didn't want to let go."

Chris started to speak, but he stopped her. "Wait, there's more. I need to tell you the whole story." He paused again as though he were trying to sort out his thoughts. The waitress returned with a couple of beers, and then left them alone. He took a deep drink and began again. "You remember, I told you about my aunt Maggie, right?"

"Yes, I remember," Chris said. "Aunt Maggie. Your mother's sister who helped raise you after your Mom died, right?

"Okay, well the thing is, my mother killed herself when I was ten years old."

"Oh, my god," Chris gasped. Her eyes filled with tears.

"I was just a kid, you know? My dad was real messed up for a while, and that's when Aunt Maggie stepped in to fill the void. Man, can that woman cook. She was always fixing up something special for me. It's a miracle I didn't turn into a butterball."

Chris laughed softly trying to imagine this lean, handsome man in front of her as a chubby preteen. "I wish I'd known you then," she said.

"Oh, I don't think so. Anyway, when I was old enough to start asking questions, nobody wanted to remember the past. Finally, I suppose my aunt just got sick of all my questions and told me that my mom had killed herself, but that was it. I had no idea why or how. For a long time I thought it was my fault. I suppose that's what most kids think when something bad happens. When Aunt Maggie finally realized what was going on, she told me that my mother suffered from depression. So I started reading everything I could about depression and suicide. I can still rattle off the facts. Over 32,000 suicides a year in America. More deaths from suicide than homicide. Over 800,000 attempts with a twenty percent repetition rate within the first three months," he said, counting the statistics off on his fingers as he spoke. Then, with a school-boy smile, he said, "Anyway, I guess when I understood that your accident was a suicide, I wanted to save you."

"Oh, Jake," Chris whispered. "I'm so sorry."

"It was like, I couldn't save my mother, but maybe I could do something to help you. I suppose that's why I became a paramedic, too. I wanted to save people."

Chris let out a small sigh, "And I became a flight attendant after 9/11 because I wanted to die."

They smiled into each other's eyes as Chris reached across the small table and took one of his large hands between her own. "Listen," she said. "You couldn't save your mother and you couldn't save me. Well, that's not exactly true. You did save me. You pulled me from that car and got me to Harborview. For that I will be forever grateful. But you could not prevent me from becoming one of that twenty percent you mentioned. That was work I needed to do alone and with the help of a good therapist. Now I've long passed those first three months. More important, I've found meaning and purpose in my life. I understand the secrets of my past that messed me up so badly. And I have every intention of living the rest of my life to the fullest."

A sly smile spread across Jake's face, accenting the laugh lines at the corners of his eyes. "Do you think maybe you're ready to let me be a little part of that full life of yours?"

"Oh yes," she smiled. "And I promise I won't run away again." She leaned across the table and kissed him on the cheek, then laughed at the surprised look on his face.

"My god, Chris. Do you have any idea what you do to me?" he croaked.

"I think the feeling is mutual," she whispered, her face as flushed as his own. "But let's take it slow. This is all new territory for me."

FORTY-NINE

CHRIS SAT CROSS-LEGGED on her living room floor, her sister's legacy fanned out around her – the large black leather artist's portfolio, the plastic case holding dozens of small journals and the oversized accordion file crammed full of photographs, postcards and letters that Beth had called her reference file.

She had awoken to her birthday in her dark bedroom on a rainy November morning only a half hour earlier. She'd crawled out of bed and put on some fleece sweats. After boosting the thermostat to seventy, she'd headed to the kitchen for coffee. She had a plan for how she would spend her birthday that she'd told no one – not Gemi or Karin or Jake. She would share her day with Beth.

She'd taken a peek at Beth's portfolio six months before, when she found the picture of Grandmother Stevens, but it was only a peek. Since then, the large portfolio had held a spot in the corner of the living room floor.

Now, she sat on the floor with Beth's journal case to her right, the accordion file to her left and the large black portfolio directly in front of her. With slow determination, Chris dragged the portfolio towards her. Climbing onto her hands and knees, she pulled the long zipper around the three sides and folded open the large portfolio. The smell of old paper and canvas, ink and oil paints filled the condo, again reminding her of the fragrances that had warmed her childhood. The smells of her sister's bedroom. Again, her sister's world lay before her in rich oils, soft pastels and dark pen and inks. Studies in every form covering a half dozen years of artistic development. Chris knew that this was what Beth had considered her best work. She knew her sister would work and rework a piece for weeks, months, until it was right. She also knew that she had never seen much of what this portfolio contained because Beth did most of her work away from home and the prying eyes of their mother. Even when she worked at the easel set up in the corner of her bedroom, she never allowed Chris to watch. She had a shoji screen that she used to hide her easel. In this, her sister had been very private, only showing a piece when it was finished to her own satisfaction, when she was proud of her portrayal of her subject.

This time as Chris paged through the portfolio, she arranged the artwork around her condo with gentle loving care, the care of a mother with her newborn child. Every surface – dining table, coffee tables, bookshelves, countertops – was soon covered in artwork. She wanted, no, she needed to feel surrounded, to be inside her sister's world, to see the world as Beth had seen it. She was transported back in time. Her coffee went cold.

Satisfied inside Beth's world, Chris sat on the edge of the sofa and snapped open her sister's journal case and took out the journals. Again she breathed in deeply, searching for the lost scent of her sister, finding only the must of old paper and ink. She forced herself to relax back into the sofa, opened the first of Beth's numerous journals, and began to read. She knew immediately this was no high school he said/she said/I hate my parents diary – though some of that was there, to be sure, but it was sandwiched between pages and pages of imagery in flowing verse and pencil sketches. Chris knew Beth wrote poetry, but she'd rarely read any of it. She remembered the hours her sister lay on her bed every evening, pen in hand, scribbling. Now and again, alone at night in their adjoining bedrooms, she convinced her older sister to read something she was working on, but not often. Beth was even more private about her poetry than she was about sharing her visual art. Chris knew that it was because of Beth's obsession with writing that she had begun her own journal. But she was never a poet. Not like this.

Chris allowed herself to float in the imagery and lose herself in time and space. The weak winter sun rose late and set early. When the phone rang, she jumped, startled back into a world she'd left hours before.

"Yes?"

"Hello, child, are you okay?"

"Hello?"

"Chris, it's Gemi. Are you all right, child?"

"Oh, sorry. Yeah, I'm fine, Gemi. Just distracted," she said as she fingered a small watercolor of vivid lavender lilacs, so real she was lost in their sweet fragrance.

"Are we still having dinner tonight, child?"

"Oh crap, I forgot. What time is it anyway?"

"It's just after four, and I'm in the south end."

"Could you come here, Gemi? I've got something I want to show you."

"That would work. I have a few stops to make, so I won't be there for an hour or so depending on traffic."

Chris was still under a spell as she ended the call. She stretched, switched on the lights, and headed to her storage closet, remembering something else buried there. She rummaged around for only a few minutes before her hand lit on the familiar object – a small leather box, about a foot long and three inches wide. Turning off the closet light, she returned to the front room where she gently set the case on the dining table. With a deep breath, she unlatched the lid and opened it. She ran her fingers over the contents like a blind woman reading Braille, remembering the warmth of the wooden stylus, the sharpness of the metal nibs and the acrid dust of the dried ink. She held the smooth wooden stylus in her hand like an old friend, a friend she'd somehow let slip away through the passing of years and the distance of age, but who still felt as comfortable as an afternoon chat over warm tea the day before. She saw the tooth marks on the pointed end and heard her teacher, Linda Wong, scolding her, "Do not put it in your mouth!"

She pulled the metal nibs from the elastic bands that held them in place. Three nibs. Two ink stained and darkened, one still boasting the golden gleam of new brass. With great care she lifted one of the darkened nibs. She felt the curved shape where it entered the stylus. Her fingernail grazed the slot that held the drop of ink. She pricked her fingertip with the sharp point. Then, with experience now only memory, she inserted the nib into the stylus.

There were two small bottles of ink in the case. One black, one sepia. "We use my ink," were Linda Wong's words nine years earlier. "You save your ink. Use it for Beth."

The two ink bottles were from Beth. For Beth. Beth's ink remained untouched. Chris fingered the small bottles, the cork top on each, still coated with hardened sealing wax. She slowly broke the seal of the small bottle of thick black ink. As the strong earthy fragrance permeated her senses she was carried back in time to the tiny shop in Chinatown with Linda Wong coaxing her every stroke, correcting, scolding, encouraging her. "For Beth."

No, Chris thought, it was not just for Beth. It was for me too, and she knew it. Linda Wong knew it was for me too.

For years the leather case, the ink, the stylus, the nibs lay forgotten in the back of her storage closet like a flute from a long ago high school band. Chris took a deep breath, the scent of memory brought tears to her eyes. Tears for a skill gained and then forgotten. Tears for a sister lost forever.

Once again, Chris returned to the storage closet. Heading back to the table, she set the box of parchment sheets down next to the stylus and ink. This is the gift she left me, Chris realized as she stood and stared at the tools in front of her, the journals of poetry on the sofa and the collection of artwork surrounding her. With newfound assurance, she dipped the pen into the tiny bottle of rich black ink.

The letters seemed to form themselves as they floated across the page, black on white. She remembered the strokes, the pen angles, the formation of each letter. But time had stolen her fluidity. She needed practice. Before she was consciously aware of what she was doing, she'd transcribed a number of Beth's poems in delicate script.

FIFTY

THE INTERCOM RANG SHRILL through the condo. Startled, Chris jumped, spattering droplets of black ink over the paper in front of her. "Oh, crap," she muttered as she set down the stylus. She greeted Gemi and opened the building door as well as her own condo door. Then she returned to the table to wipe up the ink spatters. As she looked at her work, an idea came to her as clear as a whisper in her ear. "Oh, my god," she exclaimed. "That's it. That's what I'll do."

"What will you do, child? And what is all of this?" Gemi asked as she walked into the living room.

"Hi, Gemi. This is what I wanted to show you. Just give me a second while I clean up here. Go ahead and take a look around."

Gemi walked through Chris's living room as though she were strolling a downtown gallery, taking in the beauty of Beth's work without a word. Chris wiped her stylus clean, removed the nib and inserted the cork in the ink bottle. Then she went to her friend's side.

"What do you think?"

"This is Beth's work." It wasn't a question, just a simple understanding.

They stopped in front of the table where there were a couple of watercolors, a charcoal, and a pen-and-ink. Next to each, Chris had placed poems she'd copied from her sister's journals. Each poem flowed across the parchment in the intricate lace of calligraphy. They complemented each other, the poem and the image, each adding rather than detracting from the intense beauty of the other. Gemi seemed to breathe in the essence of each image. She paused before a watercolor of Puget Sound, a dark storm in the distance. Aloud, her voice a soft melody, she read Beth's words.

Rain

From far away the gray wall comes
Across the surging sea
The falling water pounds and hums
From far away the gray wall comes

Now at last I understand
Rain's not mine but something grand
From far away the gray wall comes
Across the surging sea

"What do you think?" Chris again whispered at her side.

"I'm no art critic, and I know very little about poetry, but I do know beauty. Here you have beauty, raw, even painful beauty in the voice of a very young woman. And your calligraphy is remarkable. You still remember. The matching of poem to image is brilliant, child. Like I said, I only know what touches me, and this pulls at my heart. I think you have something very special here."

Chris breathed deeply, unaware that she'd been holding her breath. "I thought so too, but I'm biased. I miss her so much. Even now."

"Yes, child. The hole in your heart will always be there. But you have your sister here, all around you in word and image. What will you do with all of this?"

"I'm not sure yet, but I think it could be some kind of book. When you walked in the door, it came to me. This is Beth's legacy. I want to do something with it."

"You will, child. You will know what to do, and Beth will guide you."

"Thank you, Gemi, but it's so overwhelming," Chris said. "There's so much to process. To think about. To remember. Look at these." She held up Beth's plastic journal case.

"These, child? It looks like but one to me."

"These are Beth's journals. Look." She snapped open the case and took out dozens of thin, light-weight notebooks. "She never went anywhere without one of these tucked into a pocket. It used to drive me nuts. Even when we ran, she'd always wear a cyclist's jacket or vest, you know, one of those things with the zip pocket in the back.

She always had to have a journal and she'd always want to stop to write or sketch something. Check this out." Chris set down the pile of journals and grabbed one that lay open on the cluttered table. "I was looking at this one earlier today."

"A lovely sketch, child. What do you know about it?"

"I remember exactly when she did this. It was only a few weeks before her death. We'd gone running in Discovery Park along that loop trail. Have you ever been there?"

"No, I think not."

"Well, there's this long trail that circles the park and along the way there's this gorgeous old oak. This oak," Chris said pointing to Beth's sketch. "I remember Beth stopped. She told me to keep going, to do the loop without her, to come back to get her when I finished. So I kept running and left her there. When I completed the loop and returned, she stuffed her journal into her pocket as soon as she saw me. She wouldn't show it to me. Told me it was crap. But it's not crap, is it?"

"No, child, it is not crap, as you say."

"And look, there's a poem that goes with it. But there's lots of crossing out and changing. I don't know which to use, which Beth felt was best, or even if she thought it was finished. Probably the last one, but I don't know. That's why I haven't transcribed it yet. I was still trying to decide. How can I know for sure?"

"You can't, child."

"So what do I do?"

"Perhaps you could consider the last her final draft. Or, you might simply choose the one you like best. Either way Beth will be honored. May I read it?"

"Of course," Chris said and handed her the thin notebook. She watched the movement of Gemi's lips, listened to her gentle whisper as she read her sister's poem.

The Old Oak

Crooked and gnarly
The old oak stands on pronged trunk
Silent family with barren center
Stowing secrets of pain and joy

If the old oak could speak
Perhaps she'd answer my questions of heart
There is wisdom in her beauty
Peace in her enduring life

Did the old oak know grandmother?
Did grandmother enjoy her grace?
Only the two of them hold that secret
And neither will share with me

When Gemi was finished reading, the condo was filled with silence, broken only by the call of gulls over Alki Beach.

"So she knew of your grandmother at this time."

"Yes, and I think she was already working on the portrait. She was so secretive. I remember feeling shut out. I didn't know what was going on, but as it got closer to my birthday, I tried to convince myself that she had some big surprise up her sleeve."

"Oh child, I'm so very sorry for your loss," Gemi said with a deep sigh. She spread her arms wide to encompass the cluttered room of artwork and parchment. "What a treasure your sister has left you. You mentioned a book?"

"I guess. I see some kind of book here. I just don't know what form it could take. For now, I just want to spend some time with it, with Beth, with my memories. Each piece – both the artwork and poetry – and each journal is loaded with so many memories."

"Take your time, child. The answers will come to you. Now tell me, have you been out for a run today? Those pajamas lead me to think otherwise."

"No," Chris admitted, realizing that she hadn't showered or even gotten dressed since the day before. And she hadn't eaten a real meal all day. Still, she knew she wasn't slipping. There was no darkness. She knew she was okay. More okay than she could remember in a long, long time.

"Here's what I think we should do. You go put on those stinky shoes of yours and go for a run, child, one of your shorter runs, while I sit here and enjoy your sister's work. After you get back and shower, we'll go to dinner. If it's all right with you, child, I'd like to invite you to my apartment for dinner. How does that sound, birthday girl?"

"You knew?"

"Yes, child, I knew. You were my patient, remember?"

"Right."

"So how does my plan sound?"

"Perfect. I'll be quick. Maybe a half-hour run."

"Do what feels right. I have plenty to do here."

A few minutes later, Chris came out of her bedroom dressed for a winter run. She was heading for the door when she froze, turned around and walked back to where Gemi had settled on the sofa with one of Beth's journals on her lap. Her headscarf lay on the arm of the sofa, set aside as it always was when they were alone. She'd also removed her winter coat. Chris could only stand and stare.

"What's wrong, child?" Gemi finally said, a smile bright on her warm face.

"My god, Gemi. I was so wrapped up in myself, I didn't even notice. I'm not sure I really even saw you. You look amazing. You went shopping. When? Stand up and let me take a good look at you."

With a laugh, Gemi let Chris pull her from the sofa and twirl her in a circle to get the full effect of the new look.

"So, I want to hear all about this transformation. When did you go shopping? Where? Why?"

"Okay, okay, but first you need to take that run of yours. Go on now, child. We'll have all evening to talk."

"Promise?"

"Promise."

FIFTY-ONE

"I'M GOING TO DRIVE MY OWN CAR, okay?" Chris told her as the two women left the condo. "That way you won't have to give me a ride home later."

"All right, child," Gemi said. "I'll keep you in my rear-view mirror."

"Yeah, don't start driving like a crazy woman and lose me in traffic," Chris joked.

Gemi knew the invitation was long overdue. Even though birthday celebrations are not common in traditional Ethiopian culture, and almost unheard of for adults, Gemi was aware that they were important in America and decided it would be a good time to invite Chris into her home.

When she first thought of celebrating Chris's birthday with a traditional Ethiopian meal, she considered including Jake and some of the new writer friends she'd heard about. But Gemi knew that Chris's birthday would be bittersweet. It was the first anniversary of her attempted suicide, and Gemi was aware that she was treading fragile ground. Chris hadn't even mentioned her birthday. Their dinner date had been set a while back – just another of their regular bi-weekly dinners. Even before Gemi called earlier that afternoon, she'd been certain Chris had forgotten their plans. After an hour at her condo looking at Beth's artwork and poetry, Gemi realized that the only birthday plan that Chris had made was to spend the day with her sister's memory.

For her own part, she'd spent the past few weeks in preparation. She'd never cooked an American birthday cake, so after searching the web for recipes, she tried several. Determined to stick to her weight loss plan, she took her practice cakes to those patients with unrestricted diets. She was so surprised by the joy a simple cake brought to folks, she decided to invest in smaller cake pans and bake on a regular basis. In the meantime, she perfected Chris's birthday cake, decorated it with candy flowers and Amharic lettering, and added the requisite twenty-seven candles. She smiled at the thought of that pretty chocolate cake hidden in her kitchen pantry.

Over the past couple of days she'd also prepared two kinds of Ethiopian stew: *doro wat*, a spicy chicken dish, and ginger-seasoned *alecha*, in case the *wat* was too hot for Chris's palate. The ingredients for *injera*, the traditional Ethiopian bread, were measured and waiting on the kitchen counter and the green Ethiopian coffee beans were in a pan ready for roasting.

Gemi knew that so much preparation carried a bit of risk, but she had been confident that Chris would accept her invitation. The hardest part of all had been deciding on an appropriate birthday gift. In the end, she chose a *shash*, a traditional headscarf similar to the one she'd first taught Chris to tie over her shaved head in their afternoons together at Rainier Rehab. This one was a rich sunflower yellow, almost golden, silk with delicate iridescent beading around the edges. Gemi was certain Chris could use it as a shawl over a simple dress, and she knew the color would make Chris's brown eyes sparkle.

When they pulled up in front of Gemi's building, Chris hopped out of her car. "I didn't know you lived so close to Bentley's office. This place looks just like his. It's a subdivided house, isn't it?"

Gemi smiled at Chris's bubbly energy. "Come, child. Tonight I will introduce you to a bit of Ethiopia."

She unlocked the front door of the old house and climbed the stairs that led to her second-floor apartment. As she opened the door and welcomed Chris inside, the fragrance of spices hung in the air – roasted chilies, cardamom and cumin – and the soft light of the setting sun bounced off the warm walls.

Chris stood in silence, and Gemi watched as her young friend's eyes moved from wall to wall, from rugs to baskets. "My god, Gemi, I had no idea. This place is beautiful."

"Beautiful?"

"Yes," Chris murmured. "So warm and welcoming. She turned to look into Gemi's smiling face. "It's so much like you."

"Thank you, child. Now let me show you around this little place of mine and then you can help me make *injera* to complete our dinner."

"*Injera?*"

"It's a basic Ethiopian bread," Gemi said as she pointed out the living room, bedroom, bathroom and kitchen. Then, she offered Chris a kitchen chair as she combined ingredients into what looked a lot like pancake batter except for the cup of club soda she added. Chris watched as Gemi poured the batter into a hot skillet, flipped the flat bread, and slid it from the skillet to a plate for cooling.

"Here, you try it now." Gemi said, handing Chris the bowl and spatula. "I'll get the stew on the table." Gemi set the table, watching Chris from the corner of her eye, happy with her young friend's pleasure in learning the most basic of Ethiopian cooking.

"What we do in my culture is tear off pieces of this *injera* and use it to scoop up the stew. We usually use only one or two shared platters rather than individual dinner plates, but I've set two of those as well."

"Oh, no," Chris said. "Let's do it all the Ethiopian way."

"All right then," Gemi said with a smile, removing the extra plates from the table. "Then we have only *injera, doro wat* that's with chicken, and lentil *alecha*. The *wat* is much spicier than the *alecha*. Traditionally, Ethiopians use the *injera* as a utensil instead of a fork or spoon."

"Can you show me how to do it?"

"Like this, child," Gemi said, and holding a small piece of *injera* between her fingers, she picked a piece of chicken form the platter of *doro wat* and popped it in her mouth.

"A bit like the way Mexicans use tortillas, right?"

"So I've been told, child. And the way Native American Indians use fry bread. An edible utensil. Now, please, help yourself."

Clumsy at first, Chris dug in with gusto, and before long she was handling the *injera* like she'd eaten with it her entire life. Gemi smiled, contentment filling every pore of her body.

"In my country we usually have coffee at the end of a meal. And for this meal, we have a special dessert as well," she added with a twinkle in her dark eyes as she carried the empty platters to the kitchen sink. "As you know, child, Ethiopia is considered the birthplace of coffee, but we do not buy roasted beans as you do here in America. Instead we use green beans, like these," she said, holding out a handful for Chris to examine. "Traditionally the beans are roasted over a charcoal burner, but my gas stove works just as well."

Gemi threw the handful of beans back into the waiting sauce pan and roasted them, shaking the pan often to prevent scorching. In no time at all, the apartment was filled with the rich aroma of roasting coffee beans.

"Oh, my," Chris exclaimed as Gemi dumped the hot beans into a mortar and began crushing them with a stone pestle.

"There, now we have our coffee grounds. Let me just drop these into the water. We'll bring it to a boil and then let it set just long enough for the grounds to settle. In the meantime, are you ready for some dessert?"

As she stuck her head behind the door to her small pantry to light the candles without Chris seeing, Gemi admitted that she was probably just as excited as the birthday girl. Then she carried the cake to the table singing the English words for *Happy Birthday*, a song she only learned as an adult. Setting the beautiful cake in front of Chris, she said, "I feel so blessed to share this day with you, child."

Chris stared at the cake, her face a mask of utter surprise. Then to Gemi's horror, Chris's eyes filled with tears. "Oh, child, what have I done? I'm so sorry."

"Oh no, Gemi," Chris said, jumping to her feet and wrapping her arms around her friend. "I'm just so very, very happy. Thank you for doing all of this for me. You have given me so much. I love you, Gemi. I love you like a mother. Like a sister."

"Oh, child, I love you as well," Gemi murmured to the girl in her arms. Then, feeling Chris slowly loosen her grip, she said, "Now come, dry your tears and we shall see if this cake is edible."

Chris blew out the candles and then studied the words on the top of the cake. She turned to Gemi, the question in her eyes.

"It's Amharic, child. My native language. In Ethiopia, we do not celebrate birthdays, anyway not traditionally, and even now, rarely for adults. But as you know, the world is changing, and now even in Africa, some are adopting American customs. On your cake I have written *Mel Kam Ledet, Ligae*. Those first three words mean 'happy birthday.' The last word means 'beloved child' or 'dear one.'"

"It's beautiful, Gemi. I can't believe you baked *and* decorated this yourself. And that word, *ligae,* that's the Amharic word for child, the word you use when you talk to me, isn't it?"

"Yes, child. It's a custom in my country that I have chosen to carry with me. I hope you don't mind."

"Oh, no, not at all. In fact, I've always felt really special the way you say it to me."

"It is, indeed, a word of endearment in my language."

With a broad smile, Chris picked the candles off the cake, licking the frosting off each one. Then she sliced two large pieces of cake and handed one to Gemi. Between tears of laughter, Gemi told her of the many attempts – failures and successes – in the process of learning to bake an American birthday cake.

Later, as they sipped their tiny cups of Ethiopian coffee on the comfortable living room sofa, Gemi said, "I have one more surprise for you, child."

"Oh, no," Chris exclaimed. "You've gone to so much trouble already."

But Gemi was already on her feet, heading for her bedroom. A moment later she returned, a brightly wrapped gift in her hands. "This is something I want you to have, child. Something I hope you will enjoy," she said, handing the gift to Chris.

"You really shouldn't have gotten me a gift, Gemi. It's too much."

"This is something I purchased on my last trip back to Ethiopia several years ago. For some reason, I never used it. Now I know why. I was saving it for you."

As Gemi spoke, her voice gentle and warm, Chris opened the gift. As she pulled away the paper, the soft *shash* of brilliant golden silk lay in her lap. "Oh, Gemi, it's beautiful," Chris whispered. "Too beautiful for me to accept."

"Don't be daft, child. It is yours. You no longer need to cover that beautiful head of yours, but a *shash* can also be worn as a shawl. I'm hoping that you and that young man of yours might find a special reason to dress up and go out on the town."

Again tears of joy filled Chris's eyes. "I love it, Gemi. I absolutely love it. And you, too. Thank you so much, for everything."

"Hush now, child. It's my pleasure. You have also opened my world to new possibilities. We're good for each other, you and me. Thanks to Allah that we found each other."

"Amen," Chris smiled as she stepped away from Gemi and flung the colorful *shash* around her shoulders with a dramatic flourish.

"Wonderful, child. It makes those lovely brown eyes of yours sparkle. Now I'm going to wrap up your cake so that you can take it home with you and share it with Jake. I imagine you haven't even told that young man it's your birthday, have you?"

"No," Chris admitted. "I knew he was working, and besides I knew it was time for me to face Beth's memory."

"I'm sorry, child. I hope I didn't interrupt," Gemi said, concern lacing her voice.

"Not at all, Gemi. I remembered our dinner date earlier this week, but I just got distracted this morning when I got up and opened Beth's portfolio."

They chatted a bit more as Chris helped Gemi clear the dishes. As she paused at the door to take her leave, Chris took another long look around Gemi's apartment. "You know, Gemi. I really need to paint my condo. This place is wonderful. Did you do this yourself?"

"Yes, I did. Would you like some help choosing colors and brightening up your place?"

"I sure would! And I bet we could even rope Jake into helping us paint!"

"Good thinking, child. Let's put that boy to work," Gemi laughed. Then folding Chris into her arms, she whispered, "Good night and happy birthday, my child. Drive safely."

FIFTY-TWO

CHRIS PULLED TO A STOP at the side of the road before getting onto the freeway and flipped open her cell phone.

"Hey you, what're you up to?" Jake said.

"Just driving home from Gemi's."

"Driving?"

"No, I'm parked. Stop worrying."

"Hey, I've seen my share of cell phone accidents."

"Yeah, I know."

"So what were you doing at Gemi's?"

"She surprised me with a birthday dinner. It was so nice. She made Ethiopian food and she even baked a birthday cake for me. And you wouldn't believe her apartment. It's warm and wonderful, just like her, you know? And she gave me ..."

"Wait a second," Jake said, interrupting Chris's stream of excitement. "Did you say it was *your* birthday?"

"Yup. Mine. And I have a present I want to give you."

"Isn't it supposed to be the other way around? I'm supposed to have a present for you."

"Oh, but you do."

"How's that?"

"Are you off-duty?

"Yeah."

"And rested?"

"Enough."

"What about tomorrow?"

"A day off."

"Then meet me at my place in fifteen minutes, okay? You know the building."

"Sure do. You mean you're finally going to let me in?"

Chris only laughed. "See ya soon." She clicked her phone shut and drove home in record speed.

When she passed in front of her building to enter the parking garage, she saw him, tall and lean, slouched against the railing of the front steps, a look of absolute contentment on his face. He was wearing fitted Levis and a polar fleece jacket, his wavy, dark hair brushed back off his forehead, his eyes dark, scanning the evening traffic. Looking for me, she realized, and her heart skipped a beat as their eyes locked for a brief second.

She drove around to the side entrance of the underground parking and made her way to the lobby, opening the front door from the inside. With a sudden flush of shyness, she took his hand and led him in silence to the elevator. As soon as the elevator doors closed behind them, Jake's arms were around her, his warm moist lips on her own. She felt herself relax and let go. Gone was the desire to push this man away. Instead, she opened her lips to him, matching his desire with her own. As the elevators opened on Chris's floor, Jake stepped away from her. He searched her face, and she knew he needed some sort of sign from her.

"I'm ready," was all she said.

"Are you sure?" he asked, his voice husky with desire.

"I've never been more sure of anything in my life," she whispered, kissing his cheeks, his chin, his neck.

"You drive me crazy," he said, pulling away from her and sticking his hand out to stop the elevator doors from closing. "You know that, don't you?" The smile he gave her as they walked to her door sent shivers of anticipation through Chris's body.

The door closed behind them, they stood for a moment in the gentle silence, the dark evening shadows entering through the closed front curtains. Chris did not turn on the lights.

"So this is your place," he said, breaking the silence as he moved towards her.

"This is home," she replied with a smile, as she slid her hands under his shirt, over his flat stomach, and around his back.

He cupped her face in his hands like a precious object and paused before again asking, "Are you sure?"

"Abso..." but she only managed the first two syllables. The last two Jake swallowed as his mouth covered hers, his hands sliding down the sides of her neck and around her body, holding her in a tight embrace as he kissed her. As she opened her mouth to his, the kiss deepened with longing matched only by her own. They tugged off each other's clothes, fumbling with buttons and zippers.

"My god you're beautiful," he groaned, as he opened the front fastener of her lacy new bra and cupped her breasts in his hands. "Do you have a bed in this place?"

Taking his left hand from her breast, Chris led him to the bedroom at the back of the condo, wearing nothing more than an expectant smile and a pair of lacy new panties.

FIFTY-THREE

WHEN JAKE OPENED HIS EYES to the shadows, he knew he was alone. He stretched his arms, feeling the empty space in the bed, feeling Chris's absence. He forced himself awake, pulled on his jeans, and wandered into the living room. It was empty. The kitchen – empty. He peeked into the bathroom. Empty. "Damn," he muttered to himself.

The coffee pot was hot. Cup in hand, his eyes scanned the beach and running path. Then, his decision made, he showered and settled on the sofa with a day-old newspaper, determined to wait her out. She had to come back sooner or later, and he was going to be there when she did. An hour and a pot of coffee later, Jake heard a key in the lock.

"Did you want me to disappear?" he asked when she walked in the living room.

"Oh."

"You can't get rid of me without so much as a word, Chris. Did you really want me gone?" he asked as he stood up and walked toward her.

"I don't know. No, I don't want you gone. I just, I don't know, I just…"

"Hey, we don't need to get all nervous and awkward with each other this morning, do we? I had a wonderful time last night. You?"

"Oh, yes," she said as she walked into his open arms. Then she stopped. "Yuck. Sorry. I'm all sweaty."

"Doesn't bother me a bit." He held her close and kissed her deep. "Nice," he whispered a few minutes later.

"The view?" she asked, teasing.

"The view," he agreed, holding her at arm's-length as she stood before the Seattle skyline. "Can I open it?" he asked, indicating the door to the balcony. With a nod from Chris, he slid the door open wide, and they stepped outside. "Man, now I know why you love this place so much. It really is an awesome view."

"Yeah, it keeps me grounded, I suppose. Especially now that I'm at home more. But the place is awful. I really want to do some work on it, especially after seeing Gemi's apartment." She walked back into the living room. "It's so drab and boring in here. I'm going to pick some warm colors and paint and redecorate."

"Sounds like fun. Let me know if you want some help. I'm pretty good with a paint brush. Speaking of which, what's all this?" he asked. His eyes scanned the piles on the dining room table and the canvases and large black portfolio leaning against the wall.

"I told you about my sister, Beth, right?"

"Yeah, she was killed in a car accident on your sixteenth birthday." His voice was gentle. "It was her painting of your grandmother that you found, right?"

"Yeah. This is the rest of her work, her legacy, I suppose. I finally reopened her portfolio yesterday and began to read her poetry."

"Are these hers?" Jake asked, lifting one of the poems. "I don't know anything about poetry, but this calligraphy is amazing."

"The poetry is hers. The calligraphy is mine. See how the poem matches the painting."

"I didn't know you did calligraphy," he said, glancing at Chris for the okay before lifting a few more pieces of artwork and poetry from the piles.

"You should've seen it in here last night," she said with a laugh. "These things were spread all over the room. I did a quick clean-up this morning before my run."

"I was worried you might have some regrets when you were gone."

"No regrets. Just really nervous, I guess," she said, with a quick kiss on his cheek. Then, taking the package that Gemi had given her from the dining room table, she said. "Hey, check this out." With a sweep of her arms, she draped the scarf over her shoulders, encasing herself in a sunshine cocoon. She saw Jake's eyes widen. She saw the desire. "So, what do you think?" she asked.

"I think you're beautiful," he said.

"No, the scarf. Isn't it amazing?"

"Yes."

"Okay then," she said, taking off the scarf and laying it over the back of a chair. "How about some breakfast?"

"I've got a better idea," Jake said. He slowly removed her running clothes, wrapped her in golden silk and led her back to the bedroom.

FIFTY-FOUR

GEMI STOOD BEFORE THE FULL-LENGTH MIRROR where she always checked her *shash* before leaving the privacy of her small apartment. Checked her *shash* to ensure that not a single strand of long, curly black hair could sneak its way out of concealment just as her mother had taught her to do so many years before in Addis Ababa.

It was mid-morning on a rare weekday when Gemi had only one patient to check on: Mrs. Newbury. Then she'd have time for a nice walk in Volunteer Park before she met Chris for dinner. Since that first slow walk with Chris, she'd walked every day, and over time her speed and endurance had improved, and she'd lost over ten pounds. Now, as she stood alone before her mirror wearing a pair of new jeans and a sweater, her long curls loose around her shoulders, she spoke to her reflection. "Not so bad for a middle-aged African immigrant lady, I suppose."

As she reached for her dark *shash* to bind her head, she stopped. She stared at the reflection remembering the first time she'd gone into a department store and bought a pair of pants. She didn't even try them on. She knew she'd feel too exposed, even in the privacy of a fitting room cubicle. She asked a sales clerk to recommend a size and bought her first pair of loose tan trousers. She wore them in the privacy of her own apartment for several months trying to get used to their feel before garnering the nerve to walk out the front door wearing them without a long dress, a *habesha kemis,* over the top to conceal the shape of her body. It was a co-worker who had recommended it one day when they were lifting and bathing an elderly patient together. An off-handed comment really. "You know, Gemi, it might be easier to do this in a pair of pants. Don't those long dresses you always wear get in the way?"

Since that first day she left her apartment in a pair of ill-fitting pants, she'd never once worked in a *habesha kemis* again. Still she kept the headscarf, the *shash*, and it was that scarf hanging loosely in her hand that now perplexed her. She hadn't been to mosque in many years. Her lifestyle was neither Muslim nor Christian, so why the *shash*, she asked herself. "It's no different than all these Christmas decorations you see everywhere. A tradition for most, a religious belief for only a handful. So too this scarf of mine," she told her image. "My mother's tradition and that of my mother's mother. But why is it mine? Is it a tradition that I need or want to hold on to?"

She fingered the soft worn fabric of the *shash*. "A remnant of a life long ago, a life that is no longer mine. Nothing more," she whispered. She folded the large scarf into a gentle square and held it to her breast. Then, with the slow steps of a life-changing decision, Gemi walked to the dresser in her bedroom and opened a small top drawer and set the scarf inside. She gave it a gentle, loving pat, the pat of a mother to a beloved child, the pat of good-bye.

Chris set aside the used copy of a year-old restaurant guide that she and Gemi perused each time they ate together, ticking off the places they'd been and marking those yet to visit. The number of marks was growing. They had great fun writing little comments next to each listing. A personal rating system that rarely had much to do with the quality of the food served.

Today she sat waiting at a tiny place on East Lake Avenue. A classmate had told her about the great deck overlooking Lake Union and the endless menu of margaritas. Chris wasn't much of a drinker, and Gemi didn't drink at all, but the deck and the water had caught her attention.

Chris loved water, in all its forms. And she loved Seattle, a city dotted with lakes fed by snow run-off every spring from the Cascade Mountain Range just to the east of the metropolitan area. As she sat waiting for her friend, Chris imagined a map of her city with tiny Lake Union wedged between Lake Washington to the east and Salmon Bay to the northwest. She saw Salmon Bay open to Elliot Bay through the manmade canal and the Hiram M. Chittenden Locks. At the locks, fresh and salt water mixed as the mountain run-off flowed into the Pacific.

So it wasn't the saltwater that Chris sat staring at as Gemi entered the small restaurant, but still, she was lost in the beauty of the faint winter sunshine dancing on the water when she felt someone's presence at her side. She looked up into the dark brown eyes she loved, but for a split second she couldn't place them.

"Hello, child. Don't you recognize me?"

"I'm sorry, Gemi. But, my god, you look so different. You look…" Chris stammered, "You look beautiful."

"Beautiful?"

"Yes, beautiful."

Gemi pulled out a chair and sat down. Not only was she dressed in stylish trouser jeans and a blazer, but her *shash* was gone. Her long, shiny black hair was held back in a loose French braid that hung to the center of her back revealing the beauty of her high cheekbones and intelligent brow. Tiny ringlets escaping the braid framed her face, a hint of gray at her temples the only testimony to her age.

"I never thought you'd come out in public without your *shash*. You look wonderful."

After a moment of silence, Gemi spoke in a soft, musical tone. "Well, I've been doing a fair amount of soul-searching these past months, child, and I've decided that I'm not yet fifty and still have a lot of life before me. I want to feel the wind in my hair when I walk in the park. I want to open myself to new experiences and new possibilities. I don't want to hide behind a tradition or a culture that I no longer feel in my heart. You have shown me how a person can change and grow. So now that you see the new me, what do you think?"

Chris clapped her hands in delight. "Bravo, Gemi. You really do look fantastic, and not just your face and hair, but also your body. You've lost weight."

"Yes. I am indebted to you for that."

"Me?"

"Yes, child. You introduced me to the joys of walking. Even in inclement weather."

"Do you still walk?"

"Every single day. And now I need to find some more decent clothes. A kind woman at the downtown Macy's helped me put together this outfit, as well as a few others, but it is not enough. I need clothes to work in, to walk in. Just to live in. No more clothes to hide behind. Do you understand, child?"

"Yeah, if anybody can understand, I think it's me. I was hiding behind that flight attendant's uniform, and maybe even behind my running clothes, too."

"I was wondering, child, do you think we could go shopping together?"

"What a great idea! The blind leading the blind. It could be great fun! When do you want to go?"

"Would next Saturday work for you?"

"It's a date! Hey, did I ever tell you about my first visit to Victoria's Secret with Karin?"

"No, child. I think that is a story I would remember."

When a waiter came to their table, they were giggling like a couple of schoolgirls. With a quick glance at their menus, they ordered dinner.

"That is quite a story, child. I can assure you that when we go to the mall next Saturday, we do not need to stop at Victoria's Secret." Again a bright burst of laughter rose from their table. "Now tell me what else is new in your life?"

Chris felt like she was bursting with excitement. "Oh, so much good stuff. I don't know why I'm so lucky. Sometimes I'm afraid this bubble will just burst, and I'll be alone in the darkness again."

"Oh, child, you know that will never happen. And even if your bubble were to burst, as you say, you'd still have me and you'd still have Peter Bentley. And then there's Karin and your writing group. And of course, there is Jake. That boy isn't just going to burst into thin air."

"Ooh, la la, look at the hottie," Carolyn bellowed.

"Shhhh… You'll wake the neighbors," Gemi said, the sting of her scold lost in laughter. "What are you doing out here?"

"Just taking out the garbage. I made some banana bread and didn't want to wake to the smell of rotting peels. But don't try to change the subject on me. Look at you, girlfriend. What a huge decision. No headscarf. I want to hear all about it."

"Can it wait until tomorrow? I'm a bit tired," Gemi said.

"Not a chance. Come right on in here and I'll make you a cup of tea. Better yet, a martini."

At that, Gemi began laughing. "I've made some changes in my life, but I don't think I'm ready for martinis yet, my friend."

"Okay, a pot of chamomile then."

A few minutes later the two women were settled at Carolyn's round kitchen table with steaming mugs of hot tea and a fresh loaf of banana bread between them. The kitchen was rich with the sweet aroma.

"It was time," Gemi said. "The clothes were ridiculous. I should've bought some decent clothes years ago. And, now, since I've slimmed down a bit, I felt I had no choice."

"Especially after Mrs. Newbury gave you a talking to, right?"

"Yes, that opinionated old woman opened my eyes a bit, I'll grant you that. It's odd how we can go through life without seeing our own image."

"True, that explains the clothes, but what about the headscarf? That's huge."

"I suppose it is," Gemi said. She blew softly on her tea and took a small sip.

"When was the last time you were in public without covering your head?"

"I'm not sure I recall. As a child, I never wore a headscarf. But as an adult? In hospital, perhaps."

"After the bombing?"

"I imagine. After I was healed, I tried to retain as many of the old ways as I could, the ways of my mother and grandmother. I suppose it was my way of clinging to their memory and to the past."

"So why change now?"

Gemi laughed a bit, remembering when she first met Carolyn, remembering how much she loved the pushy questions of her curious, loving neighbor. "It was simply time for a change. Change is good. Isn't that what you always say? I've watched the change, metamorphosis really, that Chris has gone through. Perhaps I've simply copied her a bit." Gemi took another sip of her tea. "But there's more to this, I'll admit. In these past weeks I've seen the annual Christmas lights and decorations going up everywhere. And I've wondered..."

"Christian belief vs. American tradition, you mean?" Carolyn asked, as though she were reading her friend's thoughts.

"Precisely. This morning as I stood before my mirror, I admitted that my scarf was only a tradition that I was clinging to in honor of the memory of my ancestors, but I held no religious belief that bound me to the practice of covering my head. That's when I made my decision."

"And now? How do you feel?"

"Wonderful," Gemi said. "Simply wonderful. Light, free, alive in a world full of possibility."

"Good for you," Carolyn said. She stood to refill their teacups from the tea kettle on the stovetop. "You really do look amazing, you know."

"You should've seen Mrs. Newbury's face when she opened her front door to me this morning," Gemi said, modestly ignoring her friend's compliment. "I thought the old dear might have a heart attack right then and there."

The women giggled like twenty-somethings half their age.

"And Chris? You went to dinner with her, right? How'd she react to the new Gemi?"

"Ah, Chris. What a dear child, that one."

FIFTY-FIVE

IT WAS A RAINY, COLD WINTER DAY and Chris was happy to get inside as she pushed open the door to The Last Exit. She was early, and she wanted it that way. The coffee shop was still almost empty. Writers hadn't started crowding the space yet. Chris ordered her tea and sat down. The fingers of her right hand were stained black, and she was exhausted from hours of relentless determination to relearn a skill she thought she'd lost. She was working her way through Beth's poetry collection, reading, selecting and transcribing into script, artwork in lettering across piles of thick parchment. Lost in thought, she glanced up at the scrape of a wooden chair leg on the brick floor to see Karin's smiling face.

"Hey, Chris. Far away again, I see."

"Yeah, I suppose. Actually, I came early hoping I'd get a chance to talk to you. I've got a couple of book ideas, but I don't know what would actually work or what angle to try, and I have no idea how to go about finding an agent, or even who to go to for advice."

"Well, maybe I can help. Try me."

"You don't mind?"

"Wouldn't have offered if I did."

"Okay, so here's the deal. You know I've been working on the memoir."

"Sure. What I've heard sounds great. You've definitely got a story there."

"Thanks," Chris said, shy from the compliment. "Anyway, I finally started digging into my sister's portfolio."

"Okay, you lost me. I thought you already opened the portfolio. Wasn't that where you found your grandmother's picture?"

"Yeah, but I stopped there. I didn't look at the rest of it. And I didn't read Beth's poetry."

Chris wove the story forward telling Karin about reopening Beth's portfolio on her birthday and about digging out her own calligraphy pens from her storage closet. She told her of her obsession with relearning calligraphy and of the piles and piles of transcribed poetry she'd been working on.

"That explains the black fingers."

"Yeah," Chris laughed. "Anyway, so I've got this incredible collection of teen poetry and artwork. I'm no expert, and I have no doubt I'm biased, but I think it's good. Really good. I'd like to see if it's publishable. Any ideas how I'd do that?"

"What format are you thinking of?"

"That's the problem. I've got two different ideas."

"Okay. Let's hear them."

"Well, one idea would be to do two separate books. Continue working on the memoir and finish it. At the same time I could pull together some kind of art and poetry book of Beth's work. The other idea would be to somehow combine the two. Maybe infuse the memoir with Beth's artwork and maybe even some of her poems. What do you think?"

"I'm no agent, and I haven't seen your sister's work, but I really like the second idea. Two stories, two lives intertwined, two sisters deeply connected even after death. And, of course, the secret of your biracial heritage."

"That's what I was thinking. I've even been playing with a layout and storyline. You know, moving art pieces around, matching them with poems and scenes from the memoir. I've come up with an idea that starts and ends with the unfinished portrait of Grandmother Stevens."

"Sounds cool."

"But what do I do next? I mean, how do I find someone who might be interested in editing and publishing it?"

"Oh, the dreaded publishing process. You need an agent. Someone to represent your work to the big houses. Someone to take charge of the business side of it so you can focus on writing. But it's an almost impossible challenge in today's world. The other option is to self-publish. The publishing world is in such flux."

"I'm not sure I'm ready to go it alone. How do I find an agent?"

"Well, go to conferences, meet people, network. Get yourself a copy of the *Writers' Market* and start sending out query letters by the dozens. Then cross your ink-stained fingers and hope you get lucky."

"That bad, huh?"

The tables were filling with other writers, the coffee shop buzzing with conversation. Chris knew they were almost out of time.

"That bad. No, worse. But I've got another idea. I've never asked my agent to look at another writer's work, but I really think you might have something special here." Karin was thinking aloud. "Maybe, just maybe, I could convince her to look it over. Let me talk her. If she's interested, can I give her your number or e-mail address?"

"Of course. Thank you," Chris grinned. "That'd be so great!"

"Hey, no promises. Don't get too excited, Chris. This is a dog-eat-dog world. The chances of getting a first book published are almost as slim as affordable commercial flights to Mars in our lifetime. Might happen. Might not. But I'll give it my best shot. And even if something does come of it, you won't hear a word until early next year. Nothing happens during the winter holidays."

FIFTY-SIX

"GOODNESS CHILD, WHAT HAPPENED HERE?" Gemi asked. The condo had been transformed from the comfortable, if somewhat boring space she'd grown accustomed to, into a construction zone. The furniture, piled in the center of the room, was covered with the same plastic sheeting that covered every square inch of the white carpet, taped to the baseboards with blue painters' tape.

"Come in. Come here," Chris said. She pulled her by the arm like an impatient child. "I want to show you the colors."

"Looks to me like you've chosen quite a few," Gemi said.

"Those were just the colors I was testing. I had to do swatches on both walls because the light hits them differently. Or I suppose I should say the colors look different depending on the light. Anyway, this is the one I picked. What do you think? It's great, isn't it?"

Gemi smiled at the girl's exuberance, wondering in amazement that this was the same young woman who just a year before was so desperate that she had attempted to end her own life. "Yes, child, it is indeed great." And in the second it took to say the word "child" – a word she used on a regular basis – she knew it was no longer a simple translation from Amharic of the traditional endearment, *ligae*. Her heart felt as though it might explode, and she knew that she loved this girl as though she were her own daughter.

"I see you've prepped your space and purchased your paint and brushes and rollers, but where are all the helpers you promised?"

"Oh, they'll be here soon. Jake's probably still sleeping. He's just coming off a three-day shift. Karin and her husband will be here any minute. I just wanted you to take a look first and tell me what you think. Honestly, this whole thing is making me nervous."

Gemi smiled as Chris paced the barren, plasticized room, adjusting tape here, tucking a corner of plastic there. "It's going to be a big change, but I'm certain it will look wonderful, child. I see you have yellow on these two opposing walls, but what about the wall facing the water?"

"That's what I really wanted your opinion about. I was thinking about surrounding the glass door in a deep contrast color. I've got this great sienna, and I even found some pillows and a throw for the sofa that would match."

"Sounds awesome," came a voice from the open door.

"Hey, Karin," Chris said in greeting. "You ready to work?"

"Not so fast, girlfriend. I promised Mike you'd have a pot of strong dark coffee for him before you put him to work." With that, Karin crossed the room and extended her hand to Gemi. "You must be Gemi. It's great to finally meet you. This is my husband, Mike. Mike, Chris and Gemi. Okay, intros done. Where's the coffee? And by the way the dark accent wall is perfect – shorten the length and widen the space with light. Perfect. You'll be putting up some of Beth's artwork too, right?"

Chris laughed at Gemi's glance. "Nope, she never slows down. I don't know how Mike can live with all that energy."

"I drink lots of coffee and just try to stay out of her way," Mike said.

"Did I hear something about coffee?" Jake said from the doorway.

"Sure did," Karin said. "You must be Jake. I'm Karin. This is Mike. Cups all around before the task-master, or is it task-mistress? Anyway before she puts us all to work."

After introductions, Gemi watched with pleasure as the young people drank their coffee and got to know each other. Then, she slipped out of the room. When she returned, she was dressed in a pair of her baggy old khakis and a smock with her hair concealed in a tattered black headscarf.

"Heavens, Gemi. What happened? Are you slipping?" Chris asked.

Gemi knew the joke, though the others only stared. "No, child, I'm not slipping anywhere. I'm simply protecting my new clothes and my hair from what I assume will be quite a messy task. Now, are we ready to begin?"

"And what task might that be?" came another voice from the doorway. A masculine voice laced with a heavy accent.

Gemi smiled as Jake moved protectively towards the door in a few quick steps. The man standing there had a warm smile and a bit of gray in his curly black hair. He stood square in the open doorway. "Pardon me for disturbing you," he said. "Permit me to introduce myself. I am Antonio Meléndez. I'm your new neighbor, just here, across the hall."

Chris moved past Jake to the door and extended her hand to introduce herself. "That place has been empty for a few months. I guess I didn't realize that anyone had moved in."

"I rented it fully-furnished, so the move in was very simple."

"And quiet too," Chris said with a laugh. "I'm sorry if all my noise has bothered you. I'm usually very quiet myself."

"Not at all. I heard a little something last night, and now this morning, when your door was open, I decided to stop. Fred said a young woman lived here. I was once a father."

Gemi, still standing on the far side of the room, and feeling oddly embarrassed in her baggy old clothes and head scarf, heard his voice fade into sadness. She knew that tone and the pain that produced it. She also knew she was drawn to this man in a way she hadn't felt in years.

She felt a strong urge to rip off her scarf and rush to the bedroom to change her clothes, but she knew that was out of the question. For the first time in her life, at least in her life beyond her early years in Ethiopia, she did not want to be hiding behind her clothes. And yet here she was, stuck, with a handsome, and possibly eligible, man only a few feet away. She wanted to stamp her feet in frustration like she had once done as a little girl playing with her older brother. Instead, she watched in silence as Chris introduced her young friends. There was no escape.

"And this is my dear friend, my Ethiopian mother, Gemila Kemmal," Chris said.

Gemi stepped forward and extended her hand. She felt his warm, firm handshake, the trace of calluses on the fingertips and palm. The hands of a man who has known hard labor.

"*Mucho gusto,*" he said with a twinkle in his eyes that hinted to Gemi the attraction she felt might be mutual.

"Okay, child," she said, turning to Chris. "You said we were to get some work done today. Where shall we begin? And you, Antonio, do you care to join us? I'm sure Chris will find work for all of us."

"There is nothing I would enjoy more," he said. "Unfortunately, I was just on my way out. Perhaps I can join you all on my return later this afternoon?" He turned towards Chris, addressing the question to his new neighbor.

"Sure," she said. "We'll be here all day, right gang?" A small chorus of laughter followed.

"*Bueno.* I will see you very soon." This time he was speaking to Gemi, and she felt her face flush with the pleasure of a school girl.

FIFTY-SEVEN

THE HOLIDAY SEASON PASSED in a flurry of activities, but once school was back in session, Chris was buried in homework and revisions. She finished the first draft of the memoir. But only the first draft. She immersed herself in the process of lacing her prose with her sister's poetry and selecting pieces of artwork, for each poem and chapter.

Since first talking to Karin about finding an agent, she'd heard enough stories of agent rejections, unreturned e-mail queries, and dead-end leads from her fellow writers at The Last Exit to ever believe she'd get a call from Karin's agent. She continued to remind herself that it all came down to being in the right place at the right time with the right manuscript. Still, she kept her ink-stained fingers crossed.

She also bought herself the latest edition of the *Writer's Market* and spent several hours a week narrowing her list of possible agents and honing a query letter. Most agents asked for a query and the first twenty pages, so she had to figure out how to get top quality duplicates of the first piece of artwork and the first poem. Her calligraphy copied well, but Beth's piece that she'd selected for the opening image was coming out muddy. It had to be sharp. It had to be perfect. The first pages of prose had to be perfect. It had to grab the attention and not let go. Perfect, perfect, perfect.

"God, I'm becoming my mother. Striving for perfection just like her," Chris muttered. "I can't let this take control of me." She headed for her bedroom to change her clothes. She needed to clear her head. She needed a run.

Just as she was about to walk out the door, the phone stopped her. "Hello. May I speak with Chris Stevens?" Thinking it was a sales call, she almost hung up, but something stopped her. Maybe the "Chris" instead of the legal "Christine."

"Yes," she said. "This is Chris Stevens."

"This is Elsie Crane with Acorn Literary Agency. Karin Bishop gave me your number."

"I'm sorry. I didn't catch your name."

"Elsie Crane. I'm Karin's agent. She told me that you're working on a project that I might find interesting."

"Oh, yes. I'm sorry. Hello."

"No problem. I'd like to take a look at your manuscript. Karin explained that it would be difficult to send electronically due to the original artwork and calligraphy. Is that right?"

"Yes. At some point I'll need to digitize it, but I'm not there yet."

"No rush. I'll be in Seattle next week. I was wondering if you could show it to me then."

"I'd be happy to." Chris struggled to gain composure, her mind racing. Karin, agent, manuscript. I'm not ready, she thought. "It's only a first draft, and I'm still working on the calligraphy, but I can show you what I have and explain the concept."

"Wonderful. I'll be flying in on Thursday. I usually go to writing practice with Karin when I'm in town, so I'll meet you there, and you can show me your work afterwards."

Chris's hand shook when she closed her cell phone. She collapsed on the sofa and stared at the room around her. There were papers scattered everywhere. Manuscript pages, calligraphy parchment, artwork, color copies of paintings and drawings, scraps of paper and memories scattered around her. Oh my god. I've got less than a week to pull this mess together and figure out how to duplicate it. I'll need to show her the original and give her something to take with her.

She was walking on clouds as she headed for the running path making lists in her mind, trying to figure out how to prepare for her meeting with Elsie Crane. And how to get it all accomplished while working part-time and going to school.

The phone was ringing as Jake opened his apartment door. He rushed to answer it.

"I'm so glad I caught you."

Hearing the strain in her voice, caution flares lit up in Jake's mind. "What's wrong, Chris?"

"Wrong? Oh, nothing's wrong. Not really. Just, I don't know – shock, overwhelm. Can we get together?"

"Sure, but I'm just coming off a 36-hour shift so I might not be the best listener. What's this all about?"

"I got a call from Karin's agent."

"Oh, got it. Well, why don't you come over here? I'll make dinner for you, and we can talk."

"Dinner?" Chris laughed. Making dinner was their little joke. "Listen, it's about four o'clock now. Why don't you take a shower and a nap. I'll bring *dinner* over at about seven."

"What kind of dinner?" he asked with a grin.

"How about both kinds?"

"You bet. You've got the key. Why not bring me dessert first?" he said with a sly, but sleepy smile. "I'll be waiting for you."

"I might just do that," Chris laughed. "See you at seven."

Three hours later Jake was out cold. He didn't hear Chris slip the key into the door of his apartment and enter his front room. He didn't hear her go into the kitchen and open the refrigerator door. And he didn't hear her removing her clothes in the bathroom.

They had agreed to keep their own places, not move in together right away, but they each had a key to the other's place. Jake was the first to admit that her place was a lot nicer than his, and he knew she owned it free and clear. He was working extra hours, saving as much as he could, hoping to cobble together the funds to buy a first home. And he was close. He didn't want to live with Chris until it was in a home he could afford to buy with his own money. Maybe then he'd feel good enough for her, good enough to ask her to marry him. He hadn't told Chris about any of this and didn't plan to until he was ready to contact a realtor and start house hunting. In the meantime, he and Chris had a lot of getting-to-know-each-other left to enjoy.

He was still asleep when Chris entered his bedroom, naked but for her lacy bra and panties. When she slipped into the warm sheets next to him, he woke to the touch of her soft skin against his own, the smell of her sweet scent. He found her mouth and kissed her slow and deep with desire. He loved how she opened to him – her mouth, her arms, her body. He explored the gentle curves of her body with bold, tender appreciation, until he was desperate to be inside of her and knew her need matched his own. They made love wordlessly, only their moans of pleasure filling the small room.

Later, when they were both exhausted with satisfaction, Jake propped himself up on an elbow beside her. "So, you mentioned shock and overwhelm when you called. What's going on, Chris?"

She smiled up at him. "You remembered."

"Yeah, you sounded a bit upset. Come on, tell me."

"Okay, so like I said, I got a call from Karin's agent – Elsie Crane of Acorn Literary Agency. I felt like such an idiot. I didn't even know her name. I didn't think she'd really call, so I never even thought to ask Karin."

"I remember you told me that Karin had offered to try to set you up. That was what? A couple of months ago, right?"

"Yeah, right around Christmas."

"So this agent, Elsie Crane, must be interested if she called you, right? That's great."

"Yeah, but she's coming to town next Thursday, and she wants to see the manuscript. How will I possibly be ready in time?"

"Ahhh, Chris," Jake said, his voice as soothing as a mother's kiss. "This is great news. And you'll be ready. If anybody can pull it together, you can."

"You think?"

"I know."

She seemed to relax into the pillows, and he saw a glint of determination return to her eyes as a smile spread across the face he'd grown to love. God this feels good, he smiled to himself.

FIFTY-EIGHT

THE HOLIDAYS WERE A HECTIC TIME for Gemi. Whether it was painful loneliness or empty cheer or blatant commercialism, she was never sure. Maybe some combination. She just knew she was always swamped with extra calls and requests from her clients as well as their distant relatives. The clients needing an extra bit of attention, the family members searching for ways to assuage their guilt for not being present with their loved ones for the holidays.

She sighed, grateful the rush was over. She unpacked her basket, made herself a cup of tea and relaxed at her kitchen table, her schedule in front of her. The mid-January calm would be her own cheer. When her business line rang, she didn't yet know just *how* happy she would become.

"Gemila Kemmal speaking."

"Gemi? This is Antonio Meléndez. Chris's neighbor. We met at her condo the day you were helping her paint."

"Yes. Of course." Gemi's mind raced. Was this a business call? "Is Chris all right?" she asked.

"Chris? Chris is fine," he said, a note of bewilderment in his voice.

"Thank goodness," she said, relieved that this gorgeous man hadn't sought her out because of some type of problem with her dear young friend. But then maybe he simply needed care for someone. "How can I help you?" she asked, her voice neutral, all business.

"Help? Well, I'd like to invite you to have dinner with me."

"But I don't understand. I thought perhaps ... how...?"

"I took the liberty of Googling your name and found your listing. I hope you don't mind."

"No, not at all. I am surprised, that is all." She flipped back through her day planner. Several weeks, no, a month, had passed since the painting party at Chris's.

As though reading her thoughts, he continued. "The holidays are a busy time for most of us. I thought perhaps it best to wait. Was I mistaken?"

"Not at all," Gemi repeated, her tongue thick, her gut a knot of nerves.

"So, about dinner?"

"I'd love to."

"Saturday?"

"Perfect," she said. "Where shall we meet?" She needed her car, wasn't ready to tell this stranger where she lived despite the sparks she was now certain filled the air of Chris's condo that day.

He suggested a small Italian bistro on Beach Drive, a place Gemi had been by a number of times, but ever visited. It seemed a bit too romantic for just any meal.

"So special?" she said. The moment the words left her mouth, she wanted to grab them back.

Antonio chuckled. "Special? Yes, Gemi. Special. Do you like Italian?"

"Indeed," she said.

"Then La Rustica at 7 p.m. Saturday. Unless, of course, you'll allow me to pick you up?"

"Thank you, but I prefer to drive."

"All right then," he said. "I look forward to our special dinner."

Gemi sat in a daze, the phone still in her hand. A date? Had she just accepted her first real date? A date with Chris's handsome neighbor who she knew nothing about?

For the next four days, she tried on outfit after outfit, unsure what to wear, how to comb her hair, what bag to carry. She knew nothing about this dating ritual and was glad she'd peeked into the windows at La Rustica on more than one walk. At least she had an idea – not too dressy, not too casual. As Saturday approached, her normal serenity seemed to crumble. Still, she didn't allow herself to mention the date to anyone, especially not to Carolyn or Chris. At one point, she considered calling Chris to learn as much as she could about Antonio, but this too she refused herself. This date was something she needed to do alone.

He sat in the tiny bar sipping a glass of red wine when she arrived. She'd decided on a simple wool dress with her favorite brown boots, her hair in a loose French braid. She trembled when he took her hand in greeting. Don't panic, she told herself. Don't be Chris. She smiled.

"You look lovely," he said.

"Thank you." She just stopped herself from blurting out that he too looked irresistible. Instead, she said, "A bit better than last time?"

He laughed. "I took the liberty of ordering you a glass of Chianti. I hope that wasn't presumptuous," he said, nodding to a second glass on the bar in front of them.

She accepted, not telling him the wine, like the date, was her first. Ever. She took a tiny sip. An odd taste, she thought.

"Is it okay?"

Had her face revealed her secret? She laughed. "I'm not much of a drinker," she said. Later she'd tell him. Not yet. No confessions about dates and drinks just yet.

A waitress led them to a tiny table in a candle-lit corner. As they read the menu together, Gemi told him of her Italian grandfather, and they laughed at their limited Italian skills despite her heritage and his Spanish. They ordered a multi-course meal starting with antipasto misto and ending with tiramisu, settling in for a long evening.

Gemi relaxed. Maybe the wine helped, maybe Antonio's calm. When he offered her a second glass, she politely refused. Having never tasted alcohol, she had no idea how it might affect her and she wasn't about to make a fool of herself on her first date. She was glad Antonio ordered himself a second glass of wine without the slightest hint of discomfort.

They talked of her work as a home healthcare provider and his as an immigrants' rights attorney. They told of their childhoods, but not yet of their losses. That would come later, with time and trust. As they sipped their tiny demitasse cups of espresso, they agreed to walk Alki the following day and lunch on Capitol Hill near her home. She smiled thinking perhaps she was doing all right on this date.

He walked her to her car, kissed her on the right cheek and closed the car door for her. A gentleman, she thought as she drove across the West Seattle Bridge towards home. She thought of calling Chris. No, she decided, this is my secret. No, our secret. A secret she wanted to enjoy a bit longer, a relationship she wanted to explore a bit more, before it was shared.

FIFTY-NINE

THE WEEK FLEW BY as Chris prepared for Elsie Crane's Seattle visit. If asked, she would not have been able to describe the weather, the meals she ate, or the hours she spent at her part-time job. She took a few days off and spent every moment possible at her large table, piled high with manuscript pages. She even skipped a few classes.

One week. That's all she had, and time was running out. She knew she had three tasks to finish by Thursday and here it was Tuesday already. First, she needed to polish the first twenty pages of the memoir. It had to grab. It had to pull the reader in – not just any reader – it had to pull Elsie Crane in and not let her go. Second, she wanted to double-check that all the images and poetry were perfect. Or rather, that her memoir and Beth's work were all telling the same story. They had to tell the story in parallel forms, each feeding off the other, each adding depth and perspective to the other: two sisters telling the same story, each in two different mediums. And then there was the third task. She needed a title.

Chris stood in the middle of her living room surrounded by paintings, poems and printed manuscript pages. The hardest task of all was deciding what to cut. Chris had learned enough about writing to know that cutting was hard. It was a skill. She'd met several writers who set up a cut file on their desktop, a place to save the cuts. They felt better knowing they weren't losing those words forever, even if they never opened the cut file.

Now she was faced with cutting her sister's words, her dead sister's words. She wasn't sure if she could make those final cuts, wasn't sure if she was the right person to decide if the poem about teen loneliness in a high school cafeteria was stronger than the one about a sunset over Puget Sound from the vantage point of an eagle's nest. And if she cut a poem, then a painting or drawing had to go as well.

Chris stood, frozen in place with frustration. Small steps, she told herself. It's all in order now. Maybe too long, maybe too much, but there's a logical beautiful sequence and story here. I just need to focus on the first twenty pages, the submission pages. She already knew she had to give Elsie Crane something. She wasn't ready to digitize the manuscript yet, and Elsie had told her not to worry about it. Still, Chris wanted to show her the body of work and give her color copies of the first twenty pages. She wasn't blind to the fact that what she was creating fell a bit outside the box. All she could do was hope Elsie Crane would understand and appreciate her vision and then find a way to get it into the hands of just the right publisher.

She needed a break. The condo walls seemed to be closing in on her, suffocating her, sapping her of creativity, energy, even the simple ability to think with any definable clarity. She needed a break and she needed to see Karin.

She drove across town and found a corner table at The Last Exit. She sat, absorbed in thought, reading through another of Beth's journals, double-checking one more time for poems or prose, drawings or details that she may have missed. The manuscript was finished. And yet was it? Could she let go, satisfied that the story was told, complete and without holes? That she had reconstructed both her sister's personal and artistic journeys with accuracy and beauty?

"Lost in thought, I see," Karin said, leaning over her shoulder to peer at Beth's journal. "You've gone through all of those at least a half dozen times. You're not really still looking for more, are you?"

"Oh, I don't know," Chris said. "I just want to be sure, you know. I keep thinking I'm missing something, that there are still some secrets that I haven't discovered yet, still hidden in her words or images."

"Chris, you can't bring her back. No matter how many times you reread those journals, you're not going to get her back. You know that."

"Yeah, I know."

"So what's the problem? Why'd you drag my lazy butt in here a half-hour early?"

"Just wanted to visit," Chris said with a grin.

"Right. With Elsie Crane showing up here on Thursday, the last thing you want is a casual chit-chat. Come on, out with it. What's up?"

"I'm stuck."

"Stuck? You've got an amazing manuscript – memoir, poetry and images – how can you be stuck? That's not what I'd call being stuck."

"I don't have a title."

Karin stared at her in silence. The only sound in The Last Exit was the whooshing noise of the espresso machine, loud and abrasive over the quiet chords of classical guitar.

"A title?" Karin asked.

"Yes. A title. I don't have a title for this manuscript. I don't know what to call it."

"What have you been calling it? What's your working title?"

"I don't have one. I haven't been calling it anything," Chris said.

"But now Elsie's on her way and you need a title."

"Right."

"Okay, so let's start brainstorming. What have you come up with so far? Anything at all?"

Chris tucked away Beth's journal and pulled her own from her backpack, paging through to find the list she'd been doodling earlier that morning. "You know, I haven't really thought much about it. But it finally hit me yesterday that I had to have something so I started jotting down ideas when I woke up this morning."

"Okay, stop stalling and read me what you've got there."

"It needs to be something that includes the key ideas, the spine. It has to have words like Beth, sister, secret, running, grandmother, suicide. Something like *Beth's Secret, Missing Beth, Beth and Grandmother*. Look, I even have *B & C* in a cute little heart."

Karin burst into laughter. "Give me a break, will you? No cute little hearts, okay?"

"I know. It's lame. I was just remembering the time Beth and I carved our initials and a heart into this huge old oak in Discovery Park. It was so wrong, but we had a blast. How about *Running with Beth*?"

"Now you're getting closer," Karin said. "*Running with Beth* or *Beth's Secret*. I like them both. Either will do as a working title, I think. *Running with Beth* grounds the reader by sort of defining you and your relationship with your sister. I think you've got something."

"Really?"

"Sure," Karin said. "I'm no expert, but it seems strong and simple to me. Let me think about it some more. And why don't you toss it around with some of the other writers here or at the U? Ask that professor of yours and see what she thinks."

"Thanks, Karin. You're great."

"I know," Karin said with a wink. "So what are you working on today now that *Running with Beth* is pretty much in the bag?"

"Homework. Lots and lots of homework. I'm so far behind, I don't know when I'll catch up."

"Stop whining. If you get that contract – and I have no doubt that you will – you'll be a whole lot busier. So get used to it."

"All right, all right, enough of the lecture," Chris said. "I just wish I was as confident as you are about this thing going to press."

"You mean *Running with Beth*? It will. Just you wait. You want anything?" Karin asked as she stood up to order a drink.

"Not a thing," Chris said.

Later that evening, just as Chris was about to turn off the lights and crash, her cell phone rang. She saw Karin's name in caller ID and pushed talk.

"Hi, Karin. What's up?" she asked.

"Not *Running with Beth*," Karin said. "*Running Secrets*. That's the title."

The following day Chris typed a title page and assembled the manuscript into one tall pile of memoir pages intermixed with calligraphy pages and art pieces. She included all the original artwork that measured eight and a half by eleven inches or smaller. She photographed the larger pieces and included printed copies in the manuscript. This wasn't ideal, but it was the only way to complete the vision, and if nothing else, Chris wanted to be able to show Elsie the vision.

Early Thursday morning she packed the manuscript into Beth's prized leather artist's portfolio. She also included one of her sister's largest paintings. This was her favorite, the image she hoped to use for the cover art: the unfinished painting of their grandmother. Once certain that the portfolio was packed well enough to avoid slippage or damage, she headed to her car.

At Staples she made high quality color copies of the first twenty pages of the manuscript, packed them into the portfolio along with the originals, and headed to The Last Exit to meet Elsie Crane.

I told them about the contract with Acorn Literary Agency today. It was so cool. They were all so supportive and seemed far more convinced than I am that I can get this thing polished, digitized and submitted to Elsie. The sooner the better she said. I can do this. I know I can do it. I just have to keep at it.

Everything seems to be falling together for me. The pieces of the puzzle magically settling into place. It feels so unreal. Can I trust it? Can I believe? Or will I wake up and poof, it'll be gone. It? What's it? Gemi, Jake, Karin, Peter, The Last Exit writers, now Elsie and this contract. And Elsie said she already has somebody she wants to show the manuscript to, an independent West Coast publisher who might be interested in the book. It's just too good to be true. Why me? Why me and not Beth?

Tears filled her eyes and the pen dropped from her hand. "Because Beth is dead." She said it aloud. She said it to the walls, to the manuscript spread before her, to the runners on Alki Beach. And she said it aloud to accept the truth of it, the pain of it. To accept Beth's death and in doing so accept her own life. Wiping the tears from her eyes, she picked up her pen.

I miss you, Beth. I will always miss you. Good bye.

SIXTY

IT WAS A COLD CLEAR WINTER DAY when Gemi and Carolyn met on their front steps and headed out for their weekly walk. "I bet you miss that headscarf on days like this," Carolyn said.

"Ah, but I have it with me still," Gemi said as she pulled a wide, colorful scarf from her neck up over her head and rewrapped it around her neck.

"No point in wasting a good scarf," Carolyn said with a laugh.

They headed north through the tree-lined residential streets, past large craftsman homes. As they neared the park, the houses grew to mansions, complete with pillars and towers, visual reminders of the early years of Seattle wealth. Once the homes of local lumber barons, these beauties had sat on wide swaths of land but were now crowded by smaller houses and apartment buildings. Still, the neighborhood held its old-world grace and Gemi loved it. They circled the old brownstone water tower and entered the park.

"So tell me about this man of yours," Carolyn said.

"Antonio," Gemi said.

"Yes, Antonio,"

"It's been such a very long time. I'm not certain what to think."

"Since you've had a special man in your life?"

"Yes, precisely."

"But you're enjoying his company, right? I mean I've seen him pick you up and drop you off a few times."

Gemi gave her a look.

"It's hard to avoid, Gemi. My front window looks out on the front entrance. I see all the comings and goings."

"Our own little neighborhood security watch," Gemi said.

"Oh don't get all touchy on me. I'm happy for you, glad you've got someone in your life."

"He's a good man. I'm thankful he's just across the hall from Chris. I don't trust that father of hers."

"I hope that's not a false sense of security, Gemi. I mean, think about it, Chris could run into her father anywhere, especially since they're both living in West Seattle."

"I suppose you are right," Gemi said.

They walked in silence for a bit. They paused to look at the panoramic view of downtown Seattle and gave a nod to the Ming camels resting on the steps of the Asian Art Museum.

"Tell me more about this guy. Come on, out with it," Carolyn said.

"Would you like to take a break in our walk today? I've always wanted to step inside the conservatory," Gemi said as they approached the ornate glass building at the north end of the park. They entered the central atrium, and Gemi felt as though she'd stepped into the tropics. The air was heavy with aroma of flowers, soil and water. She spoke in a whisper as though it were a sacred place. Perhaps it was. "He is a good man, my dear friend. He has suffered and survived. Much like me, he has lost both family and country."

"I'm sorry," Carolyn said.

"He came to America before the revolution began. He was a fortunate one and now he lives with the guilt of survivorship."

"No family at all?"

"Like most civil wars, the war in El Salvador tore his family apart. But being in school here in Seattle, he remained quite isolated from the conflict. His only sister, younger by a number of years, became involved in the resistance. She and her husband had only one child. When it became obvious that their lives were in danger, Antonio sent them funds to escape."

"How? From what I read, it was almost impossible to get out once the military closed the airport."

"By land. They traveled through Central America, Mexico and across the border into the United States. Of course, they had no papers as the United States did not recognize the dangers in their country at that time. Antonio is certain that they made it into the United States.

He received a phone call. But mind you, this was a dozen years ago. Since then he has heard nothing at all. They simply disappeared."

"And he's never heard from them since?"

"Not a word. He assumed they were deported and later learned his sister and her husband were executed."

"Poor man. I'm so sorry. Even the little girl?"

"He's not certain. He finally received verification, death certificates, for his sister and her husband, but his niece is simply gone."

"How sad. Ever married? Children?"

"Yes. He lost both in a hit-and-run accident. He has been alone for a long time."

"Seems you two share a lot in common."

"Indeed."

SIXTY-ONE

EXCEPT FOR THE PART-TIME WORK HOURS, a few dinners with Gemi and a handful of evenings with Jake, Chris worked day and night on the manuscript, rewriting and editing her memoir pages and finalizing the layout. She was close, so very close.

A rare snowstorm hit Seattle in late January. The city came to a standstill. Schools and businesses remained closed for several days. People stayed home. Seattleites don't know how to drive the hills in snow and most are smart enough not to attempt it. Chris was grateful for the calm but still anxious to get the manuscript to Elsie as soon as possible. She sat at her table, the final draft before her. She was unable to move, decision impossible.

... She sees herself driving to the West Seattle Post Office. She waits for her turn at the counter and finally hands the manuscript box to the cashier. She pays the requested postage and leaves the building with a wide smile on her face. Then, and only then, does she realize that the box she just mailed is empty ...

"Real productive that is." She stood and walked across the room to the refrigerator, a faint gnawing in her stomach telling her she'd missed lunch. She knew she was close. No, the truth of the matter was that she knew she was finished and no silly fantasy was going to stop her.

After lunch, she walked to the local office supply store for the packaging she needed to send the manuscript to her agent.

"It's done," Chris said as soon as Jake answered the phone.

"Done?"

"Yup, packed and ready for the post office. I thought you might want to come with me. We could mail it and then grab some margaritas to celebrate. Are you too tired? Did you just get off a long shift? Sorry I don't remember."

"No worries. Just be downstairs and I'll swing by and get you in a half hour, okay?"

"But what about…"

"Don't worry, I've got chains on."

"Perfect."

Jake had in fact just come off a long shift. He was exhausted and still in uniform having only just walked through his own front door. But he knew this was big and he was glad Chris wanted to share it with him. He pulled off his uniform as he headed to the shower and fifteen minutes later he was out his front door.

He saw her standing in the entrance as he drew to a stop in front of the building. He wasn't sure how anyone could look so determined and yet so anxious at the same time, and yet there she was.

"Hop in, it's freezing out there," he said as he pushed the passenger door open for her. "So that's it?"

"That's it."

"Big box."

"Lots of pages."

The drive up the hill the post office was quiet. He parked and walked in with her. As they stood in line, she turned to look at him and he could see the question in her eyes.

"Yes, it's ready. Yes, it's the right thing to do. Yes, you are honoring Beth in the most beautiful and wonderful manner you possibly can. Stop worrying, Chris. It's perfect."

"And if it's not, Elsie will tell me."

He watched as she handed over the large manuscript box and paid the postage. As they walked out of the building, she laughed aloud. "What's so funny?"

"Oh, nothing. It's just that I'm remembering a crazy daydream I had about mailing an empty manuscript box."

SIXTY-TWO

CHRIS MANAGED TO MAKE IT THROUGH winter quarter, but just barely, and only with Professor Mackintosh's support. Ever since that first class in September, they'd conferenced on several occasions and Chris had taken her up on her offer to look at her memoir pages. It was to Professor Mackintosh that Chris had turned when she needed to understand the publishing contract she'd been offered and Karin was away on vacation.

When spring quarter began in April, she was determined to do her very best work ever. No longer focused on a single project, she opened herself to a broader spectrum of experimentation. It was also time for her to make a decision about her future.

She arrived at the appointment a few minutes early, but Professor Mackintosh was already in her office. "Come in, Chris. What can I do for you today?"

"Well, I have three more quarters," Chris said as she dropped her heavy backpack on the floor and sat down. "Then I'll have my BA with the Writing Emphasis."

"Good for you," Professor Mackintosh said with a wide smile. "Then what?"

"That's why I asked to see you. I'm thinking of applying for the MFA program," Chris said as she glanced around the office. "Oh, I'm sorry. I hope you're not too busy."

Sitting in Professor Mackintosh's cluttered campus office, they were surrounded by overflowing floor-to-ceiling bookshelves. There were piles of manuscript pages stacked on every surface, including the floor.

"Oh, don't worry about those," Professor Mackintosh said. "I always have piles and piles of student work to read, and then I do some editing for a few writer friends as well, so the piles never disappear."

"Do you ever get tired of it?" Chris asked.

"It?"

"The reading and editing student work. I mean, wouldn't you rather be writing your own?"

Professor Mackintosh smiled. "Oh Chris, I'm an academic. I'm one of those do-as-I-say-not-as-I-do writers. Sure, I've written and published both creative as well as analytical works in my long career. And even a few textbooks. But I'm a teacher first, and I love what I'm doing. What about you? What are your career goals?"

"I guess I'm still figuring that out. I'm glad I wrote the memoir, glad to put Beth's story into the world, but I love the work I'm doing now in my fiction classes, too. I think I just need to keep writing and learning. That's why I'm here. I've looked at the application for the MFA program. I'll do the GRE this fall, and I can use some pages from the memoir as the creative writing sample. But I'll need three letters of recommendation. Would you be willing to write one for me?"

"It would be a pleasure, Chris. And what about that teaching assistantship application? Do you plan to complete that as well?"

"I don't know. I haven't really thought about it. I mean, I need the work, of course, but I'm not sure about teaching. What do TAs do?"

"Well, you see all these piles. I don't read them all myself," Professor Mackintosh said with a laugh. "TAs do some reading and they lead some of the discussion sections. I think you'd be a wonderful TA. I've seen your peer critiques. You do strong work, Chris. I tell you what, I'll write that recommendation and you add the TA application to the packet. Then we'll have another few years to work together. How does that sound to you?"

"Wonderful. Thank you so much." Chris stood to leave, but the older woman motioned her to sit down.

"There's something I wanted to ask you about, Chris."

"Yes?"

"You've got a book coming out this year. November or December, right?"

"Yes, that's what I've been told."

"I was wondering if you'd be interested in doing a little pre-release promotion?"

"What do you mean?"

"I've been asked to do a conference presentation late summer. I'd like you to join me. It's here in Seattle, so there's no travel involved."

"Me? I mean what do you want me to do?"

"Don't get nervous, Chris. You'll need to practice public speaking. This book will take you places. You'll need to do readings. It's time to get some practice beyond the classroom walls. I'll be speaking on the creative process, on how each writer must find his or her own inspiration and practice. I'd like you to share your practice and then show your manuscript and read a bit. I realize you'll want to get permission from your publisher, but if I know the press as well as I think I do, they'll be pleased with a bit of early marketing. Also, you need to get the website we talked about up and running before the conference. So what do you think?"

"I think you're offering me a great opportunity and I really appreciate all the support. I also think I'll be terrified, but if you think I can do it, I'd love to give it a shot."

"Okay, that's settled then. Now what about that website, Chris?"

"I set up a very simple blog. I figure I'll just put up short posts about once a month or so, maybe pieces from my classes or something."

"And you'll announce all your readings and public appearances. Here's the information about the conference," Professor Mackintosh said as she handed Chris a flyer. "You can post that and I suppose you could do a post about your preparation process for your first conference. You're still keeping that journal, aren't you?"

"Yes, but that's personal."

"So is memoir. So is fiction, for that matter. Decide what you can share and you'll have plenty for your blog. Good work, Chris. Now I suppose I should get some work done on these piles."

Chris was in a daze as she headed across campus to her car. A recommendation for her MFA application and a conference. It was a bit more than she'd expected.

Sixty-Three

CHRIS FOUND A CHAIR along a wall of windows on the third floor of the conference hotel. She was early. Time to figure out this conference thing. She pulled items from the small cloth bag she was given when she checked in: pen, pad of paper, conference program, name tag and various loose papers, ads for this self-publishing company or that book doctor. She read through the thick program from beginning to end marking sessions she thought would be interesting to attend. Three full days of activities. She found Dr. Mackintosh's name and was again grateful that it was scheduled on the afternoon of the first day. Today. She had time to get used to the scene, attend a few sessions and then do her own presentation. Get it over with so she could relax and enjoy the rest of the conference.

The PowerPoint was ready. Chris knew what she was supposed to share and exactly when Professor Mackintosh would call her to the podium. She had her materials ready, in fact, she couldn't be more prepared. But still she was terrified. Half-hour until the first session, she texted Karin: *I feel like a fraud. These people are writers.* A few seconds later she got Karin's response: *And what r u? Call me after.*

Am I a writer, I mean, really? Chris wondered. Does one book make a writer? Mind a muddle, she stood to walk off some jitters, though how a few minutes along these stuffy halls would help more than her long beach run at daybreak eluded her. At least she could find all the rooms, in particular the room where she'd be speaking that afternoon.

"Well, it's over," Chris said as soon as she heard Karin's greeting.

"How'd it go? Wish I could've been there. Would've given anything to be there, you know that, don't you? I really just couldn't get the time off. Anyway, how'd it go?"

Chris smiled at her friend's long-winded exuberance. "Fine, I guess. I mean, Professor Mackintosh was pleased and I got a few questions, so I guess that's good."

"What kind of questions?"

"Oh, like why I wrote memoir instead of fiction and how my folks reacted and about my process. And then one person asked about the internal structure of the work or the mythical journey or some such thing. I had no idea what he was talking about. Fortunately, Professor Mackintosh stepped in and took that one."

"Good thing she read the manuscript," Karin said with a hearty laugh. "Well, good for you. I bet you feel a bit more prepared for the release, right? And you've got that MFA application guaranteed now. Way to go, Chris."

"Thanks, Karin. I probably don't say that enough."

"Forget it."

"No, really. Without you, without that invitation to The Last Exit, I wouldn't be here in this conference, and I sure wouldn't have a book coming out. Thank you so much."

"My pleasure. How about a beer later this evening to celebrate? Not a late one. I know the conference thing can be grueling even if you do have the presentation behind you. No. Never mind. You probably have some event to go to with your professor tonight. Tell you what. Let's get together after the conference, okay?"

"Sounds perfect."

They chatted for a few more minutes and then Chris signed off and headed to the next session. Later she'd meet Professor Mackintosh at the no-host meet-and-greet to rub elbows with all the real writers at the conference. Real writers, what a concept. I wonder when I'll feel like a real writer, Chris thought as she slipped into the session without a sound.

SIXTY-FOUR

THE RAIN NEVER BOTHERED CHRIS. She ran rain or shine, winter or summer. "It's all a matter of how you dress," she told her friends. "Just makes the air taste that much better." She teased Jake, calling him a big baby when he complained about getting soaked to the bone. "Easy for you," he'd tell her. "You're not out working in this damn drizzle all day, or worse yet, all night. You run, you go home, you get in a nice hot shower. It's not the same when you're out working in it all day."

She'd laugh, knowing all along that he was absolutely right. There was nothing worse than feeling cold and clammy in damp clothes all day. But she was oblivious to the weather when she ran. She never wore earphones, never listened to music or recorded books. She preferred the wind in her ears, the calls of the gulls overhead, and the tidbits of conversation she picked up as she passed people along the way. Today the shops along Beach Drive were decorated with bright orange pumpkins and yellow gourds. Witches flew across café windows.

She got back to the condo sweaty and invigorated, ready to jump in the shower and head for classes. She looked forward to an early dinner with Gemi when her afternoon classes ended. Her life was full. Her heart was full. She felt like a new woman.

As she entered the lobby of her building, Fred limped towards her with a brown cardboard box in his hands. "Morning, Chris. You just missed the UPS guy. I told him I'd get this to you. Hope that was okay."

"Of course it was, Fred. Thanks!"

"Can you carry that okay?" he asked.

"Sure, I got it," she said, taking the heavy box from him and stepping into the open elevator. She glanced at the return address, and her heart skipped a beat. She fought the zipper on her jacket pocket to find her key, opened her door, and grabbed the kitchen scissors from the knife block.

"Slow down," she whispered to herself. "Slow down and breathe." She took a deep relaxing breath and carefully cut the package open. She lifted six large, hard-cover books from the box and clutched each to her chest. She breathed in their rich scent of new paper and ink like a mother breathing in her newborn child before laying them out in a line across her kitchen counter. Then she chose one and walked to the sofa where she sat down and opened it. The creak of the hard spine filled her with joy. She paged through from beginning to end, pausing to examine each of Beth's images, each line of verse.

After examining every square inch, checking for ten fingers and ten toes, she left that copy on her coffee table and took the others to the table. There, she fixed a nib in her stylus and carefully uncorked a bottle of black ink. She already knew the words she would write in each book. She'd planned for this moment. She'd practiced the calligraphy. When she had dedicated each book, she closed her ink bottle, washed her stylus and headed to the shower, leaving the books open to dry.

Fresh from her shower, Chris returned to the living room in a pair of sweats and a fleece jacket, toweling her damp curls. She dropped the towel on the kitchen counter and slid one of the books towards her. Taking a slip of clean parchment, she pressed the dedication. Certain that the rick black ink was dry, she closed the cover and slipped the book into a padded mailing envelope. She addressed the envelope and slipped on a warm jacket.

There was no traffic on the hill up to the West Seattle Post Office. She pulled into an empty parking spot in front of the building in the early darkness and leaned her forehead against the steering wheel lost in thought. *What if they actually respond? What if...?* That old mind game didn't haunt her anymore. But now there was something more real that concerned her. Provocation. She didn't want to provoke her father's violence, but at the same time she wanted her parents to see the work that she was so very proud of: both Beth's and her own. She knew that they'd hear of the book somewhere, and she figured it was best if they got it from her first. It was the right thing to do. She released her seatbelt, checked her side mirror for oncoming traffic, and opened the car door. If her father got drunk and violent again, she'd just have to handle it.

SIXTY-FIVE

"I'VE GOT A SURPRISE FOR YOU."

"A surprise, child?"

"Yup."

Chris and Gemi were having dinner at yet another Seattle eatery as they continued working their way through the Seattle restaurant guide. Gemi watched Chris lift her backpack into her lap and unzip it. With a grand flourish, she pulled out a gift wrapped in shiny red paper and topped with a big bow. She handed it to her.

"It's not my birthday, and it's still too early for Christmas. What is this, child?"

"Open it."

"It's much too beautiful to open. Such a brilliant shade of red. It reminds me of a story you once told me of another gift long ago."

"You've got a good memory. Now come on. Open it."

"No, I think I'll wait until after we eat." Gemi realized in that brief moment just how much she loved her young friend's enthusiasm and how difficult it was not to tease her. She could almost feel Chris's nervous energy circling around the table. She accepted the gift and laid it on the table between them. "So this is it, child?" she whispered.

"Yup. Come on, open it. I want you to tell me what you think."

Gemi untied the ribbon and opened the heavy red wrapping. She ran her fingers along the shiny book jacket, tracing the image of Grandmother Stevens in Beth's unfinished portrait. Then she opened the book and began to page through it in silence. When she read Chris's heartfelt dedication, she ignored the tears that rolled down her cheeks. She turned the heavy pages taking in each image, each poem rendered in Chris's flowing calligraphy. Finally she closed the book slowly, reverently, lovingly and placed it on the far corner of the table away from possible spatters or spills. She dabbed her wet cheeks with her napkin and stood in silence to hug her former patient. In that embrace, Gemi felt Chris's love, the love of a daughter, and she was overjoyed.

"Can I leave now, child? I have a lot of reading to do."

"Not a chance," laughed Chris. "The reading will have to wait. We have some celebrating to do."

"I'm so proud of you, child," Gemi said. She was rewarded by the sparkle in Chris's big brown eyes and the smile that spread across her beautiful face.

Chris climbed the steep narrow staircase with slow, measured steps. She climbed without pain, only deep in thought. She knew this was the last time she would climb these stairs. She knew it was her last session with Peter Bentley. She knew she no longer needed therapy. They'd talked about it and reduced their visits over time. Now, as she took one slow step after the next, she thought back to her first climb up those stairs. She couldn't have said if the pain in her legs or the pain in her heart had been more intense.

She climbed the stairs three times a week that first month, then twice, then only once. Once a week for over a year. Then every other week for a while. And for the last few months only once a month. A gradual distancing. She was living life on her own terms. And she was happy. Yes, happy, she thought as she neared the top. I'm happy. This is what happiness feels like.

"Hey, Chris," Peter boomed from his office doorway. "Kind of slow today, aren't you? You've been taking those steps two at a time for months now. Something weighing you down?"

"Not a thing, Peter. Not a single thing," Chris said. "I'm just making every step, every moment, a memory. I want to remember this climb for as long as I live."

"Well, it's not like the building's being torn down or anything. You can always come back for the exercise," Peter teased. "Come on in. Sit down." He ushered her into the familiar office, and she walked to the window just as she'd done the first time she'd entered this room.

"So, this is it?"

"Yup, I guess so," she answered, staring across the bright blue water to West Seattle.

"How do you feel about it?"

"I'm ready," she said. Then, she turned and took her seat across from him. "I'm ready. I'm happy. I need to fly solo. But I'm going to miss you something fierce."

"You're a very special young woman, Chris. I have to confess, it's been tough trying to maintain some professional distance. You know, if I'd ever had a daughter, I would have wanted her to be just like you."

"Really?"

"Really."

"Then maybe this isn't too totally out of line," Chris said as she unzipped her backpack, took out a gift wrapped in bright red paper and handed it to him.

Peter's left eyebrow arched in a question, the gesture Chris had come to know so well. The question without words.

"Open it."

The shiny red wrapping slipped to the floor, and Chris watched as Peter held her life story in his hands just as he had held her very life on that first day she struggled up the stairs to meet him. She saw the emotion in his eyes as he leaned back in his chair and slowly began to turn the pages of her gift.

"Thank you, Peter, for all you've done for me. I owe you my life. You already know the story, but I think you'll enjoy Beth's poetry and artwork."

"I will cherish this, all of it, always. Thank you." He stood and enclosed her in a somewhat awkward, fatherly hug.

"So how are those party plans coming along?" Karin asked as the tables cleared after writing practice.

"Pretty good, I guess. I really have no idea what I'm doing, but it's just a party, right?"

"Yup, and the winery is reserved, so you don't have to worry about how many bottles to buy. And the invitations?"

"They're going out this week. And I'll bring a bunch here on Tuesday for the gang."

"Have you thought about what you're going to read?"

"Not yet, but I'm working on it. Can I run it past you in a week or so?"

"Sure, if you want, but I'm sure you can pick your favorite scenes without my help."

"Well, maybe so, but I'd love your help. And just to make it easier, I've got something for you." Chris said, as she pulled a bright red gift from her backpack.

"They arrived. Why didn't you tell me?"

"It was a surprise. I couldn't just text you," Chris said. "I owe you big time. Who knows if this thing would ever have gotten published without your help. Thank you so much! Here, for you."

"Hey, you can't make any money if you give copies away," Karin said. She ripped off the bright red wrapping to reveal Grandmother Stevens' wise, dark eyes. "Beautiful," she whispered. "Do your parents know about this, yet?"

"I sent them a copy a few days ago."

"Sent?"

"Yeah, pretty chicken-shit, right? But I wrote them a letter telling them that I was tired of their secrets. Dad can keep pretending to be white if he wants, but I'm not playing the game. There are plenty of Stevenses in the world. It's not like I fingered him or anything. This is Beth's story and mine, too. I'm sick of his games."

"You go girl." Karin said. "What did they say?"

"I haven't heard a word yet. I'm guessing that my mother intercepted the package and my dad knows nothing about it, but who knows?"

"I'm sorry, Chris. They should be rejoicing instead of acting like fools."

"Such is life, right? We all have our troubles."

"Yeah, I suppose," Karin agreed. "So, it'll be in bookstores in time for Christmas, right?"

"Should be."

"Hallelujah!" Karin exclaimed with delight. "It's time to celebrate."

"Hello, Mom. Chris here."

Silence.

"Mom, did you get the invitation I sent you?"

"Yes, the invitation, the letter and the book."

"Will you come to my party?"

She heard shuffling, a gasp, a squeak almost, then the crash of something hitting the floor.

"Mom! Mom, are you okay?"

Then she heard the slur in her father's voice. "What in the hell do you think you're doing calling this house?"

"Hello, Dad. How are you?" Chris asked, her voice calm as she adjusted the yellow silk around her shoulders.

"Very funny, Christine. You've done enough already. Just leave us alone."

"What have I done, Dad? I've learned your secret, and I've published the truth about my own heritage. You can't face the truth, can you? Can't accept the idea that your mother, the woman who gave you life, was black. Your life has been nothing but one big long lie. But you know what Dad, that's your choice. Not mine. I won't live your lie."

"Leave us alone, you ungrateful little bitch. You're no daughter of mine."

"Let me talk to my mother."

"I told you to leave your mother and me alone. Don't you ever call here again."

"Sorry, Dad, but you can't tell me what to do. And you know what, you can't tell Mom what to do either."

Silence. The phone line went dead.

Well, that didn't go as well as it could've, but at least I said my piece. Chris raked her fingers through her shoulder-length curls and shook the tension from her shoulders. She was worried about her mother, but she knew she couldn't live her mother's life. She could only figure out how to live her own. Mom's got to make her own choices. I've made mine.

Chris expected Jake. She knew he was coming and knew he'd be prompt. She'd grown to love that man, his quirks and his humor. Still, she was engrossed in her work and the doorbell startled her. The involuntary jerk of her hand sent spatters of thick black ink across her tabletop once again. "Crap," she muttered. "Another one ruined." She stood, stretched and crossed the room to the intercom in one graceful movement, the fluid movement of an athlete.

"It's open, Jake. Come on up."

"How'd you know it was me? It could've been anybody. You gotta be more careful, Chris."

"Are you going to come up or just stand down there scolding me? Besides, why don't you just use that key I gave you?"

"Be right there," Jake said.

Chris opened the door wondering about Jake's continued discomfort about letting himself into her space. After all, they were practically living together. She went back to the table to wipe up the spattered ink. She was back at work a few minutes later when Jake walked in the door. She heard him stop and knew he was taking in the scene before him. Every flat surface of her living room, dining area and kitchen was covered in small pieces of folded paper. Thick, heavy, creamy white, handmade paper. Not folded tight, not folded flat, but folded open to dry.

"What tornado struck this place?" he laughed, bending to pick up one of the papers to avoid stepping on it as he entered the room.

"Hey, you knew I wanted to do these invitations by hand."

Jake studied the black message that flowed like a gentle stream across the page. "Beautiful." Lifting another paper from the coffee table, "These are absolutely beautiful. My god, you must've put hours into these. How many are there anyway? Looks like you've got enough here to invite the whole city."

"I don't know. I haven't counted." She set down her stylus, sealed her ink, and stood back to survey her work. "I guess it does look pretty bad, doesn't it? Like some obsessive-compulsive crazy woman lives here or something."

Jake laughed. "Not crazy, just a bit too focused at the moment. When was the last time you left this place anyway?"

"Hey, I went for a run this morning. I bet that's more than you can say, so don't be getting all protective on me."

"You went out in this miserable rain? I'm impressed." He continued picking his way through the living room, reading invitations in his path. "These really are amazing, Chris. Each one is a unique piece of art. No two are exactly the same. They're beautiful."

"I suppose I need to stop making more and start addressing envelopes. The only one I've sent so far was to my parents."

"Your folks? For real? Any response?"

"No, but then I called them and my dad was drunk and vicious again. He grabbed the phone from my mom, called me a few choice names before he hung up on me."

"Do you think he'll do something stupid again?"

"Let's hope not, but I really can't think about that right now. These invitations all need to be in the mail, like now. You really think they're good enough?"

"Sure do," he said. He reached the table and wrapped her in his arms.

"Good, that's what I was hoping for. Something to honor Beth, I guess."

"Hey," he said, lifting her chin with one finger and looking into her eyes. "You've already done more than that with your book. You've told her story and your own. She'd be proud."

"Thank you," she said, and standing on her tiptoes, she kissed him. "Speaking of which, I have a surprise for you." With both hands on his chest, she gently pushed herself from his warm embrace and walked to the bookcase to retrieve a brightly wrapped gift – shiny emperor red with a large bow on top. "For you," she said.

"Your book?" he asked, hands extended in front of him like a father receiving a newborn in the delivery room, unsure how to hold it.

"Here, sit down and open it," she said, clearing a place on the sofa for him. She watched as he took out his jackknife and cut the ribbon and tape, folded the blade and put it back in his pocket. He lifted the large book from the gift-wrap and smiled at the image of Chris's grandmother on the front cover. In silence, he paged through the book, glancing at the artwork, at the calligraphy, at the memoir Chris had written.

"Congratulations. This is amazing."

"Thanks. Thank you for everything. I wouldn't even be here if not for you. And I would never have written it without your loving support. Without you and Gemi and Peter. It would never have been published without Karin's help. I'm so lucky to have you, all of you, in my life."

"My pleasure," he said, grabbing her wrist and pulling her onto his lap. He held her in a tight embrace, taking her breath away with a kiss that told many stories.

"So, are you still up for that dinner you promised me?" she whispered in his ear.

"Sure am, but maybe later," he said. Then he struggled to his feet with Chris cradled in his arms. "Are you terribly hungry?" he asked as he carried her towards the bedroom.

"Only for you," she whispered. "But give me a second to get some of this ink off me."

"Take your time," he said. He stood her in front of the bathroom door and gave her another deep, lingering kiss. "I'm not going anywhere."

SIXTY-SIX

THE SUPERMARKET WAS CROWDED with Saturday afternoon shoppers, but Chris wasn't in a hurry. She pushed her small cart up and down the aisles picking this and that from the shelves with little thought at all. The invitations were in the mail and she'd already run a few ideas past Karin about the reading. Jake was coming over for dinner. Life was good.

She had everything she needed for a simple meal of salmon and salad, but she wanted to pick up some wine and dessert. Maybe something for breakfast. Coffee, she thought, I can't forget the coffee.

As she approached the large wine section at the back of the store, she noticed a small crowd around the tasting kiosk – a regular weekend event at this store. She circled to the back of the store behind the tall shelves searching for an unoaked Chardonnay. She'd just heard something on the radio about unoaked Chardonnays being a good match for salmon and had a few local wine makers in mind.

She set her cart to one side and walked the aisle finding the section she wanted: Washington Whites. Chardonnays. As she bent to take a bottle from a low shelf, something or someone knocked into her from behind. She fell forward, but was able to catch herself on the edge of the sturdy wooden shelf without knocking any bottles to the floor.

The crash of shattered bottles that rang through the store told her that the other person wasn't so lucky.

There was a split second of silence. Even the wine tasters and shoppers seemed to stop, frozen silent. Then a slurred voice, loud and nasal, tore through the store. "God damn it all to hell."

Chris froze. She'd recognize that voice anywhere. She turned away, looking for an easy exit.

"You. God damn it. It's you. You little slut. Always causing trouble, aren't you?"

Too late for escape, Chris turned to face her drunken father. "Are you okay, Dad?"

People began to gather and gawk.

"Okay? Okay? If you gave half a shit about whether I was okay, you wouldn't have written that god damned excuse for a book. I swear if you distribute that piece of shit, you'll be sorry. I've got a mind to pay you another little late night visit."

"Come on, Dad. Can you get up?"

Mitch Stevens stumbled to his feet in his three-piece designer silk knocking another shelf of bottles to the floor in the process. In one long step, he lunged at Chris and grabbed her around the neck. "How dare you ruin my life like this, you little black whore. I should've left the day you were born."

A couple of shoppers jumped Mitch from behind and dragged him off Chris. She took a few steps away from her father and stood in a daze, surrounded by voices.

"Call 911."

"Hold him until the cops get here."

"Watch out for that broken glass."

A person with a nametag, a store employee, came up to her. "Are you, okay, Miss?"

Chris remained silent, but she didn't take her eyes from her father's face. She refused to allow him do this to her again, to reduce her to a frightened shell of a woman. When she was ready, she spoke to him in a calm, quiet voice. "You can't do this anymore, Dad. It's over."

"It's over when I say it's over," her father spat.

"No, that's not how it's going to be anymore," Chris said.

When the police arrived and took her father into custody for the second time, Chris was ready to file charges. She wasn't convinced she needed a restraining order against him yet, but she wanted him to know she was serious and she knew she should be prepared for just about anything.

SIXTY-SEVEN

CHRIS AND JAKE WERE RETURNING to the condo after a long afternoon run when Fred approached them, a large floral arrangement in his arms, his face almost hidden behind the bright yellow, red and orange of Gerbera daisies, chrysanthemums and the gentle white of baby's breath.

"Hiya, Chris. Jake. These came for you about an hour ago."

"Thanks, Fred," Chris said, taking the bouquet from his outstretched arms. "Any idea who sent them?"

"Nope. Just one of the local floral shops. I think there's a note there though."

"Great. Thanks a lot," Chris said.

Jake held the open elevator door for her, and they headed up to the condo.

"Secret admirer, is that it?"

"Must be," she said. "Seriously, I wonder who sent these. They're gorgeous."

"I thought you didn't like flowers," Jake said.

"It depends on what they're saying," Chris said. "Depends on whether they're expressing an honest sentiment. The flowers I hate are the ones that are sent just to keep up appearances."

"Good to know," Jake said. "So who's the secret admirer?"

They entered the condo, and Chris set the flowers on the table. She pulled the small envelope from its plastic holder. Curious, she slipped a fingernail under the flap, took out the small card and read it aloud.

Dear Christine,
Thank you.
Love, Mother

In silence, she read the card again. Then again and again. She stared at it, tears streaming down her cheeks. "Does it mean what I think it means?" she asked.

"That you reached her? That she's on your side? I think that's what it means."

"Wow."

"A lot to take in."

"Yeah. What's next? What do I do? No, don't answer that. I know the answer. Nothing. I do nothing. At least for a week or so. At least until after the party. Then, maybe a phone call or maybe a thank you card. I'll decide next week."

"Sounds like a plan. Man, they sure look good in here, don't they? It's almost as if she knew your new wall color."

"Okay, that's freaky. But you're right. They're fantastic, aren't they? You gotta hand it to the woman, she's got some class."

SIXTY-EIGHT

THE WINERY WAS LIT with the soft flicker of hundreds of tiny candles floating in pressed-glass votives. The fragrance of evergreen garlands and the soft rhythms of a jazz quartet filled the room. Small tables scattered throughout offered an array of fruits and cheeses, baskets of bread and crackers, and opened bottles of wine – wine that had been made and bottled on site in the back rooms of this small West Seattle winery. The owners shipped in grapes from the vineyards of Eastern Washington and filled the large oak barrels with new wine, one small batch at a time. They hosted wine-making events, inviting people to join in the fun and the work of making their hearty reds and flowery whites.

Chris had never come. She wasn't much of a wine drinker, not knowing one grape from the next. It was Karin who suggested the place. Karin who had been through this before and knew how to put together a local book-release party. Karin who stood at the front door greeting guests as they entered, inviting them to page through one of the books stacked on the small table beside her. And it was Karin and their agent, Elsie Crane, who insisted that Chris do a short reading and that a local bookstore be invited to sell copies of *Running Secrets*.

Chris was uncomfortable with all of it. She simply wanted to have a party, a celebration of life, with those she'd grown to love. But she did the reading, and the room exploded in applause. Chris smiled into the faces before her. She caught Gemi's eye across the crowded room. Her friend was stunning in a knee-length silk dress, the peach tones in rich contrast to her jet black curls, pulled into a loose French braid. Classy and beautiful, Chris laughed. And Antonio seemed to think so, too!

The moment Antonio and Gemi's eyes met that day of the painting party, they were an item. A Salvadoran, Antonio shared the pain and struggles of the immigrant experience that Gemi knew all too well. Despite their differences in continent and language of birth, despite racial and religious differences, Gemi and Antonio were perfect for each other, and Chris was thrilled for her friend.

As Chris scanned the crowd in front of her, her eyes settled on Jake, handsome in his sports coat and jeans. It had been no easy task convincing this man to move into her condo, now their condo. When he came to her with his plans to buy a "starter" home for the two of them, she struggled. She wasn't ready to leave Alki Beach, but he wasn't comfortable "sponging off her," as he put it. Over time she convinced him that by living together almost expense-free in the condo, they could save even more money. Besides, just because the condo was paid for, there were still expenses that Chris was struggling to meet on a part-time salary. Someday, when they were ready, they'd buy their dream home. In the meantime, Chris was thrilled to share the newly redecorated, brightly painted condo with the man she loved. She could almost see the children they'd have. Someday.

Chris watched Gemi make her way through the applauding crowd to reach her at the end of the reading. She relaxed in Gemi's hug and sighed with gratitude as her friend moved her away from the center of attention. "You did it, child. I knew you had it in you."

For a short while, she stood to one side of the room, almost hidden behind a large wine barrel, and watched. She saw Peter over by the door, chatting with another man, their two gray heads almost touching. She watched The Last Exit writers talking with the UW writers, the Alki runners joking with the West Seattle paramedics. And there was Jake's partner, Dave, flirting with the wine server. Jake and Karin were introducing people, making sure everybody knew each other, everybody was comfortable.

A warm, loving voice pulled her attention. "Child, what are you still doing here in the shadows? You're looking too lovely in your beautiful *shash* to be hiding."

"Oh, Gemi, I'm just taking it all in, etching it on my permanent memory. All these people, the light, the fragrance in the air."

"The love?"

"Yeah, the love. You know, I've only known these people for a couple of years and yet it feels like I've known them all my life."

"You have, child. You have."

Chris was silent for a minute, listening to bits of conversation floating around her, the soft chords of jazz in the background. "I wish Beth were here, Gemi. I just wish Beth were here."

"She is, child. She's here. Just look at the love in those faces. Look at what she's helped you find. She's here. I don't doubt that for a second, and neither should you."

Chris turned and threw her slender arms around Gemi's shoulders. "I love you, Gemi."

"And I love you, my child. Now you get out there with your guests. It's your party. Enjoy!"

So Chris circulated, thanking one and all for their support. She knew she would never have done it without them. Done it? The book or the life? They were intertwined; one could not exist without the other. The book was her understanding, her salvation, her path to the truth that freed her soul and allowed her to soar. She felt the world was open to her now. A new world, a new beginning, a life full of possibilities.

Hours later, after toasts and congratulations, after speeches and silliness, after laughter and conversation, the party came to a slow end. Chris stood at the door of the winery, Jake at her side, thanking her friends with hugs and kisses as they headed home for the night.

Peter and the man he'd introduced as Bob Treelyn earlier in the evening, walked towards the door together. Two dignified, gray-haired men, one in worn Asics and rumpled khakis, the other in tailored Italian wool. Chris watched them approach, and she knew. With a laugh, she reached a hand out to each of them, pulling them close to her.

"How long have you two been together?" she asked.

"Ah, she learned our secret," Peter teased.

"Nobody told me anything. I just knew."

"Bob and I have been together for almost twenty years, Chris."

"Wow, that's wonderful. Definitely a goal to reach for," she said.

"Well, you've certainly reached a goal today, kiddo."

"Only with your help, Peter."

"With everyone's help. But most of all with your own. Keep in touch. Maybe you'll even take an old man running on that beach of yours."

"Anytime. You know how to reach me." She held him so tight she could feel the beat of his heart. "Thank you," she whispered.

"What a great party," Chris murmured in a dreamy voice, as she climbed into the passenger seat of Jake's bright red Forester. He leaned in for a kiss before closing the door and walking around to the driver's side. She felt as though she were floating, as light as a summer cloud or a winter snowflake.

Jake headed north on 35th Avenue towards their home on Alki Beach. It was a clear, cold night, the moon almost full overhead. Chris saw the lights of the Seattle skyline twinkling in the distance.

"Wait. Stop here, Jake. Please, stop here."

He eased the car to the right. It was late, and traffic was light. He stopped at the crest of what they'd come to refer to as Suicide Hill – their private joke, their way of dealing with unbearable pain by facing it head on. The totem pole stood proudly at the foot of the steep incline, the golf course spread over the valley below.

"You okay, Chris?"

"Yeah, I'm okay. No, I'm better than okay. But, you know, it's weird, it's like I can't help wondering. Who was she? Who was that lost little girl you pulled from the battered Toyota down there?"

"I don't know," he said as he reached over and took her hand in his own. "But I know who this woman is, and I think she's pretty special."

Chris's smile glowed in the darkness.

THE END

ACKNOWLEDGMENTS

RUNNING SECRETS **TRAVELED A LONG ROAD** to publication. The earliest version began to take shape in 2005 while my first book, *The Thirty-Ninth Victim,* waded through two contracts and two indie presses before finally reaching the world. At times a distraction, at others a frustration—I worked on this first novel, set it aside, gave up on it, and returned to rewrite over and over. Without the generous support of my fellow writers, students, friends and family, *Running Secrets* would not be in your hands today.

I'd especially like to acknowledge Robert Ray and Jack Remick for establishing a timed-writing practice at Louisa's Bakery and Cafe in Seattle, WA over two decades ago and for their tireless support of emerging writers and old pros alike. Thank you also to the many writers—too numerous to name without risk of omission—who join Robert and Jack every week to put pen to paper, to share their work, to create community.

I am also grateful to the Uptown Writers for offering me a place to land each and every Sunday morning: Ella Andrews, Carol Bolt, Pamela Hobart Carter, Billie Condon, Geri Gale, Stacy Lawson, Susan Knox and Janet Yoder. And to the Uptowner we lost much too soon, Sandra E. Jones, who encouraged me to write of race even if it made some folks uncomfortable.

Thank you to my ESL students for the worldview they have taught me and for their cultural and linguistic guidance as I developed this story, to Drs. Gouri and Murali Sivarajan for their knowledge of all things medical, and to retired Fire Chief Jeff Williams for his expertise.

My sincere gratitude to Booktrope for giving *Running Secrets* a chance, especially to Jesse James Freeman who is always at his computer ready to respond to every question, concern or doubt I key his way.

And finally, this book would not be what it has become but for the dedication of my fabulous publishing team at Booktrope: Pamela Hobart Carter, Loretta Matson, Katrina M. Randall and Tiffany White. Thank you all for your generosity of talent and time.

MORE GREAT READS
FROM BOOKTROPE

I Kidnap Girls: Stealing from Traffickers, Restoring their Victims **by Pamela Ravan-Pyne and Iana Matei** (Fictionalized Biography) How a phone call to one woman resulted in the rescue of over 400 victims of forced prostitution.

Dismantle the Sun **by Jim Snowden** (General Fiction) A novel of love and loss, betrayal and second chances. Diagnosed with cancer, Jodie struggles to help her husband Hal learn to live without her. As Hal prepares to say goodbye to his wife, he discovers the possibility of happiness—in the arms of one of his students.

Dove Creek **by Paula Marie Coomer** (General Fiction) After a disastrous and abusive marriage, single mother Patricia draws on her Cherokee roots for courage. She finds her place as a Public Health nurse, but she must constantly prove herself—to patients, coworkers, and family members—in her quest to improve the lives of others.

A Medical Affair **by Anne Strauss** (Fiction) A woman has an affair with her doctor. Flattered, she has no idea his behavior violates medical ethics and state law. The novel is based on solid research of which most patients are unaware.

The Dead Boy's Legacy **by Cassius Shuman** (Fiction) 9-year-old Tommy McCarthy is abducted while riding his bike home from a little league game. This psychological family drama explores his family's grief while also looking at the background and motivations of his abductor.

Spirit Warriors: The Concealing **by D.E.L. Connor** (Fiction) Suspenseful, romantic, and awash in Native American magic, Spirit Warriors captures the tragic enchantment of the American West—and confirms the power of friendship.

Discover more books and learn about our
new approach to publishing at **booktrope.com**.